AKELA

AKELA

A NOVEL

RYAN UYTDEWILLIGEN

bhc
press™

Livonia, Michigan

Editor: Rebecca Rue

AKELA

Published by BHC Press

Library of Congress Control Number: 2018930624

ISBN: 978-1-947727-48-9 (Hardcover)
ISBN: 978-1-947727-37-3 (Softcover)
ISBN: 978-1-948540-79-7 (Ebook)

Visit the publisher:
www.bhcpress.com

To Mariana,
a lover of critters big and small
and an endless supplier of happiness.

AKELA

ONE

I DON'T recall how or where I was conceived. And I thank the universe for it. I believe everyone on this green earth feels the same way; otherwise we'd have far too many tortured souls for society to function. I never knew my father anyway. There was never even a mention of him existing in all my sweet years of life. My mother was a bit of a different story. She was always a mystery to me. I never knew her either, and yet, the very first memories I do possess are suffocating darkness and the one and only desire to find her.

I wasn't first or second or even the third one out. And I thank the universe for that fact too. From way down at the bottom of the crowded sandy pit, I could see flickering streams of light. They would suddenly pop into view, only to vanish within seconds when my face was pressed down into wet slime and pulsating eggshell. I'd turn and gasp, searching for a free space to take a fresh gulp of air. But there were just so many of us scrambling for the unknown that comfort was not in the cards.

I had never crawled before and neither had they. Flippers flapped for the first time, clumsily whacking and smacking without any hint of guilt. I'll admit I had the damndest time getting going. Sure, since

I was at the smack bottom I had the support of mushy sand and shell to press against as a launching point. But just imagine for a moment, if you will, that you have never taken a single step before. You wouldn't know what amount of force to press your flipper at or even how far ahead to put it really. It was tough; especially when everyone else used me as their launching point.

I sincerely hope the pioneers of that hatch soaked up the gentle rays of the sun while they had the chance. That would be the only minute of their lives, so hopefully they got what they wanted out of it. I tell you whoever invented this method of birth was a complete and utter buffoon. The ground to cover seemed so much farther than it actually was. For newborn flippers, it might as well have been a race across Death Valley.

Slipping and sliding about, not having a single idea what direction you were going…nowadays, odds are a pestering human child spots you and runs over ready to grab and poke. And though Mama says, "No no, don't hurt the poor babies," she pulls out her phone and clicks away like some maddening paparazzi. Crowds draw and click and flash, never seeing us beyond a thin, blinding screen. Uncoordinated toddlers make the wrong step (which at that point in my life I could sympathize with) and unwittingly smush our kin under their feet. But for the most part, everybody makes it. Nowadays there's usually some team of humans assigned to guide us to safety. Which isn't a bad thing, don't get me wrong! It's just that in my day, this particular day, there were gulls.

Oh, they didn't even have a chance, my poor brothers and sisters. One gull happened to be pleasantly perched on a branch, staring at the bobbing waves, until out of the corner of his eye he spotted the smorgasbord of a lifetime. It just started as one—this little, self-riotous monster didn't even tell his flock about the big score. He wanted us all to himself. And that's when I popped my little head out into fresh, sunny skies.

It was breathtaking—a true feeling of renewed energy I'll never forget. The sun graced my face with a delicate, warming touch. The air smelled of salt and seaweed—it was all new but I could already tell I wanted more. For now though, exploration had to wait. We all had only one goal and we'd achieve it by any means.

I still don't know why we were so determined to find Mother. We didn't know her. Were never even told about her! There was just some ready, instilled myth in our brains that she'd be waiting for us at the bottom of the sea. I wasn't even so sure that place existed. Dunes blocked my view of anything farther than a flipper. It was preposterous yet we marched on, slowly and wobbly to meet our eagerly awaiting creator. It's all we got in the beginning, a determination for family. It's all anybody's got period.

We were too slow. They were too fast. The flock of gulls had spotted their gluttonous pal cracking his way through soft shells and tearing flippers off like bananas from a bunch. While it was still only this one, some brothers and sisters had a chance. That singular gull got so overwhelmed, he tried his best just to eat everybody—nipping frantically so that scars and wounds might be the only lasting impact. His pals smelled the blood. Their eyes spotted the commotion. They flew from afar, eager to join in.

This was my introduction with the world. This was our handshake. Flying feathers and spurting blood soaking its way through sand pebbles until the beach was an alarming red. I will never erase the images of tearing and gnawing and the savage beasts even fighting each other for the privilege of devouring meatier siblings of mine. The beating sun hid behind a cloud like a frightened child, horrified by the dispute below. The world felt darker than the hole from which I had emerged. All I wanted to do was climb my way back in, but quite frankly, I didn't possess the skills to turn around. Before I knew it, I was all alone.

Now, remember when I told you I couldn't flip and flap and move so well. Who knew that would come in handy. See, I was still half-way in our little birthing hole, clinging onto the beach for dear life. I pushed and pushed and dug and stretched, but I couldn't for the life of me make it over the edge. I was stuck, perched on the side of this hole, unable to go forth to my chosen destiny—the Ocean where Mother awaited. I had to get to her. I couldn't let her down. But I couldn't move. Not even when the beady eyes of an overfed molting beast locked me in its gaze. Quick feet scampered across shells and sand like it was nothing…some kind of elegant death waltz. It wasn't fair. But if I would have been able to move, I would have been quicker than others; first in line to get devoured and last available for rescue.

Just like that, I went up. Up, up into the sky, looking down at the beach beneath me. For the first time the dunes did not block the roaring waves of the blue water slamming down onto the sand. It wasn't a gull that had lifted me; it was a human, a woman. The very first I would ever see.

Her hands seemed like an entire home—a spacious bed for me to sprawl out upon. She cupped me with her other hand, acting as a roof that shielded me from impending beaks and talons. I did my best to squirm my way out but her grip was far too tight. Oh, sure I was frightened, but it felt like a better place to be than a stomach. The woman threw her elbows about and swatted at the gulls, still determined to finish off their grub. I was dessert but this woman was equally determined to get me off the menu. With a few thrusts of her fists, the birds buzzed off—seeking shelter in some nearby trees. I could still see them through her fingers, eyes glued to me with blood-soaked feathers still raised and ready for attack. Somehow, in her hands, I could once and for all relax.

She knelt down before the water, uncaring that it flowed past her legs and soaked half of her flowery skirt. My roof was quickly gone as she gazed upon me—eyes mutually locked. Her dark skin was bruised and bumpy. Dark, circular bags hung halfway down her nose. But her mouth still presented a determined smile I will never forget. As tired as she looked, her beauty and elegance shone through. She was pretty enough to be a princess, sturdy enough to drive fear and strength into any acquaintance.

She made only one other movement with her head, a quick, worried glance behind her when footsteps neared. I did not feel jealous or shortchanged by her varied attention. I felt lucky. For one last breath of a moment, she turned her gaze to me and stroked her finger along my entire back. I really pity you humans. You're too big for a full body pet. My flippers shivered as my whole body descended into ecstasy. I can't really explain it to you other than to specify there's nothing sexual about it. It's love…a connection…a way of bonding through the simple act of touch. She smiled one last time, saying only one small word that would change my life forever.

Akela.

With a final double take, she let go. Air wisped past me until the haunting awakening of water surrounded every fiber of my being. As my rippled view of her faded further and further away, she stood stern and straight, waving as I drifted toward ground. I knew not what was coming. I knew nothing around me, only the final image of swords jousting in the hands of vicious, circling men. Their determined bodies swallowed her much like the gulls had done with my kin until she too was overtaken. She didn't fight it—she let them surround her.

"Fear not—destiny will guide you," dribbled down past the water's surface in a clouded muffle—I was positive this is what was said.

I, on the other hand, hit the soft undersea sand with a thud. I had made it to where I believed I was destined to go.

This was, and would always remain as, one of my favorite views. If you even protest for a single second that the land you call home doesn't have vibrant color, I will defy you without qualm. Flowing kelp in popping purples…anemones that stretched on like a colorful rainbow…even the critters that called this home; every color you can imagine swam past me. Every shade of yellow…pure, unfiltered blues…fuchsias and byzantiums and carnelians and…you get the picture.

But just think of all these different shades swarming about every which way. For a moment, a brief moment, I forgot about the beach. The gulls and the sand and the woman were all history at that point in time. As I wandered through the maze of plant life with saucers for eyes, I wondered just where my mother was waiting for me.

I called out but didn't harbor a single response. I called out again. And again. I was ignored. I peeked through grasses and peered into shells. I dug and dug but unearthed nobody that resembled my mother. I hadn't a clue what she looked like, and hell, I didn't know what I looked like either. But I was certain I'd know—I mean, she was my mother after all!

Concluding the search, which I must say brought my motor skills right up to speed, I found myself suddenly alone. The colors had even disappeared and a vast, empty dark blue stretched forever before me. Had she forgotten me? Had I gone to the wrong place? I refused to believe it. She'd come for me. I just had to wait. Then there were teeth.

A wriggling and winding slimy body emerged from an unseen nook with the hopes of swallowing me whole. With gnashing fangs and glowing white eyes, the beast was slender but unmistakably fierce. I didn't have time to take in a good view—I simply put all my energy into my flippers until I jolted back to narrow safety. The monstrous creature hit the ground, only collecting a mouthful of sand. As it wriggled backwards to try again, I did my best to spin around and flounder far, far away.

"How could my mother do this to me?" I wondered. "Leading me astray to this dangerous and horrible trickster of a place?"

It seemed like paradise, but that's when it dawned on me that the water was just as frightening as land…if not more. Dastardly beasts even more carnivorous than the gulls awaited me there. It was not safe.

The beast launched into another strike, narrowly missing me once more. A hollowed log seemed like the only logical place to hide in the heat of that moment. So I dug and twisted my way through a slit in the side. And just like before, on my way out of the birthing pit, I became stuck and unable to wriggle forward. I couldn't see behind me; this time I could only sense the creature was readying itself for yet another strike. This time it'd have accuracy and success. It was certain death for me while the life-or-death status of the woman I'd just met remained unknown. Her generosity and life legacy echoed through my worried mind. No matter alive or dead, I had the urge to fight for her. Possibly even avenge her. Keep at least one life afloat on this wretched death day.

My body shivered and shook until one of my back flippers made it through the crack. With one final push I blasted forward into freedom, into a dark and hollow yet safe, little bunker where I could rest. I felt the aftershock of the monster's unsuccessful crash. He had failed and for just a few minutes more, I would thankfully remain alive. Now all I had to do was wait.

And wait I did. For eleven years.

I knew I couldn't go out into the Ocean where such hellish fiends awaited me. The water was just so dark…so empty. But on land the gulls circled all day…that's all they ever did! Just circle around waiting for the right moment to strike. Mother had to be coming. I couldn't leave her anyway; I couldn't let her down…leave her abandoned.

It felt like eternity since I eked my way out from the log to grab a gasp of air. I remained where it was safe, in the midst of bright colors and docile sea life. If Mother was coming, she'd want me to be comfortable. She'd want me to wait in the most peaceful of conditions. But even shallow paradise has its crux. In those eleven years, I saw many of my own. I'd watch them swim in—high on newfound love and journeys through great mystical waters. They had nothing to do with me. Though I'd be sure to ask every single passerby if they were or knew my mother, I never was granted a positive response. It was, in my frank opinion, because I was small.

I'll never know why this happened for sure, but I have developed some hunches on the matter. It was my duty to crawl upon that sand and feel the water's welcoming splash on my own—just like it's the job of every Green, Leatherback, or what have you. If you want to live, you have to prove yourself. You have to spend every resource and ounce of passion you have to reach your goal. The woman who helped me cheated me out of it. Though her intentions were sweet, I was doomed right from the get-go—never able to reach my full potential. My second theory stemmed from the fact I was too fearful to set out on a journey through open Ocean. I couldn't seek out the proper necessities that make us grow: change, adventure, and discovery. Finally, perhaps it was simply because I slept in that tiny, hollowed log for all those years.

Whatever the case, my growth was stunted. I never grew past double my original size. You could hold me in both your hands and still see the tips of your wiggling fingers. If you're really wondering, picture a short, round child. Perhaps a rounded five year old would be around the size of my expected kind. Picture them holding a day-old offspring. I'm the offspring.

I was never bitter because I was hopeful my mother would return. I knew she wouldn't care about my size—she'd love me for who I was. But being small meant I could only travel small distances. Even if I wanted to, the open Ocean was no place for someone like me. I'd burn out before I passed the fishing boats bobbing eagerly over the coastline. And in those eleven years, I never tried.

I'd spend all my days the same, waiting patiently by a purple and beige piece of coral and then heading up to the beach for my afternoon gasp of air. The land seemed to change shape every time I surfaced. I never witnessed the woman again and would see fewer and fewer of her kind. Horses pulled wagons full of pineapples that were to be placed on steamships overlooking the harbor. Oh what a convoluted little hub the bay had become. A murky tinge blanked the water after more and more ships docked and loaded. Buildings with rising smoke lined the beach instead of palm trees. The amount of bustle made me reel in panic…I couldn't stay on the shore for long. The impending danger was too much to bear.

After a while, hope diminished and it seemed Mother never planned to show her face. I carved out a lovely nook for myself in the bay, still not completely without hope she'd one day make her grand entrance. I'm sure you understand…who among us has actually given up hope completely? Thrown a silly dream right out the coral or gave up searching for one's true love once and for all? There's always a part of you that you can never silence. A still, small voice that forever pesters you about what it is you really want. I could think my mother was never really coming back for me, but I couldn't in good conscience actually believe it.

If you're at all feeling sorry for me, I beg you to stop it! That goes for you too. We all have these moments or days or even months where we pity ourselves thanks to our situation. But the gift of perspective is a wonderful thing. The beauty about it is we all have perspective and we all receive it every waking second we're alive. If only I'd have known about the soil I'd step my flipper on…how life would unimaginably unfold…the foes I'd encounter? Again, this absolutely goes for every single one of us.

During my stay with a California aquarium, I'd stare for hours at a little sign spewing apparent facts about me and my kind. Though it was mostly bull or obvious statements I already knew, there was one fact that haunted me every day and night I stayed there and forever afterward. Only one out of one thousand newborns survive to adulthood. I can't prove or deny this but it always made me wonder. So at least I had that going for me.

Every so often I'd see a newborn plunge into the Ocean for its first time, eyes wide as saucers and flippers shaking uncontrollably. It wasn't often but I met a few beach warfare survivors as they arrived into the endless world of deep blue. When I saw their eyes, I'd recognize a feeling I had held near and dear in my heart since day one: panic. It brought me relief to know they all felt panic and fear. That they too went through unspeakable atrocities brought on by troops of relentless beaks and were now cast into a land of vast oceanic opportunity. It was overwhelming to say the least. And of course, like me, they all possessed the burning desire to meet their mothers. We were all in the same boat. But unlike me, they'd always swim on.

Conversations and adventures were few in those eleven years. Misery and loneliness were plenty. The amount of conversations had in that era had to have been fewer than the amount of southern river terrapins left in this world. But each one started with them asking who I was. How could I answer that? I didn't know my family or where I was or how I even came to be. This is where the knowledge of my conception story would really have come in handy. Over the years I'd obtain many names ranging from the ridiculous (Little Buddy) to the complex (Test Subject PH-55). And over the years I'd piece together who exactly I was and discover just where I was meant to be.

Back then, I could only respond with a nervous blurt of the one and only word I was ever told; it's all I had vocally. My name was all I had period. Each time I'd meet a new face who'd inquire about my life and story, I'd simply summon a smile and tell them what I knew.

I'd tell them Akela.

TWO

DRIFTING AIMLESS in the shallow shore presented little danger and even less excitement. Slowly I'd turn left and rotate right, one eye crazily scouting for enemies, the other peering for Mother. Dazed with drooping lids, I could feel the water's warmth building as I reached the surface. My daily mission for air was routine. I'd float about, taking in the vast changes to the harbor as I dwelled on my pitiful, lonely life. Then I'd drift back down to the bottom, planting myself by the beige and purple piece of coral where I'd keep watch for any sign of family.

It was an overly warm summer morning when I popped up for air. The sun still sat halfway along the ground like a fixed ornament. Dawn was lost on me then but it would soon become my absolute favorite. Little was stirring…no gulls, no humans, and no booming axe hacks echoing from coconut tree roots. I took in the silence until Kaimi glided into the water like a bat from hell. His rifled wings flapped, splashing disturbed water into every direction. The thing about Kaimi was he could never sit still and enjoy conversation. And if he had something to tell you—the poor Nene couldn't even land. He'd just circle around you trying to spit out what misconstrued information he had, never touching the ground for a second. That day it appeared he hit the mother lode of rumors.

"Akela. He found something. Pika saw someone. It could…it… follow me!" Kaimi's honking voice did little to rile me up. He was notorious for tall tales, but truthfully, I couldn't blame him. He was used to seeing the world from far above, so his imagination no doubt went sky high with him. Maybe he was just simply seeing the facts wrong, you know, from flying way too far up ahead.

"Slow down, Kaimi," I calmly replied. "What did you see?"

"It's her. She has all the signs. Pika's been talking to her and it… it just makes sense."

"Stay here. I'll get you your sea grass." I remember, as I listed downward to the floor, being yanked up by Kaimi's sharp, little talons until my face hovered above the rippling Ocean.

"Just come on," Kaimi honked as he flapped his way up to the sky. I dangled beneath him with only his claws gripping into my skin. As much as it hurt, it beat the painful thought of impact with solid ground below.

You're probably wondering what I'm doing with this bird anyway. Kaimi was a Nene, a rare yet celebrated goose that, like me, was solitary and full of heartache. The poor thing had an experience as a young gosling where he got tangled up in seaweed when diving for a meal. He narrowly wriggled himself out—the only real saving grace being a crab that graciously clipped him free. Kaimi was never able to face his fears and dive below the water's surface again. Even worse, he loved the taste of fresh seagrass—especially in dark depths where strangely the flavor grew the strongest. An acquired taste, perhaps, but he couldn't get enough of it in his younger days. That was until he refused to get it for himself.

I met Kaimi on one of my early morning air trips when I found him trying to brave the deep blue for his favorite feast. Naturally, I assumed I was under attack and retreated away until I saw the pathetic, skinny flapper drowning in depths that barely touched his toes. I rolled my eyes as I returned to ask the poor fool if he was all right. Kaimi straightened himself up, but he went on this long-winded rant about the dangers of the water and his plight for sweet sea grass. On certain levels, I could relate to him. I had made a friend.

As a wise bargain, I offered to pluck the sea grass and bring it safely to him whenever he asked—just so long as he kept the other birds from plucking me up for snack time. A little tough to regulate, but Kaimi was always good about keeping watch and shooing away pesky gulls. He was almost twice their size, but quite honestly they just didn't have the patience to listen to his long-winded stories. So for the most part, I was left alone by everything winged and hungry.

Yet, where did I find myself that beautiful morning? Hanging by a talon and soaring up to seemingly higher than the sun. I screamed and pleaded for Kaimi to stop.

"Stop! Stop I say—put me down! This is no place for me. We're going to die!"

Kaimi didn't listen and, even worse, for a brief second he let me go. He kicked his feet so that my body tilted right side up and I wasn't just hanging by my legs. Suspended in midair, all time froze when it occurred to me I had slipped and this was the end. I didn't count on claws locking in underneath my shell. He did it so I'd be more comfortable...even possibly so I'd get a better view. My heart most certainly stopped beating, but I suppose the Nene did have a better grip. I was perhaps going to be okay.

I don't know if you've ever flown freely before but I highly recommend you refrain from ever trying. The sheer force of wind needed to cool you down...every part of me was burning up with shock. Your whole body fights itself, arguing whether you're in paradise or on death row. I screamed as loud as I possibly could…to the point where my mouth gaped open and nothing but slime flew out.

But the view…the land always seemed to go on for miles in my mind. It was here I discovered that the land was in fact a group of tiny islands. And I could view them all. The palm trees and sugarcane fields stretched as far as the eye could see—coloring the land with a calming green. A towering mountain smoldered with bubbling lava, stewing deep within its rocky chambers. The water had no end, a theory I always pondered but could now confirm. The hustle and bustle of workers building up huts and forts seemed to overtake everything in sight. It was really too much to take in all at once. My gaping mouth finally formed a trembling smile as Kaimi huffed, puffed, and flapped his wings in a double-time swing.

"You're a lot heavier than I thought," Kaimi blew. I at first took that as a cherished compliment I was bigger than I looked after all. As we rapidly built up speed toward the pointed rocky hills, my mouth shaped itself into closed and panicked silence. Eyes as big as saucers once more, I could feel Kaimi running out of steam as his talons slowly slipped toward the edge.

"Don't let go," I begged.

"I'm trying!" he grunted.

"Don't let go!" I protested.

"Hang on, I got to land."

"Are we going to make it?"

"Me, yes…"

"What do you mean…?" Both of us launched into a fit of screaming as the mountainside boldly stood directly in front. The last thing I remember was Kaimi leaning to the left before my eyes rolled into the back of my head. Everything went white as the wisp of air ceased to stream over my face. Branch after branch whapped and slapped, catching and mangling Kaimi until one completely grabbed hold of his body and pulled the flight to a bitter halt. I slipped from his talons and glided along the prickly stump of a never-ending palm tree until I plopped straight into mud.

I opened my eyes, slowly cocking my head from side to side until I was confident I most certainly wasn't dead…or even paralyzed for that matter. The world was looking fairly upside down to me though—proven when Kaimi gently landed right side up next to my strained neck.

"We're here," he peeped as his feathers slid under my shell and propped me upright onto my flippers. It took me a moment to retrieve my breath, but once regained, I sure let him have it.

"If you ever, ever fly off with me again, I swear our deal will be over and I will see to it you'll never get your lips around a piece of sea grass as long as I live. And I will surely outlive you!"

No matter how much I shook or moved around, the thick mud that covered my body stuck on for good. And then when I stayed stationary, my insides sloshed around like they were caught in a current. Kaimi sheepishly stared at the ground, unable to look me in the eye. He knew he'd never get me to go along with him no matter how hard he begged and pleaded. As I readied myself for another batch of insults, the unfamiliar beach took away every word.

I remember it clear as day; the waves crashing down on jagged rocks, white sand winding its way through lush forest, and Pika in mid-conversation with the biggest shell I had ever seen. Extended from the humped hardback were freckled flippers faded from a long life's journey. I understood completely why Kaimi brought me without fair warning. It was a monumental moment to say the least.

Kaimi perked up as I cast him a warming smile. He gave my rear a gentle nudge to get me going. If the flight had at all made me nervous, this chance meeting could have possibly stopped my heart completely.

I slowly crept along the beach, focusing on Pika deep in conversation. He always had a stalk of sugarcane in his mouth, propped there like a little cigar. Not that he needed the sugar—Pika could scurry across the beach and up a tree before enemies even blinked. Standing on his little hind legs to make himself all the more smooth, Pika was a small Asian mongoose that sort of came with Kaimi as a packaged deal. The little guy could talk himself out of anything and chat your ear off just as bad as Kaimi. That relationship always puzzled me—there was never silence or answers to questions, mostly babble. And I never pried into their situation; Pika did eat birds…just not this particular Nene.

Nonetheless, they were my friends, constantly eager to help me feel like I belonged. I froze up again, racing through all the heartbreaking scenarios of rejection, but Kaimi was right there to push me along. As I dug in the mud, resisting every nudge, I suddenly found myself within a greetings distance. Pika turned to me with an eager, sugarcaned smile on his face.

"There's the man of the minute! Took you long enough. I know you're slow but…" All words followed by the sugarcane stick fell from Pika's mouth once he spun around and got a look at my muddy shell. I hadn't made the decision on whether I was going to be sick or not yet. "What happened to you? Excuse me, Flora."

Pika rushed up and began scraping as much mud off as he could. Licking his fingers and getting my face squeaky clean wasn't my idea of a beauty regimen. After wriggling past him, I cleared my throat and mustered the friendliest, most hopeful smile I could. Trust me—there was a lot of hope going into this encounter.

"Nice to meet you, Flora. My name is Akela."

Pika scuttled away from in between us. The old fossil craned her head up and finally made eye contact with me. She moved slowly but that was excusable—it had seemed she had witnessed everything short of the Industrial Revolution. Scraped and scratched with wrinkly ridges covering every nook, her unimpressed eyes said everything as Pika launched into his sales speech.

"This is him. The pal I was telling you about, Akela. You, what are you, thirteen now? He's been here his whole life, and I just thought you two should meet, you know!"

Even Pika's enthusiasm drained after Flora let out a gargantuan sigh that rivaled a nasty hurricane.

"You kept me waiting for this?"

Words that cut deeper than a butcher knife. How was I to respond to that? "I'm sorry?" I trembled, trying to somehow convince her I was worth the time.

"Look at him; he's one-eighth my size? I could crush him with my left flipper! He couldn't be one of mine." She wouldn't even give me the time of day. Pika perked up, leaning on his sugarcane as he strutted around me like he was showing me off for auction.

"Now wait just a minute. You said you'd been to the beach before…numerous times…and have given birth to countless little cherubs who you'd love to see. You just told me how ecstatic you'd be to meet one. Well here he is, a local boy, and now you disown him because he's small?"

"Pika, it's okay…I'm used to it." Yes, I actually said I'm used to it but the truth was I never would be. Every knock against my size rattled me to my core, sending deep debates through my body on existence and whether life was indeed worth it. Today of all days, the inner battle raged worse than ever. "If you just hear me out, I'm sure we can get to know one another. I was born in the harbor on the other side of the island. I remember everything like it was yesterday!"

"But you haven't grown. All Greens grow!"

"Well, I didn't! I am the way I am. Can't you accept me for it?"

Again, another hurricane-worthy sigh blasted from her mouth. "There is no bond. I feel no bond, therefore, you cannot be one of mine."

"Love can grow."

"Yes," she said, sighing. "But it first must be found, and you know when you find it. You do anything for it. It means never wanting to be apart."

The great behemoth shell rose up. Creakily and weakly, she began her great crawl into the Ocean—leaving the three of us to do nothing but eat sand. Everything inside me protested that she had to have been wrong. I wanted to follow but couldn't even summon the strength to move one step. I felt Kaimi land beside me, placing a wing on my back for support. No amount of full body petting could get me to forget that day though. The old bag could have just kept on swimming too, but instead, she had to turn around. She had to speak.

"Do you know what your weakness is? You think too small and spend your days searching for Mama. I bet you have never even been off this island? Where's your call for adventure? Where's your passion? Get out there and get living. Find whatever it is that'll make you stop moping around this rock. It's a beautiful place but there's more than just one type of beauty. Get out there and grow!"

"I can't go far," I said, sighing. "It's too dangerous for me."

The wrinkly shell shook in disappointment as Flora launched herself toward submersion. Her final words, "That right there is your biggest mistake," slurped through the water as it swallowed her up until she was gone.

Silence. For once, Kaimi and Pika said absolutely nothing—an unnerving feeling I will admit. But you know something? This Flora was right about a great deal of things.

For years now, the coral I told you about—all the unimaginable colors covering the Ocean floor? It had become gray to me. The sprawling lush forests, even the ones I'd see from high above that day, were already a gray memory. New colors would come with new seasons, but in the end, any reminder of my lonely, solitary days turned my surroundings into pale nothingness. Sure, I had my well-meaning friends, but their attempts to reunite me with my mother were growing thin. There was a time where they made me hike along ten miles of beach just to meet a rock they mistook for my kind. Then there was the day when they introduced me to three males who did not take kindly to the fact they were mistaken for mothers. These soul crushing adventures went on and on—I just couldn't take it anymore.

Flora's words claiming how love is found and how you'd do anything for it spun on repeat in my head. I think Kaimi and Pika could see it vibrating from my lips. I knew love was out there, far out there for me to find. What was life without a mother's love? I'd know it when I'd see it, and I could no longer wait for that love to find me. I had to bring color to my world once again. I had to go on an adventure! I had to have a purpose! I had to swim.

"Where are you going? Akela?" Pika tried to stand in front of me but I blew past him, giving no acknowledgment to his presence. Kaimi took to the air and hovered above.

"We're so sorry. She seemed like the one. It just all lined up."

I didn't stop. I hit the water and didn't even stop there. I swam straight ahead, following the same path Flora had paved.

"Come back!" Pika screamed as he turned to Kaimi. "Look what you did! If only you'd have come quicker, she'd have had more patience to talk to him!"

"What are you talking about? I flew him all the way here. If you wouldn't have yapped nonstop—"

"Oh, I'm the one who talks? You should take a good look at yourself, beak flapper."

"Takes one to know one."

That's all I heard. I'm pretty certain that fight lasted until sundown. They probably didn't even notice I had actually braved the depths. Folks, it took some doing, but on that day I hit open Ocean for the first time. Beyond the leaky, little line of rusted fishing boats. Beyond the great drop-off where the busy Ocean floor descended into darkness.

Darkness. Everywhere.

It was all I could see. Nothing ahead and nothing behind, I couldn't tell which direction went where. The waves crashed, creating dastardly undertow that flipped me from side to side. Still, I had to swim on. I had to get away. I had to search for Mother. I had to see the world. But the eyes…unimaginable fangs gnashed as the monster unfurled itself, slinking its way through the water…grazing my shell. Up ahead was a bullish great white, swaying back and forth on a hunt for prey that had no prayer. There was nowhere to go.

I tried, oh I tried to keep paddling, but I felt it graze me again. I felt the eyes of the great white lock me in its sights. Darkness surrounded me until I had no choice but to go back. But I couldn't find where back was. I circled and circled and circled. Up and down until the undertow grabbed me toes first. Like a rag doll, I was cast in a winding maze that threw me from side to side. I couldn't breathe and I most certainly couldn't see. There was nothing to grab onto—the coral was too far out of reach. I went along for what seemed like an entire life plus borrowed time until I was cast into a sandy pit just offshore.

Once again, I carefully checked myself over, amazed there was no signs of paralysis to be found. As I spit out water and sand, I shakily headed for a different destination. Though technically I was new in a place I had never been, I had done all I could to turn back. Lost and beaten and still without family, the worst of it was what echoed inside my own mind. I had turned back, purposeless and devoid of love. I had failed.

THREE

TRUDGING THROUGH wet sand and mud as the rain teemed down made me feel like a newborn all over again. I had no sense of balance, sliding every which way. The only difference was that there was nobody by my side; not any family and no enemies carrying out an attack.

From a distance, I could hear the nonstop *ting ting ting* of a hammer hitting metal. A melody of footsteps splashing past muddy puddles and clip-clopping on freshly laid wooden decks teased my ears. I was still worried about what would leap from the waters behind me. Where had that slippery monster gone?

As I dragged my heavy, disappointed body along the shore, I wondered if Kaimi and Pika were out searching. I actually believed they threw a party to celebrate the fact they were finally rid of my draining presence. I wondered how far Flora has made it out already; how come a great white had never launched an attack on her? What persevered through my mess of thoughts was the wonder if I'd ever make it off these islands. And if not, would I ever earn respect from anyone? I didn't know what I wanted anymore. And that's when we feel the most lost in life, don't we? When all goals seem useless and we have no idea which direction we should head.

Perfectly presented leather boots thankfully planted themselves deeply in the thick mud before me. As I slowly gazed up, a curious mustached smile gazed down. A man peered over the rim of his glasses, hands firmly on his hips. Curiosity got the better of him as he stretched out his eager feelers to get himself a good grab. Humans always want to grab and touch. But it makes sense. Connection!

The mustached man lifted me high above the brim of his hat, holding me steadily in the sky where rain drops could finally push away the mud. What they couldn't get, the man's fingers could dust off. There was no hesitancy—for those seconds his determination was to get me clean. What followed was the most puzzled and fascinated stare I have ever encountered. I could tell by those eyes I wasn't going to be put back down anytime soon.

He clutched me tight against the stomach of his suit jacket, trying his best to shelter me from the storm. As he trudged along, the world bounced up and down and I knew not where we were headed. The man then stuffed me under his arm, using the other to pull open a tent door. The rain stopped and only candlelight flickered, illuminating desks filled with papers and quills and maps and drawings. This would be my first endeavor indoors.

As I sprawled comfortably by flickering flame, the mustached man continued his gaze, which I have to say felt even warmer than the fire. There was something honest about him; his curious face barely faltered as he scribbled down notes—presumably what he made of me.

"Are you doing okay little fellow? Are you happy?"

This is where a feeble, young Lieutenant marched in, gulped, and desperately searched for the right words. "Mr. President," he whispered. No answer, the mustached man just could not tear himself away from me. "Mr. President, you are needed out in the shipyards."

"Look at this; I've never seen anything like it. His species is evidently Green, but his size…he does not possess characteristics of infancy. And look at this particularly odd marking on his back…"

The Lieutenant nodded, briefly looking at me but keeping his twitching attention on Mr. President. "Yes, well, we need…" The Lieutenant couldn't finish; Mr. President kept penning as he chatted.

"Amazing, isn't it? Simply fascinating. We just don't get them like this back home."

"Quite right and perhaps they could be a wonderful part of American childhoods someday…" The poor Lieutenant just couldn't get a word in edgewise. I personally think if he would have spoken a bit faster and a bit more direct…then again when the mustached Mr. President was focused, there was no breaking his concentration.

"You know, I had my own taxidermy business as a child. Oh what I would have done to capture a creature of this size. We only had small snappers back in New York." Finally, the obsessive man caught on after the Lieutenant cleared his throat and gestured to the door. "Oh, yes, right. You needed me."

He stood back up, straightening himself out and placing his thick-brimmed hat over his head along the way. As he prepared to exit the tent, he stopped himself and peered over at me with one more irresistible little smile. With a sigh, he happily marched out with me at his side.

We spent the next few hours touring around the complex, a wonder to behold. Marching men saluting in packs would troll up and down the freshly laid walkway. The inlet was to be expanded with channels running through and weaving the water inland. We, or I suppose I should just say him because I was only along for the ride, would glance at plans and point to where men were eagerly sent over to hammer and dig away. I don't know how these men did it—even through muggy rain and thick, heavy air weighing down, they chiseled and chipped and drove their diggers through the dirt. Most of them were soaked from the Ocean splashes already—the presence of rain certainly didn't speed progress up.

The mustached President oversaw everything, but his favorite view had to have been the seaside at low tide. He'd bring me with him, setting me aside as he dug around and inspected small crabs and anemones. The man generally seemed glad to be there, carefully bush-whacking and stopping to observe every plant. When he wasn't busy acting like a visitor, he dove right into manual labor and lifted a shovel himself.

There was this one afternoon I spent sprawled out with the mus-tached Mr. President and a profound sight suddenly penetrated my view. From ashore I could make out a speckled shell bobbing through the water. It was not uncommon for my kind to tread up and down the coast, but this particular passerby couldn't take their eyes off me. I could make out various splotches on their shell that seemed to form a crescent moon. As I stood, focused on the image, their eyes remained focused on me. Intense and fiery, they seemed annoyed by my pres-ence. By the time we locked eyes, they shifted and turned away.

As you can probably guess, my suspicions on who this might have been ran high. Before I could get a running start, the mustached Mr. President grabbed me and proceeded uphill. I squirmed and fought but the battle was mine to lose. I would forever be haunted by the pass-erby's gaze. But I swore to myself that day I wouldn't invest hope and energy on finding my creator ever again. My heart was just too fragile to keep that up.

Whilst in his hands, I could not help but notice a beautiful golden band around his finger. The band itself was pure gold but the glass oval was memorizing as a strand of black hair safely resided inside it. I pon-dered why on earth this was a fashion sported by such a proper fellow, but the more I studied it, the more I fell in love with its beauty. At night he'd take the ring off and place it on his bedside table where I'd drift off to sleep, staring at the glass and the light that danced within. He knew I marveled at it; it brought him joy that staring at the captured light in this thing brought me some too.

I spent a total of three days with the man, getting fed the finest greens and sleeping under a tent where it was dry and warm. Full body pets soothed me before and after every sleep. When it came time for the mustached President to leave, he had me tucked under his arm, ready to take me back home with him as he marched down the dock to his boat. After giving me a mournful gaze, I realized he knew I wouldn't fare well wherever he was going. I was meant to be outdoors and live my life by the waters.

He clip-clopped all the way down the deck and even went the extra mile, hiking through weeds and bushes still untouched by his workers. In a sandy, lonesome beach, he gently set me beside the Ocean. He was always careful to take me in and out of the water—somehow he always seemed to know when I needed to swim.

With a nod and a tip of his hat, he disappeared through the long willows as I watched and sprawled out under the newfound sun. Before he left, he placed the encased hair ring beside him as a parting gift before leaving for good. Among the things I remember from that day, the rain had stopped and droplets fell from sharply colored flowers. I will never forget that mustached President and how grateful I am for the time we spent together; I'm just sad to say I never got his real name.

While those few days were all well and good, they paled in comparison to what was to come. It was lovely to be admired and appreciated and needed and written about. I had felt a connection, an honest and true connection with a human who saw past my size. Was he a brief substitute for a mother? No, but I kept saying to myself it was a much needed, calming vacation. I had forgotten all about Flora and my failure to launch.

Now, I had no idea where he had put me. With flowers and rain-drops and lush vegetation lining every direction, I took a deep, refreshing breath before I inched forward toward the water. I had no idea where I was headed, either, but I figured I had nowhere to go but forward. I took the gifted ring in my mouth but had nowhere to store it on me, so I buried it deep within the sand for safe keeping. Whenever I wanted to unearth old memories, I could just simply do so with the retrieval of the lovely token.

I think we can all agree moments are not planned and sometimes we find ourselves in some that have seemingly no meaning. Others may define the rest of our lives. It's this mixture, a balance of the two, that creates a sustainable, memorable journey. The best moments are the ones that come as a surprise. I was placed on a beach at around eight o'clock in the a.m.—the sun had risen recently. If I hadn't been placed in that exact spot and in that exact moment, my life would not have remotely been the same. If I had just kept going into the water, minding my own business, nothing would have turned out as it did. But I was listening that day and what I heard was the voice of an angel. For once, I believed I understood the meaning of the word destiny.

"It's a shame," she claimed, "what they're doing to our land."

I froze. It hit me—those words were said in a tone of pure sugar and pleasure and bliss. I turned to see her, the most beautiful being I would ever lay eyes on. She was awe-inspiring. She was stunning. She was…my size! I had actually met someone my size! I didn't have a reply. I gulped and nodded.

"Who was that man you were with? You got an owner?"

I shook my head—words did not seem at all possible. "Just… you know…yeah." She squinted her eyes, trying to get a read on me. I searched for something to say. Anything! I refused to look like a fool.

"Well, tell him to stop poisoning our land."

I nodded, assuring her I'd relay the message. The mustached President seemed so kind and caring—I was shocked to learn he was hated in my community. Though I disagreed, I was sure to side with her. As she badgered for opinions on the matter, I shouted out, "Do you come here often?" so I could remain in comfortable, formal territory.

"I was born here. Come back this time every year. Today's my birthday, you know?"

"Well, Happy Birthday! That's…wow! How old?"

"Don't you know it's rude to ask a lady her age?"

I couldn't breathe.

"I'm old enough to see a plethora of changes on this beach, that's for sure. But I love it. I suppose I'll always come back."

I seriously couldn't breathe. I was certain I'd faint. I was unsure what plethora meant. Therefore, no response was given—I needed to conserve air. I also needed to apologize for the age question if I wanted her approval. But was she really being serious? Was she actually offended? I couldn't tell but she was smiling so I took that as a good sign. I smiled in return which caused her to stop. I think it was because I was breathing so hard. It felt like no one had said anything for all of eternity. Yet, I was comfortable. Actually, no, that's a lie—I wanted to ask her every single question that popped into my head. I wanted to know her. I wanted to hear her laugh—nay, make her laugh. And how come I couldn't remember my own birthday? It was a very complicated mess of emotions.

"Well, nice meeting you."

I missed my chance. All I could squeak out was a "you too" and "bye." I froze, watching her descend into the depths, memorizing every detail of the view until she was completely submerged and gone from my life. I couldn't move…I couldn't go after her. I was paralyzed with thoughts and fantasies. My head was spinning.

All I could do was look around at the land she held so dear. I can tell you the world was in color once again, and the view was one I never thought possible. Every ounce of unhappiness left me as I took a breath and exhaled.

My life had officially begun.

FOUR

"YOU DON'T even know her name," Kaimi squawked.

"I know that," I said ever so calmly.

"Why, you don't even know the date!"

"I know that as well."

"You're never going to find her."

I cocked my head and looked over at Pika, pacing back and forth—devouring a sugarcane stalk with every step. "I think it could work," he chimed sweetly.

"Don't encourage him—he's obviously delusional after this little trip of his!"

"Come on, Kaimi." I glared at him, trying to muster all the honesty and faith I could. There was absolutely no way I was going to let her disappear from my life. "I have never met anyone like her. This is big for me and I could use your help."

Kaimi flapped his wings and ruffled his feathers as Pika rolled his eyes and polished off his sugary treat.

"Whatever you need kid, I'm available. Romance is highly underrated. It's the very most important of things," Pika proclaimed, paw in the air.

"Like you would know," Kaimi jabbed. This prompted a glare of the highest degree. I interjected, ready to dish out a plan—I had just under a year now, but I didn't want to waste any time.

"This was two days ago, so all we got to do is find out today's date; easy as that!"

Kaimi flapped up into a low hanging branch just above—still on the fence about the whole operation. "And that's another thing—what business of hers is the time and date? That's human stuff!"

"She's cultured!"

"She's something all right. Akela, we…I don't want you to get hurt. What if she never comes back? What if she comes back with eggs to lie? What if—?"

I cut him off before one more syllable could squawk past his beak. "Because there's the what if she's my mate. Someone I can share my life with…you know, of my own kind! I have nothing without love. If I cannot find my own family to love, perhaps starting one is what I need to do. What if that could happen with her? I have to find out…I have to try!"

I saw in his face a glimmer of understanding. It was a long shot but a goal nonetheless. I believe he saw it would make me happy— even just to try…to move forward other than waiting for life to pass and family to find me.

"So, how are we going to find the date?" he said, sighing.

This part of the plan was a little more harebrained than I had anticipated. After a misinformed belief that pocket watches contained the date, I sent Kaimi to fetch one off an unsuspecting human.

The poor nobleman removed it from his pocket just as Kaimi's talons wrapped around the chain. The startled man had it clipped so tightly to himself that Kaimi got yanked backwards after setting off on a powerful flight away from the scene of the crime. The man became so frightened that his jabs and waves at Kaimi were not working that he unclipped the chain and ran off in horror. Pika opened the piece up to discover markings no one could make heads or tails of. We couldn't read English, and there was no evidence of what day we were in.

On Pika's daily waste rummaging, he came across a soggy old paper with details of the previous day's events—it had been mostly destroyed by the morning rain. While we crowded around the mulched mess, none of us could make heads or tails of the date on this either. We even eavesdropped on humans for days, but with the little English we knew—the date and time seemingly never came up. I was left with one option—permanently stake a claim on the land my girl loved. I would move from my comforting birthplace on the bay and set up shop where I knew she'd return.

It wasn't an easy decision but it really was the only answer that would lead me once again to her. I had waited for Mother long enough in the gray bay—now I could wait for the definition of beautiful to return to me outside of the mustached President's opus.

That day Kaimi offered to fly me there, but I refused to be flung up into the air like some sort of awkward passenger. He instead took my description down, flew across the island, and returned with a detailed report on how to reach our goal. I had arrived to my side of the bay by hoofing it through jungle and staying stagnant in quiet puddles of murky sludge. I only found my way after finding Pika on a routine gathering mission. He spotted me way up from atop a tree. The little bugger jumped down and scared the daylights out of my whole body because I mistook his enthusiasm for a devouring ritual.

When I got to the bay for the second time, I noticed the sun lit up the beach brighter than any spot I had visited before. Perhaps there were fewer trees blocking its path. Perhaps the water seemed all the more clear from a scenic vantage point. It was home for me now, and it would remain so until the end of my days.

For the remainder of that year, I watched the sun rise and practiced the line I would say to her when she arrived. "I've been waiting for you. I forgot the definition of beauty and needed a reminder." After a lengthy day's practice, I'd go digging for the mustached President's ring but never found it to any sort of avail. I thought presenting my mate-to-be with it would have been a nice touch. I came to the conclusion some heartless bastard stole it.

To make matters worse, I flubbed the line completely when a Leatherback emerged quicker than speed itself. He grumpily looked at me before trudging off into the bushes; imagine my horror. I was too jumpy to focus—any sign of life snatched my interest and a heart attack would nearly ensue each day. Still, I never gave up hope—there was no doubt in my mind she'd return. I would know exactly who she was once she emerged upon the sand—I'd never forget her face. And while some fine shells crawled across the beach, they never once eclipsed my sweet one and only.

"Nice weather, isn't it?" her soothing voice sang one year later. I knew it was her the moment the words left her lips. When I turned, I was aghast to discover her shell had grown bigger. Her whole body had widened in size and she had now reached her destined dimension. I must have met her in her infancy, and now she could crush me if she wanted to. Still—this only made my feelings for her grow. In my view, there was simply more of her to love. The little voice inside me claimed she'd never love me now; not with that gaping difference. But I shoved my doubt far away, spitting confused, eager words back into her direction.

"Happy Birthday!" I exclaimed ecstatically.

"Well, how'd you know that? Have we met?"

"Last year," I remarked with a hopeful smile. She looked me up and down with a confused grin. I could see it all coming back to her.

"Oh yeah…well, good to see you!"

With that short utterance, she trudged into the bushes like all the others. I didn't follow, but still I was hooked. She remembered me, and what was even better, she felt it was good to see me once again! Good! Emphasis on the good! I was on cloud nine, in a daze that left me reeling with shivers. Pika scuttled over and put his arm around me while Kaimi flapped down to my left. They were afraid to speak, but I shattered the silence with a smile.

"That will keep me going until next year," I said. "I have a lot of planning to do."

FIVE

"NICE WEATHER we're having. You came at the perfect time!" I exclaimed as she popped up on the shore one year later. As she opened her eyes and found her bearings, the first view in her paradise would be me. She smiled nervously.

"Well hello there. I didn't know you liked this place so much."

"Like it? I love it. In fact, this is where I call home."

Her mouth dropped. "You get to live here? Lucky!"

My heart pounded as my mouth sealed shut from a form of spit that had the consistency of sticky syrup. Everything inside told me to stop speaking, except a tiny, fighting flicker in my heart. I broke free and opened my mouth. "Well why don't you? Where do you live?"

"The mainland. It's nice but this...this is paradise."

And with that, she made her way into the bushes—disappearing once again. "Happy Birthday," I called out, and a sweet thank you followed.

SIX

"WHAT DO you have planned this time around?"

She thought for a second and let out an honest giggle. "Nothing really. Same as every year—just relax. Take it easy by the water. Eat a few specialties."

"Like what?"

"Well, anything sweet is my favorite. I'm a sucker for sweet. But a nice, juicy snail can really brighten the day." I gagged and turned greener than I already was. "What? You've never eaten a snail?" I shook my head in nervous despair—doubting that I should have told the truth. A flood full of lies spread through my head until the greatest words I've ever heard silenced any trace of negative thought. "Well come on! I'm sure I can find you one!"

I threw up.

Not at that moment but after—when the slime of the poor, little snail touched my lips. I hadn't thought of it much but I had been a vegetarian up until that point. Meat just never appealed to me, which was perhaps a contributing factor to my size. Although upon that realization, I began to devour meat and never gained a pound. I think my disdain for it began during my tragic birthing battle anyway—it all had to be psychological.

No, I just couldn't choke down that poor, little critter. His remnants and every other meal that week came flooding back up. My lovely lady watched me in disgust before turning to laughter. I was ashamed, determined to crawl into a dark Ocean hole and die, but she led me back to the water to wash out the taste. She was nice enough to claim that snails weren't for everybody, kindly leaving me after I became stable.

What followed, I can tell you, were some very uncertain and unnerving months of waiting.

SEVEN

A LOT of you are probably shaking your head as you read this; judging me for my foolish heart. For giving up the youthful years of my life and waiting for just a few minutes with the opposite sex. Well, then I'd simply argue with you that you have not yet found your other half. That one being that makes the sun shine brighter and brings all time to a standstill. Every moment without her was a build up to her arrival, and every moment after was peaceful reflection; joyous thankfulness that she was actually in my life.

I truly hope you get to find that figure, I really do. It's a hard, long journey, and many times it feels as though the desired pairing of you and them will not work out. Don't give up hope—I never did, but luckily, I never had to.

I'll never forget the look on her face when she washed up on shore to a pile of dead snails. She shook her head and ate them quickly so I wouldn't have to smell them for long. How gracious! That day we laughed and discussed the evolution of the beach and what she had seen on the "mainland." I wasn't certain what she was talking about, quite frankly, but I listened with intrigue—hanging on every word.

We even ventured to the top bluffs that surrounded my little homestead. The docks were in plain view, with steamships zipping to and fro. Busy men in uniform hustled every which way—some with weapons in hand and some with a hand to their head. And still, the noise increased as they worked—expanding and expanding. They worked their way inland and out at the same time. I complained how these boats honked their horns at the earliest of hours, keeping me up or jolting me awake when it was too early. They never heard me, but at least that day, someone listened!

My comfort with her was growing, and I'm certain she felt it too! Every year she came, the longer our talks would get. We'd stand closer to each other and walk further away from the bay. When she laughed at something I said or did…well, my body felt like it had curled around a warm beach fire again. There was no better comfort than to hear my darling guffaw.

Then one year…one year, I summed up the courage to ask her for her name. She grinned and sighed and squirmed and nodded. I was sure to tell her mine. She remarked how cute Akela was. Taking a deep breath, she looked me right in the eye and with a smile formed the word, "Kalea."

As she disappeared that night into the still, silent water, I found myself repeating Kalea over and over again until my mouth was sore. The magic never seemed to fall away from that name. For the whole year, I drove Kaimi and Pika insane by saying this one word every single day until her return. Internally, it's all my mind would say, period.

As I laid upon the fine sand, watching the tide creep closer and closer to my body, the familiar sound of Kalea's laughter broke my concentration. Did warm internal fires and long sunset walks ensue? No! When I looked up, I did not see Kalea at first—but a strong, masculine suitor her size. I felt confused as my heart shredded itself into oblivion. Kalea swiftly followed, keeping her loving gaze fixated on the mystery friend. They frolicked along, waltzing past me without the slightest hint of acknowledgement. She showed him our beach, my home…taking pride in every attraction I had personally showcased to her. They headed straight for the harbor where he vowed to catch her the juiciest of snails.

EIGHT

MY HEAD was buried deep in the sand for the oncoming months. Both Kaimi and Pika had families now, so my access to social conversation had diminished more and more. I was happy for them—Kaimi seemingly faced his fear of water to appease his lovely children. He wanted them to grow up on the sweetest of sea grasses—never any substitutes.

Pika was a little different. He had the damndest time staying loyal. The silly mongoose had mistresses stashed all over the island—I always felt sugar gave him too much energy, making him restless and unsatisfied. On the plus side, the amount of loving children Pika had was uncountable. I think I only met about a quarter of them…but then again, so did he.

I was back to square one, seeking happiness in a world of lonely gray. Besides plotting out the outrageous murder of Kalea's new beau, I…well, honestly, that's all I really thought about after seeing them. That, and how much I desperately loved her and needed her in my life. I had been camping out at this bay for longer than I had lived in my undersea nook. Little by little, I was getting to know the details of her life and who she really was. I wanted more and I realized that I had to act fast. A few minutes every year just wasn't going to cut it, so I was determined to do something big…something noble that showed my love. The remainder of the year was time for sketching out ideas in the sand for this culminating climax.

After a walk up the hill to take in the behemoth construction site and yell at the boat horns to keep it down, I saw a few steamers departing on manly missions to haul sugar sacks all over the world. A sweet memory dawned on me as I took in the sweaty workers loading these heavy bags onto the deck. The goal was clear and the time was near—I needed my old friends for one last mission to once and for all win over my darling Kalea.

A calm Kaimi stood with his feet in the tide as Pika failed to stay awake. The poor critter had given up sugar at this point after reaching a near overdose on the stuff. Again, I don't blame him…so much offspring! But the important fact was they were there and willing to help. We weren't sure of the day she'd arrive but I could feel it was near. I'd have to count on Kaimi to do a few rounds each morning to scout the choppy, offshore waters for our coveted guest. Thankfully, he got his kids in on the deal—training them to circle at different times.

Pika had a bit of a different job—one a little more physical that required the sharpest of teeth. He took care of them so I had the utmost faith that he'd succeed. As for me—I was Pika's ride. When we got the go ahead, I'd sail Pika out to the passing boats destined for the open Ocean. He couldn't swim so our skill sets worked out perfectly.

Imagine my panic when Kalea and her friend washed up on shore without a warning from Kaimi or his kids. They had given a few false alarms before that I don't blame them for. I tried in the most unpoetic of terms to describe her to them, but they never did truly understand that message.

Instead, my fears were realized when I saw Kalea and her suitor still together—and worse—visibly happy. I had to ask myself, could

I truly attempt to break up this relationship? Was I that hell-bent on keeping her for myself that I couldn't sit back and do what was right? Let her be happy and choose what she wanted for herself?

I came to terms with all this until I heard him speak to her from behind a palm tree later that night. His interests were put first as he pressured her for intimacy, and after, he wanted to be alone so he could reflect and enjoy the beach in peace. He didn't want her around—he was using her for a vacation. I heard her tone of voice—it was compliant and unhappy. The passion I knew in her voice had gone away, hidden past her heart and somewhere deep in the pit of her stomach. As luck would have it, Castle and Cooke had a shipment due out at the crack of dawn that very next morning. I turned to Pika that night with an eager grin on my face that radiated readiness.

"All systems go," I assured him. Pika nodded and gripped my shell with all his might.

I swam as quickly as I could, huffing and puffing as Pika sat upon me like he was the commander of a tiny raft. I could see the steamer in the distance, building up speed as it prepared to leave the bay. As we came closer and closer, it seemed the boat got further and further from us—we couldn't compete. And as I paddled my hardest, pitch blackness flooded my eyes. The beast I had once skirmished with darted across the far corners of my vision. I knew it couldn't have been real, but the strengthening current through the demonic waves very much were.

Though I was in good company, I panicked and gasped and floundered and shook, tossing Pika into the rocky waves. As he bobbed along, I tried to go forth but fear overtook me. With his calm and steady paw, Pika stroked my face and told me to go to shore—he'd take care of it. So off he swam.

Kaimi, bless his heart, led his family straight for the Captain, dive bombing him and the crew until his hands left the steering wheel.

Unfortunately, they went from the wheel to the trigger of a shotgun. Looking back now, I feel guilty for letting him risk his life this way—but luckily this man was a terrible shot.

With the boat listing in the water while the crew batted away talons and beaks (again, I couldn't help but think of my birth here. Birds are terrifying!), Pika was able to scurry up the rope and reach the pile of sugar sacks in mere seconds. I helplessly bobbed in the shallows, watching on and wanting so desperately to be a part of the event.

The brave little soul gnawed and clawed until that white gold spewed from its jail, across the deck and off the edge. I could see the water glistening with the sticky, sweet substance. Pika seemed to enter into a primitive frenzy, biting his way through stacks of these sacks. I couldn't view much of the action—I could only feel the flow of sweetness flood the water around me. And I could only hear squawks and cuss words thrown out between Kaimi and the angry crew.

Without hesitation, Pika took a giant leap off the side after he had done all he could do. After a few laps back toward land, I was able to pick him up right away and get him back to safety atop my shell. I tell you, he shook like an earthquake was bouncing him around. I had to fight the little fool from leaping off to suck in all the sweet water he could. When I saw Kaimi lead his family away, I knew the mission was successfully completed. The boat chugged along back to shore as did my incredible team. With every wave, the sugary tide made its way to the beach where I knew she'd be to find it.

As I reached the shore, Pika leapt off and darted for the forest where he could hide from embarrassment till his fur was dry. I hovered, watching a lonely Kalea stare at the water like I so often did. I must say, it was beautiful—watching the tide creep closer and closer to her mouth. I giggled when a strong wave finally smacked her right in the face. She was startled at first, but could quickly taste the surprise on her lips.

As she lurched forward, slurping and rolling in my sugary creation, she looked up to see me watching from afar. All she could do was smile. In fact…that's all both of us were capable of doing.

"You're a sucker for sweet," I said calmly as I let the tide carry me over. Now face to face, she turned to look at the beach one more time. Kalea seemingly searched for her old life, scanning for any reason to go back. Thankfully—nothing was found. She smiled too, swimming forth until our heads touched.

"What now?" she wondered softly.

Frankly, I hadn't thought that far ahead.

NINE

SOME EVENINGS later, the beach was lit only by shining moonlight and adjacent twinkling stars. Lining the sand were rows of plumeria flowers and carnations…I'd notice sometime later that humans seemed fascinated with them too, often wearing strands around their neck. I can see why—the colors are vibrant and happy. You just can't be upset when you're facing a carnation. Thanks to Kaimi, my "best man," the beach was colored with them. I'll never forget that sweet smell.

Now, our wedding traditions are quite different than a human ceremony. We don't sign anything and there's no binding legalities stamped and sealed by some appointed official. We just stand in front of each other and agree to never have another mate as long as we live. To never migrate without consulting each other first. To share food and space equally without competition or quarrel.

Kalea emerged from the bushes, looking more beautiful than I ever thought possible as she waddled along the carnation pathway. Her shell was waxed, casting a glare from the moonlight that seemingly added an additional layer of radiant beauty. Our eyes were locked on each other and would never have to settle for a gray and lonely view any longer. We had barely known each other, but after Kalea decided to stay in the bay with me all we could do was talk about life.

Again, I led a wide search for that damn ring, thinking this was the most opportune moment to give it to her, but I couldn't find it for the life of me. The only gift I could offer instead was myself. So I told her about my birthing experience and living under the Ocean in a fearful hole. I told her about the mustached President and how I got washed over to him in a frantic ploy to journey far away.

I learned about her experiences on the mainland…humans everywhere! She described the roar of motor vehicles speeding down roadways, instantaneously smushing anything that dared to cross its path. She told me of food she had eaten and friends she had made on her journeys back and forth through the open Ocean.

I asked her many times if she was frightened, to which she always—surprisingly—admitted yes. But that was what made the experience so grand—the higher the risk, the greater the reward. She often so lovingly referred to me as her reward, while she frequently labeled our relationship as destiny. It was meant to be that our paths would cross on that beach. While I did not know the forces that made it all so for us, I agreed.

There was just this connection I hadn't felt with anyone before. I could often feel myself on the verge of blurting out how proud I was for sticking out those lonely years and winning the love of my life over through subtle conversation and a sugary mess. But I didn't. I would instead just smile and rub my face with hers. We were rarely far from each other now—often snuggled up as close as one could get to another. It's where I wanted to be most in the world. It's where I felt comfortable.

Our ceremony was beautiful. Kaimi and Pika and their families came out to witness the event. They stood next to us…I could never thank them all enough for what they did to bring us together. I'm glad they were there. Kalea invited a few friends she knew who just happened to be passing through around that time. I didn't know them but the more the merrier I suppose. They didn't seem to be there in support of us though—mostly to have an excuse to shout and celebrate. Nonetheless we said our lines, agreeing to share and to love and to be together until the end of our days. Pika shot straight up in the air and cheered like a wild nut when it was all said and done. Kaimi led his family in an under-rehearsed song.

We agreed to remain on the same beach; it was too important to leave now. And while we were certain the mustached President's project would overtake us one day, we would fight until the bitter end. Our land was sacred to us as if it were the hallowed stage where our lives were to play out.

Our friends departed, but the moon glowed like a spotlight, searching out lovers to shine its approval upon. I wanted the whole world to see us. These are the days when you feel like you are the protagonist in the world's plot. May you get to experience, at the very least, one of those days. I find there's an important balance though; too few and you feel forgotten, too many and people want to forget you. I would never forget that night.

In the oncoming years, we'd frolic through the wet sand—moonlight aglow as our radiant smiles pressed against each other. Fire dancers in grass skirts waved around in a hypnotic pattern while gentle strums made beautiful music. The sound of the waves crashing down provided the perfect accompaniment.

Kalea and I made the point of coming to this celebration every chance we got. As they feasted on swine and covered themselves with frightening but astonishing color, we couldn't help but feel in love. There was something about the music and people that surrounded us—they even saw us join their celebration but happily let us be. Some actually scooped up a few bites of their meals and generously flung it our way.

Days were fueled with tiki and drums and spacious, bright skies. We walked and talked, pondering life and the fantastic odds that we found each other. If time could have frozen that moment precisely, I could have been happy forever. But my friends, this is not the way it can be. It has been decided there must be an up and down for everyone. Kalea and I were too busy snuggling and talking to notice. Regretfully, marital strife happens to the best of us—despite days of music, fire, and spoon-fed poi that will seemingly never end. I'm sorry it's not better news; I truly am.

TEN

LIFE CHANGES—that's one notion I am positive we can all agree upon. And it changes for the better or for the worse, no matter whom you are or what it is you are anticipating. The fact is, we get older and sometimes we get sick. This was true for Kaimi, whose life span was significantly less than mine. And though I had met him while he was at a fairly young stage, no matter what time you have with a friend it's never enough.

I did not want anyone to gobble up his body for an easy meal. We spent the entire day digging a hole in a secluded, shady spot. While mine and Kalea's life together had just begun, Kaimi's time had ended. This was exactly what was said in our condolences when we placed his body inside the hole. I would miss him always, but the memories of our flight and his infectious generosity would forever remain. I was grateful to have those memories for the rest of my days.

In that period of my life, death was sad but expected. It was commonplace in the animal kingdom, and as troubling as it was, you were typically destined to be food. Though—as you know—I rejected feeding on flesh, I had not yet given a single thought to what came after your life was over and all that remained of you was excrement. I assure you that changed me!

Sadly, Pika and I drifted apart—a family first mentality has a way of phasing out friendships. While we did our best to keep in touch, it was a big landmass to cover and an even bigger family for him to care for.

Again, a friendship always remains alive as long as memories are preserved. No friendship is ever unnecessary; that's one philosophy I've learned in my life. Each one gets us through to wherever our next chapter of life is set to begin. And we become slightly richer or slightly wiser by having experienced that friendship in our life. It was to Kaimi and Pika that I owed my very relationship with Kalea in the first place.

Even today, I still miss them all dearly.

ELEVEN

AS YOU might have guessed, size difference was in fact an issue. Though Kalea was gracious enough to never bring up the subject, we did encounter some battles, especially when it came to having children. Without getting into too much graphic detail, we were simply incompatible. Having children was not in the cards no matter how much we tried.

This was a shattering blow to both of us, especially Kalea. She had dreamed of the day that her children would emerge from the sand and stumble toward her at the edge of the bay. She'd be waiting for them and she'd make sure nothing ever happened to each one on their journey. I so desperately wanted to be there beside her, but for us, it seemed children would never be so.

I suggested, with a heavy heart, using a different mate to make her dream come true. She protested, claiming we had each other and that would always be enough. I had never given children much thought, truthfully, but my "disability" cemented the fact that it would never come to fruition. Sad, yes, but I worried more for my heartbroken partner. It dimmed the passionate energy I had come to know and love over the years. This was perhaps the beginning of our problems.

The next blow was when I sought to cheer Kalea up. I wanted to reclaim that spark, so after much debate and mind wrestling, I decided to take her to the mainland to visit friends and familiar sights. Again, she protested when she saw my fear and doubt. But I knew it was something she desperately wanted. And I knew she would never go without my accompaniment.

I feared the deep blue, for that forthcoming journey would be the furthest I'd ever traveled. I shook my head when I remembered that was where great whites lurked; the very place where monsters swim and contemplate their sneaky attacks. Where darkness surrounded you for days with no chance of refuge. How Kalea did it all these years I just could not understand. All I knew was that she was strong.

In the upcoming weeks, Kalea would ask if I was sure I wanted to try this, and she suggested we go someplace else, like the other side of the island.

This didn't sit well with me. She already doubted that I could carry on with the trip. Her faith in my abilities was smaller than my size. She was worried on the surface, but below, I could tell she was ashamed.

So on the morning of our launch, I was obviously a nervous wreck; shaking and shivering and unable to just sit still. We departed and obviously she had always been a much faster swimmer. She had to tone down her strides just so I could keep up. The first while wasn't bad, but I suppose that was because I had made it that far before.

When we hit open Ocean, I stayed behind her, using Kalea as a beacon of hope and guidance. Darkness still found a way to wash over me. A great white swam underneath me, plotting out its kill. I continued to tell myself this wasn't real but I refused to believe even my own words. Out of every corner, all I could see was impending death penetrating through the darkness. I couldn't see Kalea. I couldn't see myself. I had to turn back, and regretfully, I did.

It was an exhausting swim to say the least—I was out of breath, and the reason I couldn't see her was because even at her slowest stride, she would paddle miles ahead of me. As a last resort, she offered to pull me along. I begrudgingly accepted after much prodding but the same feelings were there. I was too frightened to face the deep. I blamed it on bad grip.

So we were bound to each other in a stagnant life on the beach. No friends and no children, it was just her and me. Resentment grew, her against me and me against myself. Even the very fabric of how we came to be had me in pain every time it came to mind. It was not I who spilled the sugar sacks and treated her to a sweet surprise. I organized the plan, but when the moment came, my deceased friends were the ones who braved the mission to make it so. I could feel after all those years that the end was coming. Too many differences and too many problems to overcome—once again, I was a failure with little to give or offer.

TWELVE

I WILL never forget that morning, and I have come to understand that many others feel the same. A morning filled with obliteration and unforgivable anger—an inexcusable attack. The bay was calm and the sun ascended with warmth and beauty. My chapter in this story began with a fight.

Oh, it had been culminating for years. Kalea kept her feelings inside while I buried mine until not even my subconscious could find them anymore. We still ventured alongside the bay and swam together and feasted upon snails (well, that part was all her—truth be told they always sent me into violent spirals of shame and disgust). If this was the worst it would be, then I had no problems to even speak about. My feelings for her never wavered, but there is of course that little golden rule that many choose to ignore. You must love yourself before you can love another.

"Why don't I make you happy anymore, Akela?" she begged. I didn't have an answer, only protest.

"Of course you make me happy. You are all I ever wanted, Kalea—don't say that!"

"I don't give you all you need. That I can see!"

I protested more and more, choosing to ignore words like "purpose" and "weak." I watched her stare out into the bay, way out to the clouds where the sky and sea met in a wavering dance of pale blue.

"When did we give up on ourselves? Did we not have drive for adventure?" she pondered.

"You do! You always have." I protested more, listing as many positive qualities as I possibly could. Kalea didn't dispute them; she just repeated her chosen answer over and over.

"When you love somebody, their happiness becomes ingrained in yours. You do not seem content nor do you seem happy."

I swallowed hard and joined her in a view of the bay. The gray had returned.

"Because I hold you back. Your dreams and passions, they are gone because of me. Because of my size."

"That's not true," she cried sternly.

"You can't convince me otherwise. I can see it. Perhaps honesty is then our toughest foe."

Silence. I remember a long silence between us that lasted for eons. I knew the thought formulating in Kalea's head would no doubt shake everything to its very core. Instead, a question followed.

"What is it you want in life, Akela?"

"You! I want you!"

"You have me. So there is obviously more. As well there should be."

Honesty is a fickle fixture of any relationship. In order for one to thrive, you need it. But it is rare that both parties are truthful about the same hope or belief. Chances are either way, your mate is going to be unhappy. Working around it is the challenge. I wanted to take a swallow and a stab that morning, to tell her of my hopes and dreams. I drew a blank. Honestly, I always thought it was her that I wanted. Her and nothing more.

"Well, Kalea, if what you say about ingrained happiness is true… all I want for you is to be happy. And I will never believe that I am not holding you back."

"Whatever problem you may think you have, we will work it out together."

"You remember the sugar?" I inquired, with a quivering lump in my throat. She assured me there would be no possible way she'd ever forget. With a sigh and a deep breath, I spoke the truth that had eaten my insides whole since many years ago when it had happened. "It wasn't me who dumped the sugar for you. I couldn't brave the water to reach the boat. Not even our beginning is because of me. But I will be sure to be responsible for the end."

My heart pinned me to the ground—refusing to let my flippers turn at any angle. Kalea's tears dribbled onto the sand, but her gaze remained fixated away from me and out to sea. I knew silence and isolation would be the only act that could follow.

Kalea protested as I broke free of my paralysis. I turned slowly as she whimpered and cried and called for me to come back. I did not look behind me now, only forward as I disappeared into the palm bushes that had thinly separated us from the harbor. I was silent inside and out. Figuratively speaking, I had become a shell of the being that first laid eyes on her.

I walked the busy beach that stretched over and under the massive harbor. Unsure where to go, the only destination that could actually penetrate my thoughts was the volcano I once saw during Kaimi's flight. The urge to plummet into the bubbling chasm was disturbingly overwhelming. My flippers guided me as I secured the mountainous sight and began to head in its direction. Unsure of my plans, testing myself by hovering over the rocky edge seemed like the perfect activity for that moment's state of mind.

Oh how the land had changed since I first arrived. Construction had amplified over the years, with more and more identically dressed humans marching up and down the docks. In those recent times, large ships lined the inlet, bringing more and more humans to and from the port. Massive were these grand destroyers that echoed in my ears and often blocked my views of the Ocean. Painted with strange titles like "Sphinx," the vessels were always preceded by "USS." They seemed like their own impenetrable worlds which I had no desire to visit.

I wandered and wandered, realizing just how miniscule I was. But I effectively ruined one life, so that had to count for something right? I had held back a beautiful, sweet, caring kind soul that had the right to travel and have a family of her own. I felt that all I had worked for and dreamed of was slipping away because of my overwhelming faults and shortcomings. I had no meaning…no purpose but to cause negative effects. Why oh why was I the one out of all my brothers and sisters to survive?

As I trekked forth, a spotted shell rose out of the water as it splashed along the bay. Their face turned and shot the most comforting smile my way. Their eyes refused to leave; they watched me as they passed, studying my every move until the smile vanished and concern forced their head straight again. That's when the crescent moon on their shell became perfectly visible. Old feelings came back—old goals and old hopes. The majestic stride of this particular swimmer had me hypnotized. I felt I knew them…there was some sort of connection, though we had never spoke. Yes, I found myself repeating the phrase "Could it really be her?"

I ran, oh I ran like I never thought possible along the sand, screaming "stop" yet they kept on swimming. I made a sudden turn, tromping through water until my flippers jetted off with the force of the day's intensity behind them. I was careful never to let the crescent moon out of my sight.

"Stop! Stop! Come back!" I yelled, but still, they could not hear me. They could swim faster than the wind blew.

As I gasped for air, I found my own thoughts were being drowned out by monstrous roars from afar. The water was too shallow to produce such a vicious, hungry creature, so I peeked into the sky to find the horrid culprit. In the distance, a flock of birds flew in a menacing formation—determined to make their presence known. But the hum, the unforgettable hum and rumble of these attackers was overbearing. I looked around for my newfound friend but they had gone way into the distance. They were too far away to warn. My new goal was to find shelter but producing rational thought amidst this noise was unthinkable.

As the earth vibrated, up from underneath the shivering sand came a gold band with a glass oval. It was the very ring I had buried, arriving beside my flipper with a sudden desire to be found. My thoughts returned to my sweet Kalea—our wedding and our many walks along the beach. I had to finally give it to her and profess all my love. I had to apologize and find her as soon as I possibly could. I grabbed the ring and scanned for shelter.

As they swarmed closer, I could see they were not birds and what was dropping from them was not fecal matter. The contents hit the water with such force, waves and plumes of frothy whitecaps mushrooming across the beloved bay.

The whole Earth trembled and then everything went black.

THIRTEEN

AS I twitched, my sand-encrusted eyes opened to a blur. The wreckage that surrounded me was simply indescribable. Wood and metal met in startling piles that had torn down palm trees and ripped plants from their very roots. The ground was as red as when I had first met it. The water washed ashore with a light brown tinge—and in it bits of ship and dock. The ring was once again missing in action, nowhere to be seen.

I couldn't tell you what happened, but it took some doing to scramble back onto my flippers. Being propped up on your shell is no laughing matter. With a piercing ring in my ears, I couldn't even hear myself call for help. I rocked back and forth so violently that I managed to flip onto my side, dizzy. It took me a few moments to recuperate from the violence of my own swing.

I called out for Kalea but there would be no chance of hearing a response. I gawked but my vision was sickly, blocked by tears and mud and blood and dirt. I stopped dead in my tracks when a human ran like mad for nowhere. They looked just as confused as me—running in circles and screaming. Worst of all, they were covered in blood and shrapnel. It made sense that I too may be covered with an array of cuts and scrapes. So I peered in the calming tide that carried on without a hint of despair or pain—that somehow made it okay. But the water was so polluted I could not even make out my own figure. I refused to plunge into the infested unknown and kept moving forth along the coastline, trembling. I know now this was my biggest mistake.

Retracing the steps of my angry walk before, the fight with Kalea was forgotten and, more importantly, meaningless. I had to find her at all costs and tell her just how much she meant to me. I had to tell her that she was absolutely right—her safety, not mine, was my biggest concern. And even though I was small, I would protect her with all my might. It dawned on me that I may have survived that day solely because of my size.

As I carried on, humans began to emerge from the trees, confused like they too awoke in a different land. No one seemed to know just where to go; embracing each other looked like the only action that made sense. They paid no attention to me as I marched on, stumbling toward the opposite direction. The mustached President's harbor lay in ruins. It had spent many years in the making—I guess humans could only really stop and stare at the defeating destruction.

I moved slower than usual, sore from the events that took place during the blackness. Though I'll never truly know, all signs pointed to a surprise flight into a palm tree. Maybe I flew so high, the impact from torpedoing to the ground was a step below death. Still, I walked day and night, calling for Kalea. Even when my hearing returned, all I could hear were horns and tears.

I did not stop to eat, only to rest. When I finally reached our home, it was crushing to find it in complete ruins. Trees, plants, and driftwood formed a clustered pile. I searched, moving what I could as I feared the worst. There were luckily no signs of Kalea underneath, but her whereabouts still remained dishearteningly unknown. Determined to find her, I set out inland, toward the center of the island where I hoped she feasted upon snails and awaited my return. Instead, I was raised up to the sky by human hands for a third time.

I should have turned when I saw the man in white, dressed in a thick uniform that was topped with a full covering mask—you couldn't make heads or tails of his face. I wasn't even completely sure if this being was human at all. Before I could turn, they lifted me high—observing and touching and checking my body over. For a split second I thought this could be an advantage that doubled my searching speed. But the cold, rough edge of their gloves made me realize otherwise.

As I searched around for help below me, the vantage point did reveal a holy sight. Kalea poked her head from between bushes in what looked like fear and curiosity. I screamed for her.

"Kalea! Kalea, you're alive!" I rejoiced—as did she—when our eyes met for the last time.

"Akela! I'm sorry. I love you!" she called back as she ran toward me. As inspiring as her intentions were, I knew she could do no good.

"No! Stay there! Hide!" I cried. She stopped, shaking her head with a will to fight my captor to the death. But with my last words, I pleaded for her to go. I cried to her that I loved her and that everything would be all right.

Without warning or reason, a blue box to the left of the human was opened. A small pool of water sloshed around the bottom. I spread my legs, desperate to latch onto the side and stop myself from going in. The white human was too strong. I knew there was nothing I could do—it was certain I would be placed in the blue box and carried away somewhere. With my last ounce of strength, I gave one final, warming smile to a tearful Kalea as she vanished from view.

"Love! You know when you find it. You do anything for it. It means never wanting to be apart."

The lid closed and all was black again for a long, long while.

FOURTEEN

CONFINED TO a lonely tank, I could hear nothing. Only the splashes brought on by my twitching body and the echoing thoughts of my frightful mind. At least this prison was glass and I could see my captor's daily actions while I waited for answers, and quite honestly, death. It was so cramped that with any other company I'd have gone mad with claustrophobia.

Day in and day out, I'd peer from my prison and watch men, cigarettes hanging from their mouths, crowding around a long metal table. Dim lights swayed back and forth from the ceiling. Knives and weapons hung neatly in a long row. Surrounding the workers were tanks filled with other unfortunate Oceanic creatures.

Every day the men would enter and light themselves a fresh cigarette. They'd slip on a white jacket that covered their entire body, hanging just above their feet. After pounding back a cup of coffee, they would reach into the tanks and retrieve an unlucky victim.

I saw them once pin down a helpless starfish with needles and swab its body with some sort of cloth. A small, yet razor-sharp knife scaled the poor fellow, prying off a fair layer of his lower left arm. They chucked him back into his little enclosure and carried away the piece like it was the holy grail. They then disappeared for hours, only to return with freshly lit cigarettes, coffee, and the tools to do it all over again.

The room featured a strange variety of critters from poor, little zebrafish that came out of the tank and were never put back in to crabs that were crudely pulled apart from their shell and swabbed to death by forceful hands. Once dead, they were placed under some sort of viewing tube where the men would watch for hours, scribbling down whatever they must have thought.

There was even a sharp-toothed, little alligator that squirmed like the little girl in *The Exorcist* every time he was taken out. It became a horrific wrestling match where one man would hold him down and the unfortunate second soul wrapped his mouth with tape. I'd watch in hopeful excitement every time I saw him being taken out. I knew blood would be drawn and these soulless meddlers would receive an ounce of pointy comeuppance. My heart would break every time the gator would be put to sleep, thanks to an injection of some noxious tonic. I feared that would be his last moment and he'd never wake up. If he couldn't survive, what chance would the rest of us have?

My plan of action was to comply with whatever it was they wanted from me. Compared to some of the poor victims I saw get manhandled, I didn't have it all that bad. Usually every few days they'd sprawl me out on that cold slab of icy metal and shine beams of light directly into my eyes. And with some stinging substance splashed onto a fuzzy cloth, they'd swab away and rush out the door, carrying the cloth to some unknown but surely important destination.

Needles were painful but cigarette burns were worse. Ashes would occasionally and accidently fall off onto my neck. I'd squirm, but thankfully they'd dust the remnants off and settle me down. I liked the black-haired man—he'd actually give me a couple full-bodied pets to put me at ease whenever he sensed fear. Small shards of my shell were occasionally collected and filed away—those days were preferred. No pain, little loss—that I could live with. They seemed very intrigued with a certain spot on my back right side—perhaps a wound from the violent explosion that wouldn't heal.

I still to this day don't know exactly what it was I was doing there. All their prodding and poking and testing made me wonder if I was sick. Every session mysteriously began and ended with the term "Subject PH-55." I'd watch fish flop around and die after being yanked from water, and I'd see salamanders make a run for the door, only to be caught and displaced in a yellow bin. You didn't want to go into that yellow bin—you were only put there if you were stunned, still, or gave the men all they could take. One man would haul it out once every few days and bring it back empty. My heart shudders when I imagine where the departed were thrown.

Most of the time I'd just shiver in my little glass box, trying my best to shift around and find comfort. For the first time in my life, I felt big and hoped I wouldn't actually grow. On second thought, fantasies of becoming so big and strong filled my brain during this time. I dreamed that their testing made me grow at a rapid speed. Nothing could stop me, not even the glass! I'd burst through and continue my growth spurt as I stormed over to the villains and stomped them to death with my gigantic flippers. I'd destroy the tops of our tanks and take us to safety. No one would ever have to endure pain and prodding and awful invasive examinations again.

Sometimes, I'd imagine I'd grown so big I'd simply just have to look around to spot Kalea. She'd be there waiting for me—and now there was nothing stopping her love and respect. I was the biggest! The strongest! And my love for her was unmatched by any beating heart. It was the largest heart to grace this green earth. And it was all hers because she deserved it.

Oh my Kalea, how I missed her. I thought about her every waking second—glad it wasn't she that was being subjected to these terrors. But I did not know that for sure. What if she was put in another box? What if another white-suited human combed the bushes and collected her for…I refused to believe it! I would close my eyes and whisper to the world to please tell me she was okay. A calm stillness hushed over my untouched and unchanged water. Silence represented peace in my mind, so I decided she was okay. The hard part now was being away from her.

Her beauty was indescribably radiant while her internal sweetness completely rivaled any sugarcane field. Sometimes that's all I called her—the sweetness, not only for her love of the perky substance, but for her all-around pleasant manner. Everything about her was pleasant. It was in that tank that I realized how lucky I was to have her in my life. There were horrible days where I felt she was better off without me now, but I managed to chase them off with an outweighing number of warming memories. We had plenty and they were worth fighting for.

So I made up my mind right then and there that I'd do anything to get back to her. I had to rub my face with hers at least one more time. I had to share sugar with her and catch snails for her and walk with her along the sun-setting beach. I'd swim with her and offer all I had. She made me happy, happier than I could ever be stuck in a little box in a dark laboratory of death. The first step of deciding what to do was easy; carrying out this plan was going to be an immense challenge.

To begin with, I had no idea where I was. I had lost all track of time being hauled and swished and trapped in the dark. Perhaps I was still on my home island, or perhaps I had actually made it to the coveted mainland Kalea had spoken so fondly of. I knew little of the topographical region the mainland boasted to begin with, just secondhand stories that mostly took place at bays and shores.

There was no water in this place; I was lucky if my water was ever changed at all. I think in all that time, the tank was cleaned only once and cold water was dumped in the removable roof above me. Every so often they'd splash some powder in that looked like sugar but certainly did not taste like it. Actually, those were good days…it tasted like home. I was fed processed flakes that most definitely did not grow in the sea. I was rarely hungry to begin with, so they would just fall down to the bottom, creating a scummy, mossy layer of filth I'd have to lay in till new water came along.

When my tank was clean, I could make out some writing that was printed on the outside of my glass. Unable to read, I would stare at the image all day long, trying to make sense of the inscription. While even to this day I still do not know what it meant, I will never forget the imaged burned into my mind.

TCEJORP NATTAHNAM bordered the circle top at an arch. Below it, an A symbol covered most of the real estate with NAM TAF underneath; subject PH-55 was scribbled on just below.

When I wasn't in agony and when I wasn't thinking of my sweet Kalea, I puzzled over what this meant. It was displayed on all the tanks and printed on many of the tools. I promised myself I'd try to get a glimpse of it on my way back to the tank after each operation. No matter how hard I tried to do so, I was always simply relieved that I had survived another testing. My eyes were always shut with exhaustion as I fell back into my pool. I'd forget all about the cursed marking and would find myself staring at it once again until the next go-around with the white-coated men.

Nights were the worst because the swinging light would be shut off completely. We were left to sit in the dark, all to our lonesome, in pure silence. Yes, if you were going to ask if I tried to escape, yes I did. There were a few dark times where I'd stretch out and push the top of the tank and there was no movement. The men had locked it tight, counting on escape attempts and preemptively stopping them completely.

Now, there was one and only one successful escape attempt I can tell you about. For many nights the only noise that I could hear was a faint *tap tap tap* against glass. All night, every night, I could hear it rise up from below and pierce my own segregated, little fortress. I'd peer into the night but nothing was there—no sign of movement or commotion.

That was until the tapping stopped and a single piercing shredded the glass completely. I had to squint, but I was sure something scuttled across the floor, bumping into chairs and table legs along the way. I could make out the shady figure when it leapt up and reached for the doorknob. I think everyone in that room could see him there jumping as high as he could for the handle to freedom. I thought maybe we had all finally lost our minds, but a collective gasp and cheer filled the room when it was evident the escapee lifted the latch.

Were we a little mad that the alligator didn't do his part to free the rest of us? Sure, but honestly, what could he have done? He earned his freedom, along with our wild screams of praise and celebration. He flung the door wide open and clip-clopped down the hallway to the great unknown.

You should have seen that room; for once, I could hear pounding as fish and crabs and even birds fluttered around their cage. If it did anything at all, it gave us hope that something like this was possible. That we could in fact escape if we put our minds to it. Maybe he had an advantage, what with the teeth and claws and grip he could produce with his fingers—but it was possible! We could be freed! The door slammed shut, blocking out all light and silencing the room just like before. The noise died down but the message was clear. Spirits were lifted as every single prisoner plotted their own disappearing act.

I was coming for Kalea no matter the challenge. All I wanted in that moment was for someone to tell her. Deep down, I knew she already knew.

FIFTEEN

OH YOU should have seen it! The puzzled men searched the gator's tank for hours and then every single other tank in the room to make sure he wasn't accidently stuffed into the wrong slot. They must have opened up the yellow bin about fifty times, somehow believing that they kept missing his curled corpse on every inspection. Once they agreed the gator was officially missing, every person who entered became hilariously on edge. Some men who I once knew, like the black-haired man, never returned after that. Guess they were positive the little nipper was waiting up in the rafters for a chance to attack.

While I did squirm so hard one day during testing I fell off the table, I ended up landing smack dab on my shell. I writhed liked a seizure had taken hold but the fellows were in no hurry to help me back up or stop me from my dastardly dash to the door. They just went on yakking and casually lifted me back up to the cold metal slab. It seemed my escape attempt wasn't much of a concern.

That little room was where I picked up all of my little tricks for future endeavors though, so it wasn't all just wasted time. An iguana managed to thump up and down so violently he lifted the latch right through its lock. Out he went, but sadly, he wasn't too lucky with the door. The men found him the very next morning, huddled underneath the metal counter bottom.

During testing, when the men weren't looking, just about every critter tried their best to roll away. Most were caught just in time, others were slapped down upon the hard, painful floor. The fish had it the worst because their tanks didn't seem to be locked. There was a streak going where once every night someone would flip up and out. But fish don't live too long without the old H2O surrounding them. Into the yellow bin they'd go the next morning.

The long string of copycat escape attempts grew thin—everyone was unsuccessful and, worse, dying in the process. I knew my limits but, still, that didn't stop me from dreaming about escaping in the most ludicrous of ways. Every day I'd think of Kalea and wonder what she was up to. Did she have company or was she all alone? Was she out searching for me or had she already moved on? It had felt like eons since I'd actually seen her last. Time went by slowly in the glass jail— the time and date was foreign to me so I can't actually tell you how long I spent waiting.

The tipping point came when a very different man came zipping along one morning; all the men were eager to show him their animal selection and every darn crevasse of the room. I had never before seen his device, a chair with two massive wheels attached at both sides. He'd spin them along with his hands, wheeling over to wherever it was he wanted to go. The man was certainly stern and evidently respected— the other men couldn't keep their eyes off him. Well-dressed in a suit, he scooted over to our tanks until he stopped at mine of all places.

He adjusted his glasses, peering over the top as he drank me in. I froze, expecting the worst that was evidently going to come when he pointed at me. After a couple painfully loud taps on my glass, however, he moved on to the table where the others had prepared some sort of papers and sheets.

I can tell you this was the busiest our little room had been. Though I couldn't see my fellow prisoner friends, I could tell everyone squirmed to find out just what he was reading. All I could make out were circles: red, orange, and yellow. The wheelchaired man pointed at it as did all the other frantically excited men. With a long reach into his pocket, this feeble gentleman lit himself an elongated cigar before rolling out of the room with eager hands pointing where he was to visit next.

I knew this was the beginning of the end—the experiments stopped and the men entered less and less frequently. Alone in the dark glass box, I was beginning to lose my grip on the truth. I'd often rock back and forth, wondering just what was to become of me. Fresh air was scarce, water was sludge. They seemed to no longer care whether the tanks were cleaned at all and if we got fed. My insides rumbled and false images flashed in the corner of my eyes. I knew it wasn't possible, but the monsters of the Ocean had seemingly followed me to my little tank too! There was no comfort, only warm memories of Kalea to keep me company.

Psychosis was starting, to the point where I'd twitch every time someone entered the room. Every so often, a fish was plucked and never returned. Sometimes they'd storm in just to find a tool, but their frantic movements made me all the more on edge.

Finally, the day came when the dreaded yellow box returned and blue water sloshed around the bottom. I could hear snaps and creaks as lids flew open. One by one, we were pulled out and flung into this dank excuse for transportation. No one had any idea where we were headed. The hopeful side of me celebrated that perhaps the testing was done and we could go home. I stuck it out and would now be reunited with my love. The anticipation of the long, dark ride made me weak.

And then my tank was lifted open and a hand swished through the water and latched around my body. I left the tank for the final time;

oh what a blessed bright side that was. I can remember my eyes blurring as I gazed up at the swinging lights one last time. The door swung open, revealing a long white hallway. And then our blue box swung shut and darkness concealed us. We were lifted up, rolling around from side to side once more.

I was angry and still remain angry that I never did get to escape from that dreadful room on my own terms. But nonetheless, I would escape and be en route to my home and Kalea. That's my little lesson I'm going to keep hounding you about, over and over. Perspective is a wonderful thing, but when you're in the thick of it, fear of the unknown can consume you. It almost did that to me here, but I thank the universe for sending me my friend Earl to stop that from ever happening!

The feeling of fresh air…I tell you, I felt like a whole new being when the warm breeze surrounded my body. The blinding, white shine from our old friend the sun prevented any possible grip on my bearings. As happy as I was to feel its stinging warmth, it stunned my every sense, to say the least. That's what you get for being cooped up in a dim, windowless room for an unknown chunk of your life. The feeling was warmer than what I remembered, certainly dryer and unlike what I had ever experienced before.

When the worker sat me down, I was brought back to life when the warm sand beneath me burnt the very soles of my flippers. Unlike the sand I was once used to, this crispy, hard-packed soil refused to move. There was no chance of burial whatsoever. It was so dry; evidently there was no water in any nearby capacity. So there I sat, burning, hot, and blinded by the elements. Still, I preferred this to my slimy glass box.

As my vision returned, I was stunned to see miles of nothingness. The crispy sand lacked any sort of life—dead vegetation sprawled out in ugly brown patches. Rolling dark hills stretched far into the distance. Croaking beaks flew in a circle up above, expanding their feathery wings so almost all of the hopeful blue sky was blocked out. They looked as though they could eat a gull in one bite for breakfast.

Before I could pump my legs fast enough to get moving, a half-circular metal cage dropped over me so further steps could not be taken. With me was a poor crab that raised his claws and hid tightly in the opposite side. Through the slits, white feet where visible—circling the metal dome dungeon until they were satisfied with the position.

I peered up and up, following lengthy legs until a white human (exactly like what I had seen before I was taken from Kalea) came into view. He scribbled something down on a board before grasping the blue box handle and dragging it through the sand. I watched him move in a rectangular path as he slid along to the next destination. What followed him was a motorized vehicle, carrying about a dozen more half-circle metal dungeons and blue containers. As shocked and hurt as I was, I was mesmerized by the sheer speed of the contraption.

Unable to squeeze through the holes or lift up the bottom, I just watched the vehicle drive into the distance, dropping metal dungeons over carefully arranged critters in the sand. The white-clad human would scribble down what was done, and then they'd move on down the desert until they were no longer around.

How isolated this place was…hauntingly quiet and sprawling on forever. Pigs were the only proprietors of sound, squealing from towering boxes that perched on some sort of supportive tripod. Some were free range in confines like mine. The others, narrowly slipped into the raised boxes, wore some shiny silver outfit.

"Do you know what's going on?" I asked the shivering crab. He just shook and looked in the other direction. For having such a powerful defensive tool, they sure always seemed scared of the unknown. I guess I could relate. But all I could do was wait and wait…like always.

No one came back for us so we'd move with the sun, hiding under the little shade our dungeon cast. Any direct contact with the sun and you'd start to cook. I was feeling quite dry as it was. Water was needed, although I was ready to settle for a plain explanation. Was this the final test? Were we ever going back inside? Where were we in the first place?

"Hello? Hey you? Little Buddy? You alive?"

This raspy voice rose up from nowhere. I looked around and saw emptiness—no possibility of an owner. From the top of the domed dungeon, the escaped gator pounced off onto the sand. His every move was fast and fluid. He was quick, filling my view, startling me. Shocked to see him, I rushed to the dungeon edge for a better view.

"You? But you escaped! I saw you leave."

"Well that's right, Little Buddy, I got out. Made it all the way out into the parking lot before I realized I'd never be happy until I freed the whole lot of you—and well, if that makes me a commie, then so be it. Come on; let's get you out of here."

The gator wrapped his little fingers along the bottom slits, pushing up with all his might.

"What's happening? What is this?"

"You ain't in the strike zone but that's just what they want. To see what them there chemicals do to ya. Awful, just awful stuff I tell you."

He didn't make much sense to me but his claws and good heart were helping me escape and that's all I cared about. I helped too, pushing upwards, trying to use my shell as leverage. The damn little crab just stood there and watched. I felt we could have been out of there a whole lot quicker if he would have pumped his claws and helped out. We finally tipped the dungeon over so it rolled on the sand like me if I were turned over on my back. The gator nodded, giving me a formal greeting.

"Name's Earl."

"Akela!"

"Pleased to meet you, Little Buddy. Now let's get the others."

I was perplexed why he bestowed that name on me—really we weren't that far apart in size…plus I had just told him my given name. I turned to wave the crab on with us but he just stood there, shaking in a confused, frozen state. It was a million degrees out but he looked like he was huddled up in the arctic.

"Come on, what are you waiting for?" I screamed. That didn't get him moving any faster. I went back to nudge him along and that's when he raised his little clippers in defense. To hell with him I decided; I turned around and chased after Earl to the best of my ability. To this day, I am certain the poor, stubborn soul died right there in the desert. Hermits…can't convince them to do nothing.

I reached the second domed dungeon just as Earl had flipped it over. I felt I wasn't much help, especially when he took off for the next one and I was already out of breath. I looked over at a shriveled slug, restricted to move at an even slower speed. Once Earl realized this, he thankfully turned back around to instruct us further.

"Take him in the opposite direction. There's a river there—biggest darn one you ever did see. That's gonna get us all to safety. I don't know how many more I can get but just head that way. You won't miss it."

"What about you?"

"I'll make it, just head for the river!"

With that, Earl bounded across the sand toward farther dungeons, tipping over the pig towers along the way. I looked down at the slimy, little companion who sheepishly buried his head in embarrassment. I understood completely. I also continued to doubt that a body of water was going to magically appear in the middle of dry, deserted dust.

"Come on!" I flung him with my mouth right onto the back of my shell, where he planted himself in tightly. I took off like a mad bat out of hell toward the direction Earl had told me. Bless his heart for turning back—we were all sure he was living the good life in some far-off lagoon. He was probably one of the greatest creatures I've ever had the pleasure of knowing; second or third below Kalea, of course.

The idea that I was on my way to see her allowed me to glide over the hot sand until the drowning sounds of the pounding river blocked any rational thought. Sure enough, it was a darn big river. It was not the Ocean, but it was a start!

I placed the slug hitchhiker to wait atop an onshore stone and I jumped straight in, too preoccupied to care about any impending river threat. Oh what an icy chill that was. Careful not to get too far out into the current, I spun around and joined an ever growing line made up of saved critters. I peered up the rocky river slope. One by one, the newly saved came stampeding into the flowing water as if they were washing off the past and embracing their new life. It was a rebirth, a cleanse that washed us all clean. While a few stuck around to wait for Earl's return, others flew down the flow of river, disappearing instantly around the first bend.

I was hesitant about whether I should get back out and check on poor Earl, but before I could decide either way, he suddenly hurled himself from the riverbank edge and right over my shell. Frogs and toads and salamanders and crabs poured into the mixture, falling over the edge and soaking up the icy freshness of the surrounding stream.

"We go now! Now!"

"Did you get them all?"

"I did my best," he assured me, slithering upstream with one arm waving us all on. I nodded, picking up my little friend from his rock and fighting the current to go forward the best I could. Everyone splashed and thrashed as they searched for good grips and calm waters. I could see Earl just up ahead until he found himself a muddy patch and dug in deep.

"Come on, no time!" he urged, instructing everyone to do the same. And to the best of their abilities, everyone dove as far down into the earth as they possibly could.

With all the wiggling and fighting, it was hard staking a claim on a safe patch of mud. I was dwelling on the irony of what I was doing when Earl put his arm around me and shot me a smile.

"Put your head in your shell and hold on tight."

"I can't do that, Earl. I'm from the sea. I'm not like that. I'm not a regular—"

Suddenly, it felt like the entire Earth shifted on its axis. Dirt and dust flew like mad through the sky, clouding up the plain view with rolling ease. I buried deep into the mud but the great shake sent me skidding into the water—probably a safer place than any other. I eventually poked my head out, vaguely seeing others do the same. And there was Earl; oh I wish you could have seen Earl, perched on his behind with one suave arm leaning against the bank. His eager little grin said it all. One by one, we all joined together with a collective smile.

"Well there you have it, folks, we survived!"

SIXTEEN

SURE, THE moonlight glowed that night but it was nothing in comparison to our glowing faces. After a swim upstream, we managed to find a valley with grass to feast upon (mosquitoes for the bug eaters) and fresh water in a calm bend to lounge about in. Yes, some carnivores were present, but in the spirit of the evening, everybody was able to put away their primal urges and just enjoy each other's company.

My little slug friend was so excited, he couldn't keep still. He'd race from one rock to the next, exploring at a ridiculous speed (especially for his kind) just to make up for lost time. Sal the rattlesnake instead shook a beat with his tail, providing pleasant rhythms for all to enjoy. Boris the bullfrog was determined to let his voice be heard, croaking loud and proud and hopping higher than any of us could dream of reaching. In fact, I remember there being a competition on who could jump the highest. Sal cheated and insisted his long reach counted as a jump…we ruled it did not. I think you can guess I failed at that game.

There were so many excited faces, from lizards to amphibians. We were still unsure why we all ended up together, but at least we had a few habits and needs in common. Some left the party early, eager to get back to family since they knew it was going to be a long journey home. The pigs certainly didn't stick around; they had no manners or voice of reason. Just about all of them darted out in all directions, frightened in their freedom. One joined our crew, but for the most part, he ate his own meal off to the side.

I understood—they had their own clan, kept in a different room for a longer time probably. Maybe they were even bred and born together so it made sense they didn't want to make any friends at that moment. It was emotional for us though, hugging and rubbing, finally getting to meet after watching helplessly through glass for all that time. We had all been through tests and saw each other get pulled back and forth onto that horrible metal slab. Ah, but it was a distant memory now so we had to move on. There was a vow that night not to speak of anything we saw or experienced during our time in the room. Anytime someone pondered why it happened, we'd playfully shush them and move on to another game.

It was a wild night—two frogs who had never officially met went off into the bushes to mate. Others fell asleep, exhausted from fear and ready for a comforting nap under the stars where they rightfully belonged. I tell you, it was like being reborn—your whole outlook on life and the time given to you was reawakened. I knew I certainly wouldn't waste another day waiting around or hiding from bad weather. I needed to be outside in the sun or the rain—regardless of the sky. I needed to be in the open…with my Kalea. I shook with excitement; that was now possible once again.

Then there was Earl, calmer than a cucumber. He refused to be thanked or worshipped or rewarded with interspecies love. He just insisted on having a nice rest, floating around on his back with his little arms behind his head. Sometimes amidst conversation, we could hear him hum to himself or sing a tune under his breath. I remember desperately wanting to thank him for his bravery but I understood he wanted peace. Hours had gone by until it was only me, Boris, and Sal left awake. Finally, the gator flipped over and crawled onto our grassy, little shore. Earl's mere presence brought existing conversations to a halt and a switch of topics.

"Earl, my dear friend, we just once again would like to say—" Boris croaked as Earl quickly raised his hand to cut him off.

"No need, baby, no need. Just talk normal. How's everybody feeling?"

"Superb," Sal hissed.

"I feel amazing. Free! I can't stop moving…wiggling my flippers," I replied.

"Good. Good. That's the whole idea. Everyone should be free to stretch their legs as far and as long as they please."

"That doesn't sound like communist talk to me, Earl," Boris commented.

Earl just laughed as he settled his way into our little circle. "Maybe I'm just a little bit of everything then. A little spice, a little rice, a little naughty, a little nice. Now that's the way we all should be."

I couldn't argue with that logic. I also felt a little starstruck being in Earl's presence. He just seemed larger than life, like some sort of celebrity, only no one knew it until he escaped out the door that night. I just wanted to make him smile. Make him feel proud and happy and appreciated. I wanted to thank him profusely. I figured the best thing to do was keep my mouth shut.

"Where did you come from?" Sal asked.

"Oh, all over—Everglades originally. See, there's a network of pipes that connects you to just anywhere you want to go in this world. They got this thing called a toilet—one flush and I'm on my way to somewhere new."

"Any favorites?"

"Chicago's cool. Oklahoma has a nice spice to it. How 'bout you? Where y'all hail from?"

"Desert country, west Texas I think," Sal answered.

"Here and there—wherever there's a lily," Boris croaked happily.

"Lily? Is that your wife?" I mistakenly interjected. Boy, did they get a real good laugh out of that one.

I played it off as a joke but they could tell I was really that naive. Turns out lilies are what some folks call those floating green water leaves. Shame on me I guess for not understanding the regional dialect. Very quickly, I was feeling out of place and ill-informed about the world. I had no clue where west Texas was or what kind of spice Oklahoma had. I froze completely, stammering like a fool when Earl's eyes landed on me.

"I…well, I don't…palm trees, bay…" I could see Sal stifling a laugh as I mumbled.

"Let me guess," Earl said with a calm smile. "Sunny shores and sugarcane fields. Bright carnation flowers strung around people's necks."

"Yes! That's exactly it!"

"You're lucky, Little Buddy. Do I know of that place? Heard it got hit pretty hard before I got scooped up to this darn prison cell of ours. You feeling all right?"

"Oh yes. Fine! Fine! Earl, where is this place? My home?"

"Far. Folks call it Hawaii. Beautiful landscape. But very far."

My heart sank. I knew I had been taken a great distance but it never did dawn on me just how far it was. But I kept repeating that word to myself over and over, letting the piece of information sink in. It was such a pretty word. Hawaii. Hawaii. Hawaii. At least knowing where to go was a start.

"What was all this about? Government conspiracy—some sort of cosmetic testing? Why were we—" Earl once again raised his arm to silence Boris.

"Now we ain't talking about that tonight. Just relax and let it all fade out into distant memory."

"It was just such an ordeal though. I can't believe we were—"

Once again, Earl silenced Sal with just a simple look.

"How about instead of the past, you say where it is you want to go now."

I think we all sensed pain emanating from Earl's voice. He wanted to move past everything, which is really what we all just needed to do. Forgive and forget and move on. Then I thought of Kalea...sometimes there is just a past and memories you don't give up on.

"Just find a nice field of lilies, to be honest with you. No matter how long it takes, I'll seek out a nice, wet, sprawling field of lilies."

"You know this land really ain't so bad, except for all the darn terrible associated memories with it. I'll head east maybe; see what kind of soil I can find."

Then once again it came to me, hesitant and uninformed little old me.

"Well I...I...I have to get back to Kalea. She's my partner. My one and only. We had fought before I was taken. I just need to know she's okay. I need to know that she feels loved. I need to see her again."

Silence. Boris couldn't even look me in the eye after that cathartic release. Sal was uncomfortable, twitching his rattle to take his mind off everything. Earl, dearest Earl, showed his nasty fangs in a wicked grin. Anyone who didn't know him would surely take off running in the opposite direction.

"Love, Little Buddy, that's all there is when you get down to it. You don't see a lot of true love these days either. Couples are just about an ideology of the past. She still in Hawaii?" I nodded. "Oh, now that really is a long journey. But let me tell you something, it is worth every step of the way and then some. She something special?"

"The best! I spent the better part of my life trying to win her over. I'm not letting her go without a fight."

"She look just like you?"

"Bigger?"

Earl playfully licked his lips and wagged his tail. The others didn't care, they just faked a laugh to impress Earl and remain in the conversation. Their thoughts were elsewhere. They were different. But that's okay.

"You got to get her, Little Buddy. At all costs you got to find her. Hold her! Let your past guide you and drive you. Love, baby, it's all there is when you get down to it."

I agreed, flashing a confident smile over at the other two. A little triumphant gloating, if you will, after proudly winning over Earl's interest and respect.

"How about you, Earl?" Boris chimed in. "What are you going to do?"

The playful smile disappeared as Earl stared past Boris and into the darkness beyond. As we leaned in—eager for a response—a long sigh was there to greet us.

"I think I'm going to call it a night."

Though it was a wonderful sleep, I still had this burning drive to get myself going. I needed all the time I could get if I was to make it back to Hawaii…believe me, I said that word about a thousand times under my breath, trying to understand it correctly. How did I never know this before?

As I stretched, I found the only other one who was awake in the darkness was Earl. He looked down at the wind blowing through sparse blades of grass. I suppose he had lied about calling it a night—he just didn't want to talk anymore.

"Eager to see her?" he said calmly. I had barely moved yet somehow he knew I was restless and awake.

"You have no idea," I whispered as I made my way over to him. "What are you still doing up?"

I could see it in his eyes. His mouth remained closed. Somehow, he was more intimidating without his toothy smile. Earl didn't look at me; he remained still and focused like his thoughts were carefully displayed out in front of him.

"There's so much anger among humans. They're angry, Little Buddy, and that's exactly why they did this to us."

"But there has to be more to it than that. I've known some pleasant humans."

"I'm sure you have. There's good all around us too. But because of them angry few, innocents like us got to suffer."

"Why were we there, Earl? I won't tell anyone."

Silence. A long, struggled silence.

"If you feel sick or weak you tell me okay? Won't you do that, Little Buddy? Tell me if you feel bad. That's just what they wanted to find out, you know? But they can't hear answers cause they don't listen."

I didn't know what to say or how to respond really. I looked back at the rest of the newly freed—it was best if I didn't say goodbye. It was easier if we all just went our separate ways before real friendship set in.

"You going?"

I gulped and sighed and eventually nodded.

"I'm glad for you. It's going to be one hell of a journey. But you'll do it. I know you will."

"If there is any way I can repay you—" Before I could get going on a heartfelt thank you, Earl silenced me with a raised hand like he did everyone else. I smiled and readied myself for the long walk ahead. "I do not know the way."

Before I could take the first triumphant step forth, Earl's raspy voice held me back.

"I never did either, but that was the fun of it all. At least you got a goal, Little Buddy. Something to work toward."

I turned.

"Why did you save us? Why didn't you go home? Go to your family?"

Tears trickled. He had seemed so cool—so collected and strong and guarded. But there was something burning deep inside his heart that was yearning to get out. As much as that sight pained me, it was relieving to know others struggled and strived for some unattainable desire.

"I had the chance to go to Hawaii, but I settled for Savannah instead…I'm unsure if that was the right choice. I've done a lot of navigating and swimming over the years—seen a lot of changes and a lot of roadblocks. Guess what I'm getting at is that I know a way. I can get you to the Ocean, Little Buddy, if you'll have me along, that is."

I was speechless; my first inclination was that I'd of course have him along. But his pointed fangs had me thinking otherwise. What if this was all just a ploy to have a righteous feast? Perhaps he freed us to eat us? I couldn't be left alone with a potential killer that could rip me to shreds before I could yell for help.

I would go it alone…where a variety of hungry mouths could also ingest me with very little effort. Perhaps a set of protective jaws was just what I needed? He did seem to have a built-in compass that could guide me home a lot easier than my ramblin' guessing could. Maybe he was lonely and just in search of a friend. He did save us after all—earning the top spot as respected group leader. I was honored to be chosen as his perspective acquaintance. Perpetual, crushing self-doubt made me wonder why anyone as inspiring as him would want to help me. I decided teeth and all, I would find out.

"You know I'm not that little," I informed him with an eager, adventurous smile. "I can do everything others can too. How about you just call me Akela on the journey? Is that a fair compromise?"

Earl's grin returned. I winced as he slobbered and licked his twitching lips. "Good night," he said, rolling over instantaneously. I was too eager and jittery to fall back into slumber. I watched him all night and it seemed to me he had the best sleep of his life.

SEVENTEEN

IT WAS a bit of an uneasy start for me that following morning when I asked Earl just where it was we were. He mumbled a few different answers before changing the subject and trailing off as he gazed out into the distance. It was pretty evident this was going to be an improvised journey, though I was banking on Earl remembering at least some of the way further down the road. I doubted his previous tales and promises were completely built on fabrications. We yawned and stretched in typical nonchalant Earl fashion as the sun rose up and cast down a sweltering blanket of heavy heat.

Sal slithered on down the hard-cracking dirt, determined to wind his way to a cozy new home. Boris jumped at the chance to journey with us up the river a little—he'd exit the company when a lily-filled swamp came into view. The others cheered us on, some desperate to follow their fearless alligator leader and some still in a daze of opportunity. Freedom was sometimes overwhelming—I think an iguana ate himself into a coma upon escape.

So there we were; a motley group of water-based critters swimming upstream to arrive back at my home in Hawaii. I was the embarrassingly slow member of the group, squirming and struggling against the current with all my might. Within the first few hours, I tuckered myself out and made the entire party stop for a rest. I insisted they all go ahead without me but that of course did not make any sense.

This rest offended some of the crew, forcing two upset salamanders to abruptly rush off in an angry storm. My speed was just something they absolutely could not put up with. Boris would roll his eyes and mutter some bitter comment to Earl when he thought I couldn't hear. Even when I couldn't, I could make out his grumpy expression—full, pouty lips hanging in disapproval as he watched me flounder about.

Earl only said words of encouragement but he never really seemed to be in a rush to get places anyway. I feared he would abandon the journey only days in after realizing how long the whole swim would take. I wasn't afraid like I was in open Ocean. It lacked depth and changed patterns every couple of strides. Mammal life was rare and dark pools were few and far between. I was exhausted but rarely detrimentally fearful.

I'd think of Kalea and power on for a few more hearty strokes before gasping and having to stop again. What really caused me problems was the taste of the water—how different it was than the kind I was used to. Sure, it was blistering warm outside but somehow this stream was cool. The feeling took some getting used to; I remember being wide-eyed and alert whenever I was first submersed.

But there was some strange feeling I simply was not acclimated with. My flippers sliced through without hardly any resistance, causing me to have to flap three times as hard to get anywhere. The swim was just lacking in comfort or familiarity, which thankfully Earl could plainly see. After witnessing me spit out a small geyser, he came up with the perfect solution.

"Little Buddy, are you salt or freshwater?"

"I, gee, uh, don't know…"

"Coming from the open Ocean, I'd peg you as a salt gulper, wouldn't you say?"

I hadn't given it any thought really. Back home I had always figured that water was water but evidently that was not the correct assumption. I nodded.

"I saw back in our little hold up that them pokers and prodders kept a box of it for the salt gulpers. You remember any of that going into your tank?"

I thought long and hard and most certainly did; the taste of home, it all made sense now! Earl promised to fix that little problem the next time we floated on through civilization. Every so often we'd skirt through a row of buildings but were hesitant to journey up and see what was inside. We could hear triumphant spirits singing and shouting and marching with tubas and drums at hand and mouth. Some towns would simply ring a bell for the entire duration of our passing—probably longer. From what we could see, people were hugging and face rubbing and embracing one another. Laughter echoed across the river valley as did amplified speeches from embraced dignitaries and uniformed men. I could never make out the words though; the excitement was too vibrant and overbearing to actually hone in on.

It was inspiring to bear witness to all this celebrating, prompting me to wonder if humans were always like this on the mainland. Here, parties and excitement filled town streets almost constantly with an accompanying victorious spirit. This made the need to remain inconspicuous on Earl's missions for salt all the more difficult.

We waited on the shore when Earl assured us he could get the stuff we needed. By this time the group consisted of just myself, Boris, and the mute, little slug. We just sat in silence after Earl slipped himself through a pipe that led up to a row of shops. I don't know why Boris didn't care for me—it's not like I ever did anything to him. And I was trying my best; he was just never willing to cut me some slack. Luckily, this was the final straw for him—Earl came bounding out, sure enough with a box of salt and some kind of thin, red string.

"Here you are, Little Buddy, a taste of home. We gotta care for all of us, even the salt gulpers, don't we?" Earl turned his attention to the slug. "You might want to step back a little."

Sadly, our slug friend could no longer continue the journey as long as salt was involved. He rode upon my back where this box was now tied with the string wrapping tightly around my middle. Earl carefully bit two dainty holes in the top where it could shoot out as planned. I offered to nix the idea once I learned our little friend could no longer come along. Boris claimed he had enough of us all, so the option of riding on his shoulders was out. The grumpy, old bullfrog hopped away to go it alone. We'd bump into each other along the trail every now and again, but usually we'd take a different turn once we spotted him hopping along the bank. I got the sense Earl didn't like his downbeat attitude either.

We did a trial run with the slug hanging onto Earl's shoulders as I trudged along behind. Every lurch forward after a flipper stroke jerked a sprinkle of salt out of the holes and into the water ahead. Once I reached the water with floating salt particles, I'd get a rejuvenating taste of home and my stride would oddly increase a slight hair. It did however only work for a few minutes.

The box deteriorated almost instantly, leaking salt and clumpy cardboard all over the place. Earl made the judgment that glass might be the better way to go. In the next town, he bravely scurried through a restaurant to pick up a glass shaker. It was smaller, and evidently stealing was going to become a habit of ours in each town we passed. Earl luckily enjoyed the thievery rush while I benefited from the salty sprinkle. It was a win-win that kept us going. Little comforts go a long way.

In no words at all, the slug assured us he'd be fine on his own and wished us luck on our adventure. With a grateful smile, he left us when he found a nice, quiet nook to call home. I regretted not having him along but what could we do? At the pace I was going we'd never make Hawaii (in my lifetime at least). Now that it was the two of us, Earl assured me we'd have to go forth as quickly and bravely as we could. I'd have to strengthen myself along the way to keep up and keep going. I don't know if it was Earl's words or the salt or the repetition of swimming upstream all day, but you know something—I did!

With every day that passed, I could feel myself getting stronger. Sure, there were times where my flippers couldn't even move and I had absolutely no energy to swim a single stroke ahead. There were days when I begged Earl to slow down or take a breather, and usually he would; but then he would begin to vocalize my most private of thoughts. He'd mention Kalea and speak in poetic soliloquies about love and passion and being together with our one and only. I'd perk up and nod and get right back in the water. Salt would pour and my mind would race.

Usually, Earl would babble about some story that happened to him, like getting chased off porches with a broom or lounging about the Everglades in murky, hidden swamps. He'd occasionally sing too; oh, how I will never forget his singing—particularly this one verse that he'd hum and belt out over and over when the sun rose.

I would tire and grow sick of them and then suddenly once again rejoice in their beauty—maybe it took me way too long to understand them. But they would make me ponder and keep me going; the fighting pain of swimming would retreat to the back of my mind. He was a soulful spirit that Earl, and I'd give anything to hear him sing those songs again.

No being has more luck than the sun
Because when the day is over and done
It goes down in defeat on a defensive retreat
But it always rises up for more fun

If only I had daily chances like him
So when life looks dark and quite grim
I'd come out on top and won't have to stop
How lucky he is to brighten and dim

After a while I could keep up with old Earl; my stride improved with every sunrise. I have no idea just how many of them I witnessed but I assure you I simply couldn't get enough. The bright glow over-top an empty desert was often the only fixture in the sky—not a cloud to budge in its way. The horizon glowed before us like it was the very destination we sought after. The nighttime sky was just as bright with-out it—stars glistened around the majestic moon; I'd always ponder the past when it took its crescent form. But I loved mornings because I knew it was another chance to gain headway. It was time spent getting closer and closer to my dearest Kalea.

When Earl wasn't busy shouting out some limerick, I'd fill him in on stories about her and my years spent waiting in the bay. I wanted to get back to that old, stagnant spot—knowing the name Hawaii gave it all the more prominence and beauty. But sometimes neither of us would speak on the matter; we'd watch the sun slowly slip away.

Mountain peaks looked large and looming but a dipping sun hid-ing behind its sharp edges made it seem like we had arrived at the edges of its lair. The first time I heard wolf howls I spun and dug a hiding hole as quickly as I could. Earl laughed and smiled, assuring me they were friends proclaiming the serenity of the land around us, asking the sun to return so we could once again bask in its visceral beauty.

The grass was a dark, calming green, sprawling for as far as we could see. I don't know how long we journeyed to be honest—access to the time was not at our hand. It felt like we'd strived toward a location for eternity; it was almost sad having to just pass through.

If you are gripping the pages, anticipating a lengthy waterfall scene where we take a wrong turn and plummet into a misty, rumbling pool below—I'm sorry to disappoint. We were careful; Earl had a sixth sense for these types of obstacles, carefully guiding us through rapids and speedy, tumultuous curves. Whenever a steep incline or a straight drop advertising certain death came our way, we would find another path down. Mind you, for most of the trip, we were heading upstream so we always knew what was waiting ahead.

As my stride grew more powerful, so did my appetite. Mossy grasses and weeds were bountiful in these rivers and streams but they never did fill me up. The taste? Remarkable. They were not sweet like what I was used to, but instead an oaky, bold, cleaner flavor. I couldn't get enough and evidently, the same went for Earl. All during that lengthy adventure, I never once saw him eat a single bite of meat. Surely that comforted me—for every day that I saw this, I was certain I wouldn't succumb and be his next meal…so long as he didn't relapse.

I asked him why and he would just sing away and mumble his limericks. Occasionally he'd spit out if he didn't care for the taste. And while that applied to me as well, I needed something extra to keep up my strength. It felt strange to let Earl see, so I'd sneak the odd snail or dragonfly when he wasn't looking. I felt strange about the act of eating too—the taste and texture was appalling as were my murderous actions. I would just tell myself it was the cycle of life and it was required in order to keep moving. After I gulped whatever poor creature it was down my throat, I'd wonder how exactly Earl was managing on just grass and weeds. I thought back to the villainous gulls who murdered my kin—I was no better than them.

Of course, I completely retracted that cycle of life statement when a grizzly bear came bounding out from some bushes one afternoon. Actually, here's a little scene of frightful action for you! This angry, hungry, miserable bear of a bear was determined to make us his predinner snack but blessed Earl wouldn't let this be so! He stood his ground, gnashing his fangs and arching his back! I would have helped but once again there was nothing I could do.

Paralyzed with fear, I was certain the bear's paw could smash right down through my shell if he wanted to. I was completely dependent on Earl to survive. But truthfully, it was me, embarrassingly, who saved our lives that day—the bear looked over and saw my salt shaker contraption, sending him into convulsing laughter. I tried to defend it, adamant it helped me swim more comfortably but this only sent him into further hysterics. He left us alone but the mental damage from this was done. I tried to throw the shaker right off me but I had to depend on Earl to remove and fasten it. He laughed and thanked me for my bravery before we kept on.

Oh, here's another good close call you might enjoy. One night when my salt had run out, Earl insisted on replenishing the supply by sneaking into a bustling party held in a nearby building. I in return insisted to go with him this time, which was something he didn't take too kindly to. He warned me to keep my distance as the humans swayed away. All I wanted was to see Earl in action and observe the activities mainland humans enjoyed.

I poked my head in as Earl kept to the wall edge toward the food table. I watched uniformed men flash around medals on their chest as they lovingly flung women with gorgeous curls about. All of them seemed to drink steadily as some absent but lovely voice sang something about dancing cheek to cheek.

It looked like a wonderful time until one of the humans spotted me and they began passing me around, tossing me about so everyone got a turn to grab. Earl growled as he saw this wild game of pass around on his way out with the new shaker. Some giggly woman let me slip through her fingers, which caused my rough landing upon the ground. They became so enthralled with laughter and locking lips, I was able to slip away untouched. It took Earl a long while to forgive me for that one.

The rolling canyon hills that seemed as though the world had become wrinkled in that precise spot—that will always stick with me. Looking high up and never finding the top, it felt like these towering red waves of dust and sand wound forever. It didn't seem possible. I felt as though we would be alone until the end of time.

It was here my supply of salt ran short. One real challenge we faced was being completely blocked by a dam; a literal sturdy cement dam that ended the river without guilt. Up the jagged rock peaks we would have to go. I don't know how much you know about me and my lack of coordination and grip to climb with. If open Ocean terrified me, this was certainly the next level that threw me into an all-out panic. I'd look down to find solid, hard ground waiting for my body to fall back onto it. I shivered and shook but found escape in Earl's songs. I joined in to form a rousing chorus with him, putting one flipper in front of the other, one vertical step at a time.

When you climb a mountain face,
there's a trick that you should know.
Face the challenge with some grace
and the higher you will go.

Just know that you will come down,
To the bottom you will slide.
Throw away your frightened frown,
There'll always be another ride.

Before I knew it, we made it to the top, although my shaker wiggled itself loose and plummeted straight down to the rocks below. Hearing it shatter into a million pieces was really not a comforting sound. But the warm bask in the sun made it all okay. Earl's persistent cough, however, sent my worriment into a spiraling growth. He'd been hacking away since the canyon but dismissed it as dry air. Watching him huff and puff atop that cliff had me on both a literal and figurative edge. He looked bloated and pale. His determination to keep me going had me thinking otherwise.

Ready to replace my shaker, he entered the nearest and most intriguing place he could find. Bright, flashing pink letters had me hypnotized as I waited in the nearby fountain. As I paddled along, minding my own business in a moment of much appreciated peace and serenity, a man in a checkered suit marched hastily down the sidewalk, followed by two other similarly dressed associates. They all wore the same fedora-type hat. The followers scribbled down just about everything the lead one shouted out. He stopped dead in his tracks when he passed me floating in apparently his fountain. He looked back at his men.

"What is this? We got livestock floating around my hotel now? Does this look like a zoo?"

He shouted as both dumbstruck men looked at each other in fear. As I watched, one of them turned to apparently clear me out, but that's precisely when Earl came bounding out the front doors with a salt shaker in his mouth. His eyes were as wide as saucers—pupils swirling every which way. I can only imagine what he saw in that bright, flashing behemoth of a building. All three men watched Earl scurry along past their feet and into the pool beside me.

"I want all animals gone and out of the Flamingo. I need a break I tell ya. By the time I get back from Beverly Hills, not one more animal in my hotel! Got it?"

The men nodded, both scribbling down the heated words as they stormed over to the door. That, I remember, was a real close call!

After leaving the strange central desert town, Earl had some trouble finding his bearings. We had seemed to have run out of river, prompting him to wonder if we overshot our exit and had to go back. With no real sense of direction, all Earl really knew was that we were looking for the Ocean and it was nowhere to be found. We couldn't just ask someone either—I'm afraid it doesn't work that way in the wild. We'd walk for miles on the side of dirt roads, asking scorpions where they led but no one truthfully knew (or cared). It was hot and that made them all short-tempered and unwilling to help. That also made Earl all the more confused and angered by his lack of an inner compass.

We tried rivers and lakes but most of them seemed to abruptly end while others would be reminiscent of ways we already passed. Going in circles brought out stress and weakness in Earl I never thought existed. He didn't have anything riding on this journey other than helping me achieve my own goal anyway. Why me, I wondered? Why would he help little old me?

I often pestered poor Earl to find out just how he had heard of my homeland. If he hadn't been there, what critters bestowed the glowing recommendations of the beloved sandy beaches and waving grass hula skirts? Earl just assured me it was common knowledge that spread through animal folk—especially well traveled ones like him.

When we were lost in the desert I asked again. It was there he confirmed some flirtatious Greenbacks told him one day and made him pick out a pineapple to prove their land was best. Earl fell in love with the taste and apparently both of them. That apparently began Earl's shoplifting missions as well as an unusual, frowned upon relationship between species. He'd do anything to satisfy them, including the odd pineapple recon mission, until the great blue waves of home called them back. That was all I could ever get out of him.

One night after we decided to go off to bed, I awoke in the desert to find nothing but a long string of blood soaking the soil. It evidently wasn't coming from me so I carefully followed it, fearing my travel companion had been claimed as a meal or, worse, took his own life out of frustration.

After following the trail behind a man-shaped cactus, I found Earl sitting there. He whimpered and moaned in frustration, blood dripping from his chin—splashing when he coughed. By his feet sat the remains of a dessert cottontail, devoured almost completely besides its bones and stomach sack.

Earl couldn't look me in the eye, nor could he look at the murderous mess he had made—shame covered more than just his face. Being lost had me in a tizzy too, but not enough to spill blood like that. I just smiled and sighed, mustering a sympathetic look of hope and help. The taste of blood could get him lunging toward me next but I felt I knew Earl better than that. As I sat beside him, he remained still—staring far ahead at his past.

"Oh, Little Buddy, I feel like it's been an entire lifetime since I've tasted gristle and flesh between my teeth. Far too long for any beast of my stature but for me not long enough. I didn't mean it, honest I didn't. All of 'em, I didn't mean it. I still remember the look in his eye…the screams I worked so hard to silence as quickly as I could. I killed 'em all, Little Buddy, just to get the taste of meat again and my belly full. And the boy…he was just a boy wandering close to see himself in the water. I didn't want to do it but there was some flash of another being that took over me. Some primal anger inside me that propelled me forward, Little Buddy. Not a day goes by I don't think of that family. Of every family I went and ruined because of an uncontrollable appetite. I owe 'em all life. So that's what I got to do. I got to give you life and get you to that Ocean to make it all worthwhile—to make it better. I got to keep making it up to them."

Tears streamed down his face, dribbling past his nose until it met the splattered blood on Earl's jaw. I took another step closer. "It's okay. It's life." As the words left my mouth, I had to think—was that true? Was it just life, those horrid, flapping gulls dive-bombing my brothers? Was it natural that they were to be gobbled up so carelessly and quickly?

What had I become then, sneaking bugs when Earl wasn't looking? The life cycle was the most vicious beast of all but who were we to deny our animal instincts? Did that apply too to the humans who took us? The ones who spent days carrying out experiments and the ones who suddenly snatched our land back at home? Was this all part of the life cycle or were there limits?

Here I was, sitting next to a mass murderer who perhaps even claimed victims of my own kind. But Earl never seemed bad to me in the least! He was helping me get home, after all, and had risked his life for others about a thousand times since I first laid eyes on him. Perhaps it was because I had gotten to know him—made it past the claws and fangs. Maybe my human captors were misunderstood too and I was only studying them from one biased view? Maybe, just, maybe, the same went for the murderous flock that finished my family. Maybe that included the entire Ocean.

I smiled and invited Earl to come with me to Hawaii. There, he would at least have one true friendship that was not built on heroism or fan worship or worst of all, fear. He shivered as he smiled, eagerly thanking me between each "yes." Sometimes, you just need to forgive and move on.

And we had been moving all right—traversing through rivers and canals for the better part of five years.

EIGHTEEN

EARL WAS even more relaxed and good-natured than I ever imagined possible after that night. There was a difference between him feeling he owed everyone good gestures and him just doing it strictly for you. He was adamant about filling my salt shaker, though neither the opportunity nor water came up through our latter travels. His songs felt cheerful and his demeanor more hopeful, despite the plain fact we were lost.

There was no clear path to the Ocean that Earl could recollect, and no one seemed to point us in the right direction. I could have been mad that the silly gator got us mixed up in a weaving maze of sand after claiming he had traveled the route many times before. While in fact he had, toilets and sewers were the preferred method of motion. I took pride in the fact that I could not fit down a toilet bowl—I was actually too big for something!

Unable to locate a proper river or a sewer pipe, let alone one big enough, we found ourselves in the ditch of the famed highway Route 66. Earl had told me all about it along our trip and how the "Oakies," as he called them, used it to seek out a better life just a few years before.

Now, we watched elongated fins and rims of near coral colors fly by with families of four crammed in next to suitcases. Angry fathers glared out at the road while their wives flipped through frivolous fashion magazines. Their children sat behind where they smacked each other and the seats and the windows and everything around them in a release of spastic boredom. I swear to you, this was every car!

This is where Earl got the harebrained idea to hitch a ride. He figured about half of them were headed for the California beaches, which was apparently where we needed to go too. So the question of the matter became how do we flag one of them down? Surely, they weren't going to just stop and offer us a ride—humans and reptiles don't get along that well for some reason…because of the teeth I think.

Earl tried first, lying down completely in the middle of the road. Trust me, he botched the idea a few times, racing off the road before the car came in contact. A few actually seemed like they wanted to hit him or something. Eventually, he worked up the courage to stay put but the car just went right around. Then I tried, feeling a tad braver than he, thanks to the confidence-boosting layer of protection on my back. They all drove around me without the slightest dip in speed.

The plan's crescendo came after we both decided to lie together on the road, blocking the entire lane. Vehicles would have no choice but to stop and move us or simply drive on overtop. At least we'd die together if that was the case.

Low and behold, a Plymouth came to a wobbly halt right before my head. I know it was a Plymouth because the lettering nearly pressed up against my face. We were so astonished a car actually stopped we weren't even sure what to do! As the door swung open, Earl charged into action and tried to slither in between the man's legs and into the seat where he'd find us a space to stow away. We didn't count on the man having a squeamish fear that caused him to step on Earl and flee back to his car. He took off faster than any car I'd seen before or since.

We repeated the process, figuring the interior was a no-go zone for us. We would have to settle for the rooftop, but neither of us could get ourselves hoisted up there. Earl managed once but he couldn't reach to pull me up with him as the car sped away. He had nothing to reach for either so he went flying backward, completing at least three or four bounces across the pavement. The car was already halfway down the road but I could hear them all scream bloody murder when they saw Earl come rolling down off the trunk. This is when we realized our plan wasn't going to work.

So there we sat, dehydrated as all hell in the ditch of Route 66. It had been days since we had a dip of water, and the sun decided to be extra cruel that afternoon. The beam of hot, heavy heat extracted every bead of water from our bodies, drying them out until we were jerky with eyes. I could feel my drooping skin crack and slump into near liquid itself.

We tried to retreat back to water, any water—the fountain at the Flamingo would do. But we couldn't move; we were so weak and sickly. I craned my head to look above, where sure enough, three vultures circled in a determined counterclockwise descent. I rasped and croaked to Earl, who only mumbled and coughed without any movement. We had come so far but it seemed our number was up. The end was official this time and ironically, it was the opposite of the Ocean that would do it to me.

I awoke to the refreshing coolness of water splashing upon my face. I whisked along at sport boating speeds, skimming atop the crystal clear lake. Massive talons gripped me from all sides like the constrictive bars of a prison. Above me was the brutish body of the ugliest vulture you ever did see. A dried out, beet red, drooping face stared out straight ahead as it ascended from the water. Its wings blocked out all sunlight and any possible view—they were astonishingly massive.

A second one did the same with Earl, caging him in its grip as it flapped along. I worried Earl had already left us until a burst of coughing flew out of his toothy grin. I called his name but he could not answer. Weakly, I watched the third vulture guide his friends out and front until I fell back asleep.

I think I didn't really care about flying high this trip because I was so fixated on what was to come or where we were headed. I did not feel dizzy nor did I think I'd plummet to my death—the vulture had a tight, secure grip. I'd imagine being picked apart once we finally got to our destination by thousands of rapid birds. Every few hours the vulture would dip me in a stream or lake and make sure I was fed. I was certain they were just keeping us alive so we'd be fresh for the feast.

I awoke several more times, less and less groggy each time my eyes fluttered open. Typically we'd be out in mid-flight; sometimes, we'd be perched on the side of the road. The vultures would be having a feast, surely devouring a dead carcass while Earl and I waited off to the side.

When I really got my strength back, I shook Earl as violently as I could; now was our chance. Poor Earl was much too worse for wear, so no matter my poking and prodding, he refused to get up. I told him we had to go and that now was the moment of escape. I even tried to sneak away but knew in all good conscience I couldn't leave my travel companion to die. So I crawled back to my dusty spot and nervously chewed on dead grass as I waited for my number to come up.

"There he is! Bright eyed and bushy tailed."

"Hello, hello! How ya feeling?"

I cowered as the vultures crowded round me—pecking with questions and eager eyes.

"Where are you taking me?"

"Well, where is it you want to go? We've been waiting to hear from you and we're open to suggestions."

I was puzzled. What out-of-their-mind bird does such a thing as offer rides like a taxi service?

"Away from you!"

"You sure? The both of you don't look so hot. We'll take care of you, we swear!"

"You don't want to eat us?"

The vultures cackled and flapped as they waddled around the desert floor. Something about my distrust made them roar with laughter. Poor Earl lay there in pain, watching the entire hysterical scene unfold.

"No, pal, we don't want to eat you. We're here to spread joy and cheer."

"We're the Good Time Gang, at your service."

"But you're vultures!"

"We're changing our image! Helped a little ground squirrel get across a river last week."

"Delivered a pair of frogs to a nice bog just a few states over one month before that."

"Our work is never done."

I still didn't quite register what they were doing. I could only respond again with the fact that they were vultures.

"That may be true, but with all the troubles that have been going down these days, pal, I think the world could use a few straight-shooting birds like us."

"Well, what do you eat if not the dead or dying?" I inquired curiously. The third and silent one, the one who had not carried us through the sky, pulled something from his molting feathers that looked like green-clumped grass. The other two went crazy for the stuff and began pecking it right off the ground. The guardian of it all had to slap their heads a few times and push them away to keep them from gobbling it all up.

"Humphrey here found this delicious plant just thrown away behind a government research station. He had to peck through a few layers of packaging mind you, but we got it and it sure does cure the mind and soul."

"Looks like your pal is really hurting. He could use some of this miracle plant, you know! It's great for what ails you!"

I had noticed we had been flying crooked for most of the journey but I had assumed that was just how it was done. They stopped to eat quite frequently, just about anything they could get their mouths around. Rocks, bark, fish, cactus…there were no limits to what they would munch on or carry out in absurd actions. There were quite a few nosedives to the ground and bumps into tree stumps. But they weren't going to eat us so what did I care how they flew.

"The Ocean! Can you get us to the Ocean?" I screamed. All three looked at each other and snickered with delight.

"No worries. Just sit back and have a good time." They collectively pushed the green grass over to Earl who had enough sense to chew it up and go back to sleep. Still to this day, I don't know really what it was, but Earl hadn't sung like he did that night in the whole time I knew him. I only munched on a small bit, but once we hit open sky, my world was changed. The colors I had first discovered in the Ocean were surpassed. A few times I could have sworn I had wings of my own.

Still, my winces and shivers every time a bird claw came toward me didn't help our trust issues during the journey. One of them actually pulled me aside one night after the others had all fallen asleep. He could see—despite the fun I was having with them—there was a deep, inner part of me that simply could not let go.

"What is it? What's got you down?" he inquired. After ten dismissals and four changes of subject, I took a breath and recounted my birth to him.

"My family—all of my brothers and sisters and maybe even… maybe even my mother were eaten. There was no hint of mercy. There was no sign of guilt." As I got worked up and ranted louder, he shushed me and stroked his wing along my shell in a comforting, full-body pet.

"I know. I hear you. I was like that once too. I broke up families and ended prosperous lives all for the cause of a midnight snack. But let me tell ya, they do it cause their cowards. They prey on the weak. Birds are more afraid of you than you are of them."

"Well, then what chance do I have? Look at me."

"Yes! Look at you! Impenetrable shell. Bulky, muscular flippers. Birds like food but they hate movement and they hate to work for their meals. I'm sorry for the pain my kind caused you. But do not fear us; stand your ground. Just give us a swat and you'll be fine."

I gently raised my flipper in mock defense but the gentle vulture just shook his head and corrected me with a wave of his wing. "No, no, no. Like this." For the remainder of the night, we laughed as we swatted our way through lessons in bird defense. I began to smile as his wacky movements showed me only a gentle heart beat inside him. Though I couldn't forgive the flock that devoured my family, this was a start.

The journey became kind of relaxing for the most part. Flying didn't bother me so much after that night, and for the day I'd typically lay back in the vulture's claws and watch the scenery go by. The rolling hills filled with crispy, dead grass didn't seem to offer the greatest of views but it did stretch on for miles. Sometimes the peaks were so jagged I couldn't understand just how they came to be.

One day we even flew over a movie set. An honest production with old-fashioned wagons rolling along that I hadn't seen since the first time I washed up on shore. Embarrassingly enough, I thought it was all real until the vultures pointed out the bulky, black cameras that captured the rough-and-tumble cow folk. I had never seen a movie yet in my life but that would drastically change in the years to come. The vultures swore we made it into the shot but I wasn't so sure. I was more focused on the man with one eye, yelling and waving a tin horn in his hands—the other eye was blocked completely by a dark patch. The movies looked like a bizarre place to be and I simply did not understand. Again, believe me, that would all change.

Most of those days consisted of the Good Time Gang flapping their way to the Ocean and dipping us down for water and food. We'd camp out at night and tell stories and chat. Earl was really on an honest route to recovery thanks to the mysterious plant they were feeding him. Plus, all the resting time during the day helped him conserve energy.

We really lucked out on this one and I swear I tried my best to repay the silly birds, but the group was "out patrolling for good and serving the animal kingdom the best they could." They were funny cutups who I wished a long and fruitful life. If only the rest of the world had discovered their strange, stolen grass—perhaps there would be a lot more spirit and sweetness among humans if that were to be grown and sold on the market. Either way, I was beginning to trust birds more than I ever thought I would have in my lifetime.

Out of seemingly nowhere one day, a bright white sign perched up in the hills that read "Hollywood" came into view. Studios and bungalows and pools and palm trees stretched as far as the eye could see—you can be rest assured this bird did in fact dip me in some poor human's backyard swimming pool.

Oh, and then there it was—the Ocean that stretched on until the end of time. Beautiful blue and green water with swaying whitecaps; how I had missed it! Earl awoke with confusion, peering from side to side as we neared contact with the big blue. Without word or warning the vulture let go, sending us straight into the glistening water—now that felt like home to me. Earl joined me with a thrashing splash; the cool water did him a world of good. We watched them circle in the sky and head back in the direction they had just come.

Left with directional choice, looming vessels, and familiar droves of saluting men in green, the mission for home continued and was just about a near success.

NINETEEN

THE WATER silenced Earl's coughing while the sight of nearby ships rejuvenated all hope and light in our eyes. I couldn't actually believe it—I had made it to water, to the brink of home and Kalea and all that I held dear. I was so happy I absolutely had no idea how to conduct myself; all I could do was flip around the familiar liquid—salt infused, of course.

"Well, Little Buddy—let's get swimming. Times a ticking and we have a long journey ahead."

I gulped—amidst the entire journey's hours, it had never dawned on me we'd have to swim across the dreaded open Ocean to get home. My delight faded as I shook, watching Earl happily splash forward into the bay.

I knew the darkness was coming—enemies and monsters would overtake us, no matter how wide and vicious Earl gnashed his teeth. I would not be protected and I would not stand a chance in a fight. I would be alone in vivid nothingness until something gobbled me up. I swam the rivers but I was no match for the Ocean. It was too far and too treacherous to move forward. There had to be another way.

"Earl…I can't." Without question or protest, Earl turned to see me struggling to keep up once again. He saw the fear in my eyes and ripples expanding after every shake and twitch. Bless him, he never asked why or how or told me to stop. He simply nodded and looked around for options.

Surrounding the pier were rows of women in dim dresses, waving handkerchiefs and frantic hands toward the green-clad men rising up the vessel anchor. Children stood stern, staring out toward their uncertain family futures. Lips pursed against hands while music rose from a small marching band parading in the background. Much was happening but it was safe to say all focus was on the departing ship.

"Them there boats are headed out to sea, over to the biggest naval port in the Pacific." I nodded, unsure just how their route was going to help us. "That would be over in Hawaii, or so those island critters told me," he added. "I think we've earned a break from swimming all this time. All we got to do is hop aboard and enjoy the ride."

Confused but relieved, I agreed to give it a try and followed Earl to one of the massive, flat-deck ships that vigorously honked a familiar sounding horn to clear its path. I was reminded of my old home in the bay—I'd hear that sound echoing all day long. Perhaps this was the best method to get back. Perhaps this is where they had come from all along.

Earl assured me this was his preferred method of transportation, although it wouldn't be pretty. It would take some getting used to but it would be fast and we'd at last be fed and watered. We'd just have to be brave. So we slunk to the ship and dove down deep (its bottom seemed to stretch forever).

Inside a small hatch, Earl weaseled his way until he disappeared completely. With a deep breath, I followed suit but found myself stuck halfway. It took a lot of yanking and pulling on Earl's part to get me through. I wondered if I was getting bigger but that of course was wishful thinking.

Through a slimy, dark maze, Earl scooted along the wall edge with excitement radiating all around him. I could hardly see but I could feel and most certainly smell. A foul odor wafted through the darkness, stinging every sense with a horrid, rotten scent. Every step squished and slid under my flippers. Slippery and sickening, I couldn't help but wonder if it was old kelp decaying under coats of fuzzy moss and algae.

As I did my best to stop the odor from penetrating seemingly everything, including my thoughts, we came to a wheel; a strange contraption that spun upon touch. Earl climbed right in which forced it to turn and carried him to the other side. Nervously I followed, spinning into a dark mystery until Earl once again came into view. Then up we swam, swam and climbed until the vile water was no more—only a chamber above us with a plain hole for entry and exit.

Earl hoisted himself up and leant a hand to pull me up with him. With all his strength, it still took a few tries until I was able to propel myself forward through the water and up into the tank. We both laid back, gasping for air after a job well done. We had made it to our hideaway until our destination arrived.

"How are we going to know when we've gotten there? We can't see a thing!" I inquired. Just then, the ship took off on a rocky, swaying journey into rough waters. We swished about, slime and hardy liquids splashing back and forth from one side to the other—and us along with it.

"Once this feeling stops," Earl replied, "they'll blast the horn and we'll be still."

I watched Earl make himself comfortable like he'd done exactly this before. The gator had seemingly done a lot of traveling through sewer lines and pipes buried deep down in the ground.

This was his world, but for me, it would take some getting used to. The constant, violent rocking would take a long while to acclimate with. Then there were the seeping, dripping, horrid, semi-solid piles of waste that surrounded every corner. Not to mention a steady flow of new batches flooding down the pipe above us. I wondered what kind of pleasant comfort humans were treated to in other rooms of the vessel.

I got the idea to plug it up so no more could enter, but whoever was above always found a forceful way to dislodge it all through. At certain times, the contents would be sucked through the hole below us where it was all spun and churned and stored and sent away to the sea. We were very careful not to go out with it, usually claiming one nook of the hole as our own little safe spot. At first the smell was enough to physically sting—surely I passed out a few times, but as time went on, I just put up with it. Really, it was our only means of survival.

I asked Earl why this was the place of all places to stow away and he assured me humans would toss us overboard without hesitation or mercy if they were to find us—and that might even be the kindest act they'd carry out. There was no water or food that he knew of onboard that we could help ourselves to without risking capture. What we had wasn't glamorous but at least we had liquid to soak in and sip. As for food, half-digested meals and scraps thrown down the garbage disposal became our only option.

Occasionally, there would be lettuce bits or corn or even small bugs that found their way inside our chamber. But I really got a taste for human food for the first time that consisted of mostly meat off bones and potatoes prepared in various softening ways. The scraps weren't much but at least there was variety. String beans were the closest comfort to a home meal for me, while sweet sugary substances became a rare treat. I always thought about Kalea when that came flooding down the pipe.

Earl ate everything without qualm or concern. But little by little I noticed his appetite was shrinking. In all the time spent blinded by darkness in the chamber, I could feel Earl's body shriveling up. I could hear vicious coughing fits and spit up splashing onto the floor. After a while I rarely heard him eat anything at all. Sometimes I didn't hear him speak or even move for what felt like days.

It was a lengthy journey that should have made me feel like I was right back in that tank again. But the hope of seeing Kalea was so close I could almost reach out and touch it—the nearing proximity helped pass the time and kept me grounded.

I'd blabber on about her, describing her beauty and rehearsing just what I was going to say to her once I saw her standing there. I'd tell her how much I loved her and how the moment we met defined me. How I thought of her every moment I was gone and how she was the driving force behind my return. How I ventured and braved the elements to see her again. My wonderful sweet Kalea was all I needed. Earl agreed that it was perfect.

We'd talk about life and love and sometimes Earl would get enough strength to sing. We had nothing else to do so we had to pass the time through conversation, games, and near-psychotic sing-alongs. I spy in the dark was out of the question.

Some days I couldn't contain my excitement as I sloshed around, while others I couldn't stave off boredom, wanting still silence in the chamber to finally come. It was maddening never seeing the sun or knowing the time of day—all I had were my thoughts to occupy me this time. But it was still vastly different being cooped up in smelly darkness when you were there on your own free will.

"I wonder what everyone who escaped the experiment is doing now. Spreading love and living life to the fullest I would hope." Earl gave no response. "I still wonder what it was we were all doing there.

What did the humans want with us? Why all the ships and celebrations?" Still nothing. "That Boris was really something, wasn't he?"

"What do you think we're supposed to do while we're here, Little Buddy?"

"Well, nothing, Earl," I replied. "Just wait for the ride to be over. What can we do?"

Earl gave a little snort, finding something about my innocent reply amusing. "What happens when it's over? Life! Did I do enough to redeem myself?"

"You've done so much! You've helped me get back home. You saved everyone from that room. Animals will live for generations because of what you've done."

There was a long pause in the haunting dark.

"What if it wasn't enough? What if I started doing it all too late?"

"Too late for what?"

Another snicker followed by a haggard cough and a long sigh.

"Don't you ever think there's more to come?"

I'd been so blinded by the goals of finding Mother and earning Kalea's love and getting home, I never thought about what came after it was all said and done. I was confounded by what the gator was actually getting at—the idea that there was more after death was incomprehensible to me.

"How can there be more once we stop existing?"

"I heard humans talk. Down in the Bijou they'd be chanting and singing for days on end about the big place in the sky. One respected old fellow, Bud Elmer, drowned after fishing around too deep for crawfish. No one took a nip at him; he just fell and couldn't get back in his boat. For days on end they cried about his absence, but these people, I saw them down on their knees begging for forgiveness to nothing there. Forgiveness for Bud and all the fish they took from the river. I'd be shot ten times over if they didn't put down their rifle and get down on their knees first. Guess they wanted to do right by this invisible human. They said they didn't wanna harm me so they'd see Bud again. Clean conscience or something along those lines."

"And they spoke to someone?"

"One all-knowing, wise man that glows with such radiant light—one you can't see with your bare eyes. They created it all and judge who gets to live forever in peace or in strife. But I don't know a critter who knows this more than secondhand! Does it apply to us too? Do we get to see the fallen once again?"

While I reveled in the chance that Kalea and I could be reunited forever, the concept of it all seemed unbelievable to me. I had too many questions that I feared would poke too many holes. I was certain I'd seen no evidence of an all-seeing human and their afterlife paradise.

"Well, where is this place?"

"Far away, Little Buddy, too far to find. But I fear I do not hold the key to entry. I seen that Bud fold his hands every day and give thanks, and I never seen him kill what he didn't have to for food. If people were concerned he didn't make it there, what chance do I have?"

"What concern is it of yours? Earl, this is human stuff. This doesn't apply to us."

A long silence passed. I sensed no movement in the dark. Only the growing puffs of air filtering through Earl's flaring nostrils. I remembered hearing my sentence uttered to me in a disapproving warning before.

"Guess you're right. I just liked the idea that there was more. More than just being a consumer of others, more than just being destined to be somebody's meal. Something to look forward to. I had a family I'd like to see again. Good folks, my ma and pa. Don't you have someone gone that you can't get back?"

I immediately thought of my brothers and sisters, of every single one of them; I had only blurry visions of their frantic panic. I wanted to know them more and discuss with them the ones who created us. Maybe they too had made the long trip to this faraway place.

I thought of Kalea. Kalea who was mere hours away from me now—I had worked so hard to get her back. Of course I had my purpose; something to look forward to. I could not bend to the pit of my stomach where a growing fear of life worth gathered. Her love was everything to me and Earl's guilt wasn't going to change any of that.

"There's nothing, Earl; what you see is what you get. And I have it. Love for Kalea. It's all I ever needed to give in order to feel good. I'm sorry you don't have a perfect partner but I assure you, you deserve one. Once we get off the boat, we'll take a look around for—"

"Come on, you're telling me this love of yours is so strong there's nothing in this world that can break it?"

"Not distance or time or self-doubt. I just swam rivers and walked deserts for her—nothing can ever keep us apart. Now, I don't know about your afterlife or your forgiveness, but I do know I have a purpose to be the love of her life. That's why we found each other, that's why I'm making it back to her, and that's why we'll spend the rest of our life together. It's destiny!"

Earl's hissy laughter made every bit of my body tense up with anger, ready for attack.

"Don't you think you are leaving a whole lot out there, Little Buddy? Just focusing on one tiny part of life and forgetting the rest. Does loving her really make you that happy?"

"No, I don't. You'll see when we meet. Our love is all that matters. In fact, you said that!"

Silence again. Without the laughter, Earl's wheezy voice turned to a blend of coughs and sighs. I could tell the sickness within him was spreading, and while it took over his voice and lungs, it even seemed to touch his carefree spirit.

"Well good for you, Little Buddy. True, I did say that, and while I admire your determination and certainty on the matter, what if you make it back and find she's dead? What if this beauty of yours has moved on with another partner? Or worse yet, what if you never find her? What kind of purpose is that for you? Wouldn't you want to believe in an afterlife then? Wouldn't you worry your efforts to get you there didn't pay off? What would you do?"

Before I could answer with an ill-informed defense, a grand echo vibrated through the chamber as the water and sewage came to a standstill. The horn let out a stern, elongated blast as the vessel suddenly came to a grinding halt. What would I do indeed!

TWENTY

FRESH AIR was just what we needed in that moment. I sucked in pleasant, gentle odors I'd been craving ever since we crawled up into the chamber. You get used to the pungent smell but a trip outdoors reminds you just how sweet and flowery and wonderful air should be.

Earl let in a few gasps as he rolled around, eyes glazed and stomach swelled. Hitting the icy cold water below and reveling in the rain pelting down from above, he became renewed to a small degree. I think the smell and lack of fresh…anything had made him sick along the journey. I nudged Earl along to the land, thinking he was going to need all the help I could muster to get to shore and find home. The toothy grin was back as he splashed along to my home.

"Welcome home, Little Buddy."

At this point he still could not speak very clearly, only mumble or hiss. His persistent cough had turned into wheezing and gasping but the gargling of fresh water cleared it all away. With my head, I pushed him along up the muddy slopes and to a grassy patch where I feasted on sweet, familiar blades.

While it was a dreadful, intense situation, I could hardly contain my excitement. We had achieved our goal and made it back to my home—to Hawaii. All I had to do now was journey back through the familiar and find my darling Kalea. And sickness be darned, Earl was coming with me.

We would stop every little while for Earl to catch up and rest but thankfully his strength seemed to be building, and sooner or later he began to keep a steady pace. When he got too tired, I would push him along or even pull him a few steps by letting him rest atop my shell. The pounding rain made it much too slippery for him to stay on for very long, though.

I'd point to familiar trees and tell him the history of what I knew. Carnations once again grew freely on budding stems around us. The water tasted like it always had and now I knew the reason why—salt. It was home all right, a familiar, wondrous place I had spent years trying to get back to. And now I was here! I was back!

As we wandered along the water, I couldn't help but notice men unloading in the quickest of fashions. Some took smaller boats while others raced to shore on foot. They all wore dark green helmets and carried long guns with the barrel pointed up as high as they could.

I wondered why they didn't arrive to the mustached President's docking base since that's what it seemed to have been used for. I feared we were far away from that side of the island, or worse, the neighborhood had changed more drastically than I imagined. But there were simply no remnants of what had been built for all those years—perhaps Kalea had moved to another place.

As we marched on through rainfall, I screamed Kalea's name with hope and excitement. There were no creatures stirring no matter where you looked. As I gazed on, I saw the grass inland had been trampled and burnt while trees leaned crookedly—some even wilting under flames. As I frantically searched for help of any kind, a pair of shivering, wide eyes caught my attention. A gecko retreated as far back as she could as I eagerly bounded toward her.

"What is happening? Where is everyone? Can you tell me what part of the island I'm on?" No response. The gecko looked around, eventually locking her frightened stare on Earl. "He needs help. Do you know of anyone? Do you know Kalea?"

As the earth below us rumbled, the gecko made a mad dash past me under a pile of rustling leaves. The calming, green color that had returned to Earl's face vanished as the trees swayed and the ground shook like thunder. We shared a look, a mutual passing of concern and fear. I wondered what had happened to my dear home and Earl wondered if he would in fact make it through this ordeal or not. With a couple gasps of air, he nodded and gestured ahead. Now was the time to run.

We crept over soggy leaves and hurdled over broken branches. We fought and dragged ourselves past the elements, determined not to give up now. But if there is one item that can stop you dead in your tracks, it's a bullet.

Gunfire erupted from the trees as greenery seemed to move on its own free will. Men from either side of us moved forth, aiming their weapons in frightened haste as cigarettes flew out of their mouths and helmets bounced up and off their heads.

As shrapnel came bounding over, a circular medal with red atop blue landed by Earl's feet. He let out a bothered sigh after a glance at the supporting Hangul.

"Communists," he grumbled.

In the piercing and bustling battle zone, I felt the only reasonable place to go was back to the water. The storm of newly arrived men seemed to push their way inland.

Earl's eyes were wide as his head bobbled from side to side, scouting out danger. His coordination had diminished from our river floating days but he managed to slip past racing feet tromping all around us.

We raced between men's legs who collapsed beside us like freestanding gelatin. One of them, recently made headless, fell directly on top of me. With all his weight over me, I squirmed but could not get myself free. Earl pulled with all his might until I popped out as the force of another fallen man rolled the other body backward. Nearby explosions made them jump up into midair from sheer force anyhow.

We continued to weave our way to the water, bathing in fresh pools of blood as we crawled. As I turned to make sure Earl was still with me, a bullet went ahead and grazed my shell, taking out a small chunk on the top left side. I did not feel any pain, just the shocking force of the graze that chipped my beloved cover. To this day a white mark is still visible in that spot. I remember Earl laughing at that occurrence—actually laughing behind me in bewildered hysterics.

"What a crazy, lucky little critter you are. Did you see that?"

"No, but I felt it. Just keep going."

"Okay, but do you think we got time for me to invest in one of them shells?"

We weaved our way behind men and blockages they quickly set up using branches and sandbags and any tools they had. I desperately wanted to stop, only for a second to understand what was happening. When I tried, Earl would yell and push me on.

I wondered what had happened to my homeland. Why in these past years had such fiery explosions been the common thread of danger in my life? What type of advancements were happening in the human world, and more importantly, why were there conflicts? It was then I wanted to ask Earl these very questions, who I was certain would have a strong opinion. But my mouth was full of mud and bits of flesh while my heart raced quickly; I lost track of all thoughts and a logical grip on our surroundings when the noise became much too overbearing.

It was then I saw the point of a gun barrel from far in the distance and a human racing for cover beside us. His feet nearly stumbled over Earl, but his uncoordinated dance made him fall flat a few flippers away.

The gunman missed his target but hit another. An unrelenting bullet put Earl out of his misery. Lodging its way through his stomach and tearing through his wounded insides, blood spurted out as his breath drew to a halt and his eyes rolled shut. I let go and screamed in anger and sadness for what felt like an eternity.

I gripped his body, holding it as close to mine as I could. I did not want to let Earl go; he was the very reason I had made it this far. The one I owed my very life to for saving me back at the room. It's funny how after someone you know dies all of the bad memories or little irritants you had against them disappear without a trace. You hold them up in the highest esteem and beg for more time with them.

For the first while you can't believe they are actually gone before you move into the hero phase where you praise and cherish every little action they took. I wished he had decided to stay on the mainland, which prompted me to think of ways time travel could be accessed. Whizzing bullets, one after another, made me snap out of another wave of wishful thinking and realize that I was still alive, and better yet, unscathed.

I opened my mouth the widest it could go, filling it with Earl's cold flab to try and drag him along. The journey would be too slow. I had to leave him. I checked at least one thousand times to confirm he was in fact no longer with us. Searching for some kind of error, hoping that he would bolt up with fresh breath and a witty joke, I saw no life in his eyes.

I scampered a few flippers away, only to return to him. I repeated the process about a half dozen times—getting further and further on each attempt. Finally it came time to say goodbye, which I uttered through tears and slime masking my blubbering face. He would not be forgotten and certainly he would not go unrewarded. I would pass on every song and limerick and heroic deed I ever saw him do. With a deep breath, I made a break for the water. I heard bullets disturb and churn the very ground I so recently left beside his body. With one last look, I said goodbye to dear Earl.

Alone.

Alone is how I felt when I returned to the water. Unsure and frightened of my next move, I tried to retreat to the vessel but there was no way I was climbing back into the chamber. Every decision was now up to me, which was both freeing and completely terrifying. I didn't know where to head so after a few circular laps offshore, I returned to land and headed up the coastline. Men stampeded from that direction too. They were everywhere.

I looked up and saw spinning blades carrying metal rooms in the sky, casting men out to the ground via large blankets on strings. One by one, they came crashing into the water as the sky vessels circled around on a retreat. Others went straight ahead, dropping water that seemed to create a vicious explosion of smoke and fire when it reached the ground. I couldn't escape and I certainly could not fight. My only option was to hide.

With no time to bury myself in sand and no place to get through the forest wall, I had no choice but to use what I had. A fortress of sticks and rocks and broken trees would have been the solution here but there was no way of penetrating the safer side. So I retreated into the accessory that saved me moments before; my shell.

Some of you have probably wondered why I hadn't hidden there before this point while others might be a bit more astute on the subject. Being what I was, my kind actually lacks the ability to go inside. It acts merely as a cover and not a home like so many other species use it for. But I chose to defy that basic logic and try my damndest to make it work.

I folded my arms and legs underneath me—yes it was painful and the circulation was nil. But they were covered and guarded, only leaving my head. Sore from the cramped chamber, it was extra work retracting inwards, but bit by bit I was able to bring my head in until I could see darkness overtop. Creaks and cracks and shooting pain were only a temporary ailment. I desperately wanted to see Earl at all costs. I hoped he was right. I had to see him again. And where was Kalea? That's what kept me going—I had to find Kalea.

But there was this sneaking suspicion all around me that tipped me off I may not be home after all. There was no way such a peaceful land could be ripped apart and ravaged by hateful battle.

So many questions to ponder…that's all I had. My questions blocked out the exploding wreckage and screams of pain. I shut my eyes and quivered, fearful and stiff. My shell provided comfort but answers to questions would have shielded and comforted me in the moment all the more. I waited for absolute silence before I allowed my head to return outwards. I ached all over—inside and out.

TWENTY-ONE

SILENCE IS often a goal many seek to find answers or peace. They take solace in a break from the grinding noisemaker that is society. But it can also be the calm before the storm; the simplicity before the complication.

I had endured silence for much of my early life and it calmed me then because it seemed as though monsters could not reach me. But I have grown to fear it, thinking there is most certainly some kind of striking danger lurking in the quiet. I had come to distrust it. Perhaps it was a sign that there was no one else around. Everything, big and small, miniscule and life defining, was now up to me.

Silence surrounded me as I crept along the bodies, past the broken artillery and through shredded pieces of bark and leaves. At least the rain had stopped. As I looked out at calm waters, the sight seemed distant and unfamiliar—I did not connect with the sun like I always had. I turned my back and sought answers through the trees. I spent hours searching for a way in and finally found a path that revealed itself past a blockade of locked branches.

The sunlight wove its way through the trees, illuminating small patches of the forest floor. The first sounds were songbirds chirping sweetly. I did not fear them; it sounded innocent enough and even welcoming to my ringing ears. Marching forth like I was placed in a trance, I wandered, searching for clues and answers. Everyone seemed to remain in hiding.

After another struggle through plant life, I came to the most beautiful of lakes. Small and nearly perfectly circular, this space had little blockage so the sunlight reached it and lit its entire surface.

As I dipped my left flipper, a calming warm surrounded my skin—the water relaxed every muscle and pore. I dove in completely, embracing the gentle boil of thermal heat. Steam gently rose up to the sky. The only sound was the kicking splash brought on by my eloquent stride. Drained of all energy, I nearly fell into a relaxed slumber as I drifted along, careful not to stray too far toward the deep darkness.

Movement in the bushes awoke me within an instant.

I looked around and sure enough caught wavering weeds off in the distance. A chill went through my body as the silence was broken by something, or someone, walking through the woods. As I shivered on the lakeshore, dripping wet and still in a daze, I remained still.

I felt as though I was living in a dream, disoriented and unable to get myself straight. I felt like I would collapse at any moment, and in fact, I wanted to. Without knowledge of my whereabouts or a friend's assistance, I had few resources to help fuel the final leg of the trip. As I debated whether to move a flipper forth, those making all the noise surrounded me from each side.

They looked like me—most likely distant cousins of mine. But their backs were flat and damn near square…it was very bizarre. Their heads all were tiny except for their prominent noses claiming most of the space. Then there was the sheer fact of their size! These beasts could have crushed me with one swat. A bizarre wonder to behold, their penetrating, little, yellow eyes beamed at me as I cowered. There were three of them slowly closing in to my right, left, and directly ahead. There would be no escape.

"Why have you come here?" the biggest bellowed.

"Shelter," I mumbled. "Did you not hear the attack?"

"Are you part of the war efforts? Did you come with the invaders?" the second spoke. He seemed smaller and spinier than the others. I hesitated to respond to his question, shaking my head in my truth that I really wasn't part of this war effort that plagued them.

"Are you alone?" the third inquired. Her voice had the most worry and sympathy as her curious eyes watched me cower. I felt comforted by her speech so my gaze fixated on only her when I was called upon to answer. I nodded sadly in response to her question, tears streaming from my eyes.

"But that is my very goal. I need to find my dearest love…my home. What has happened to my beloved beaches? Where is the colorful coral? What has happened to Hawaii?"All three looked at each other, confused by the words I had uttered. "Is this not the island?"

The plumpest and eldest slowly moved forward with a proud look flowing through his face. "This is a land of freedom for all. One shall lead while none shall be left behind. There must only be peace and unity, not violence such as this. I do not know where you stand but we cannot have you here. This is our lake and our home; a balance must be kept to create order. While we hide too, you may not hide here."

"Must you be so cruel? Hear him out!" the female advised. "I am Byeol, and this is Chul and Hyeok. We are the keepers of the lake. Tell us how you have come here."

I could sense by their voices they were old; grander and wiser than I, holding wisdom and tradition of past generations high above all else. They were elegant and hauntingly mystifying, and I was afraid to speak or even remain in their presence—yet I wanted to learn more. Byeol's curiosity toward me calmed me so. I took a breath and stepped forward, desperately pleading my case.

"I have come from far away. I was traveling with an alligator (I remember wowed gasps upon the mention of him) who fell ill and has died in battle. We did not fight; we were desperate to flee. I was taken by strange men who ran tests and kept me locked away for years. But I have escaped and traveled through mountain and desert. I have flown with birds and stowed away in boats. You must help me."

"And who do you seek?" Chul hissed.

"My dearest Kalea; the one who brings me all of life's meaning. I cannot die without her knowing how much I love her and need her. I must be with her. I must get home. It is destiny!"

"There is no Kalea here," Hyeok uttered, his words piercing like a blade. "You have been misled," he continued, until Byeol silenced him with a stare. "Do you not realize what you have done?"

"Where am I then? Where can I go?" I yearned for answers as their bodies swiveled like grinding boulders in the dirt. I followed as they turned—I was desperate for help.

"You have entered our lake, fouled it with your presence. The slightest outside influence can disturb and unfold all we have worked for to achieve peace and unity."

"Come now, I was hardly there. If you won't help me then let me leave. I'm wasting time!"

Angry and weakened by the string of constant setbacks, I turned to leave—finding only the serene lake as a pathway onward. I knew I'd create a fuss if I were to dip back into it. And believe me, as mythical and wise as these beings acted, I did not want to invoke any further kooky conversations. It certainly was not home and I was desperate to carry on. The trees and bushes ahead blurred together in a maze of confusion and trickery.

"I can help you only if you help me. I have traveled to this place you call Hawaii many times as a younger spirit. I can guide you there only if you complete my chosen task."

This is when I turned with newfound rejuvenation for the mission to find Kalea. "Name it! Anything."

Chul grinned. "You see my lake? The very one you have tainted with your presence. You must fill it with sand from the Ocean. Fill it with pebble and rock and sand until the lake is no longer. Then you must build a new one of the same size and proportion in its place."

Of course I didn't bother to respond; I trudged past them with utter annoyance propelling my legs. I knew I couldn't have been too far off course from home if they could easily guide me there; it was simply a matter of finding help. I knew not which direction to go or if the very place I stood was an island too. My eyes met Byeol's at last as I weaseled my way between her and Hyeok. Sympathy clouded them and from her face it seemed as though she wanted to volunteer to help. Chul's watchful eyes kept her silenced.

"It will serve you well."

"No, it is pointless and will take me years—if not lifetimes. I will go it on my own."

"So be it, but unkind spirits and fortune will surely surround you in your travels if you deny what is required of you. It is not only I you have upset by swimming where you should not have gone."

I was not one to believe in spirits or curses that day. I had no interest in, or better yet, had no further evidence such forces surrounded us and controlled our very lives. If that had been true, I would have been cursing the world for putting me through this journey every second I had been taken from Kalea.

I was always under the assumption I was in the wrong place in the wrong time and that was the end of the story—I now just had to fix that problem. But if you recall my chance meeting with the mustached President, you know that surely wasn't just chance at all. That was the very incident that created who I was—the same went for my birthing struggle that left me fearful of the deep and dangerous. Perhaps it was destiny we were together, but if so, why had destiny now forsaken us and led me astray? As I marched into the jungle alone, it hit me that, in the blaze of gunfire, I was the one who had survived and not Earl.

Survivor's guilt is a destructive force that tears up your very soul. As the rain poured down, I huddled alone in the miserable cold, wondering why Earl was taken and not me. My brain sent me on tangents, searching for connections and patterns in my lengthy life. I had survived too many explosions and attacks to even fully account for, causing me to wonder if there was some sort of guiding spirit after all.

Earl seemed so alive and happy despite his painful struggles with appetite. Did he really commit such atrocities that his life had to be taken in such a horrific way? Were we that different, and was I doing something right unintentionally that caused my spirit and very self to deserve living on? Or was I reading too much into everything and we die when we die, by accident or by old age? It was mere flipper holds and pacing that separated us from life and death. There was no meaning to Earl's or my siblings' deaths; they simply now ceased to be.

For days I wandered, lost and alone. The grass had a strange taste that did not appeal to my stomach. I felt sick and full—but I was certain that feeling was the guilt filling my body. I couldn't shake my thoughts on fate, for if I wasn't destined to meet and be with Kalea, what chance was there for me to see her again? The chance that we would ever meet was low and the universe would be quite content with letting that happen. Without our connecting love for each other, I had no purpose.

So the question became, are we in control or are there external forces guiding us—using our past actions as a scale for where to reward or subtract? Was it my choice or the invisible person in the sky Earl mentioned?

As I ran like mad from some hairy, brutish forest swine, I couldn't help but think of all the hate and carelessness I had encountered—especially among humans. What did this constant attacking and fighting get them, since primal instincts for sustenance didn't have to exist in their society?

They ate us instead of each other, therefore no blood needed to be spilled. Yet, buckets full of red flooded my beloved bay and now even this dark, forsaken land. I took cover under a patch of soggy leaves, which was easily enough to outsmart the frothing pig. In the end, no one gets what they want and everyone wants to kill each other, in the animal kingdom or otherwise.

But I couldn't bring myself to think like that for long. I needed something to believe in—whether it was an afterlife or a present life I could be proud of. After asking and searching, I found no one who would help me, and worse yet, I couldn't even find the Ocean. I thought of Earl's last conversation with me, pertaining to his thoughts on the afterlife. Did he know he was going to go or is it something everyone has constantly demanding attention in the back of their mind? Disappointment loomed no matter the choice and hope looked grim and far away.

There were times I realized I may never reach my goal but my hope was only truly diminished if I gave up searching and trying completely. So I trudged back, trying my very best to follow old trails until I found myself back at the steaming, circular lake.

I wondered why me and not him. I too was exposed to the tainted air that surely killed him. Why was I so fortunate to have not been affected? I wondered about that with all my siblings as well. I was weak after all—afraid to even swim to the very center of the shimmering water before me. There were far better choices than I when it came to surviving, but yet, there I remained. So I was destined to return to Kalea with that point of view. But I also understood what Earl was getting at now; if destiny selects, it is most foully cruel.

Chul lurked across the water, speaking every intention with only a smarmy smile. Maybe he knew something after all, directions home and directions for life. All I could do was shove my philosophical breakdown aside and stick to the only purpose I knew—returning to Kalea.

I nodded, as did he, solidifying our agreement. He pointed to some trees behind me where sure enough, I found the Ocean. I picked up a slimy stone with my mouth and waddled back to the lakeshore. I dropped it and watched the pebble ripple and wade to the bottom; I would repeat this process for years to come.

TWENTY-TWO

THESE WERE the most exhausting years of my life. It mostly consisted of walking up and down a well-beaten path to the Ocean. Each trip would take me around seven minutes one way. Eventually, I got it down to five and finally four after my flippers became pure muscle and I could walk the trail with my eyes shut.

I had a particularly small mouth because of my size, so I couldn't fit more than three or four pebbles inside during a trip. Mouthfuls of sand were the foulest because you'd lose half of it by swallowing or by simply breathing. The real fine bits just seemed to eek their way out of my mouth no matter how hard I puckered. I think I lived off sand and stone during my journey in all that time; a large quantity seemed to fill up my stomach each day I worked.

But I needed something hardy to keep me going back and forth for all that time. I carried pebbles and stones and sand over every single day before the sun had risen until it disappeared below the trees. Not once did I take an intentional break and only stopped to eat a few blades of grass or to linger in the Ocean to have a drink of water.

There were days when men would scour the surroundings in long, symmetrical formations. They'd march with their guns forward in the air, scoping out bits of jungle to lay claim to while looking for more enemies to slaughter. I'd simply hide when they'd march through, carefully scanning to see if I could pick out which one killed Earl. They'd move too fast, though, and I never got a good look to begin with. After a while, these marches became so frequent I'd just keep on working as they moved past. They'd never do anything to me anyway, sometimes just point or stare. Gunfire and explosions often rang out minutes after their march through.

Chul would watch me every day, making certain that I was doing the job right. He'd interject some days and tell me the stones I was throwing in were not apparently suitable—I'd have to fish them out and bring them back to the Ocean. Some days I doubted the legitimacy of what I was doing, certain Chul would break our deal. And it just felt so tediously pointless, especially during the beginning when the lake seemed as though it could never be covered.

I was exhausted most days, wobbly and forcing myself to continue on—others I blinked and missed completely. Focused on both the past and future, some days I labeled this as my punishment for surviving instead of Earl. Every day I'd think of Kalea.

My images of her were slipping—getting fuzzy as well as the sound of her voice. I couldn't recall her exact tone while cherished miniscule memories sometimes never surfaced no matter how hard I tried. And when I made the conscious decision to stop my task and tell Chul to forget the deal, Hyeok calmly told me the lake was freshwater and contained no salt of any kind. I hadn't noticed and thought fondly of the funny, little salt shaker that had sat on my back during the great river journey. Maybe I was growing stronger after all. And perhaps Kalea would want to see me after all those years. Perhaps she'd see someone tough; a provider.

Bit by bit the lake filled up until my pebbles stretched over toward the deepest and darkest depths. I dreaded having to toss pebbles down where I could not see. Perhaps the lake weaved down forever, deep into the earth, and I'd be stuck foolishly tossing pebbles in for the rest of my life.

Faced with this dilemma, I knew I'd have to flounder my way down there to see just how deep it really was. Even the thought of answering that question left me nervous until bubbling curiosity finally got the better of me. I carried a pebble inside my mouth and plunged down until the sunshine no longer reached.

As I went deeper and deeper, shadows danced and bubbles wandered like eyes. I needed out—something vicious could still lurk in the black sand. I squirmed and raced back to safe shores until the pebble fell from my gasping mouth and sailed on down toward the floor. Gently but surely, I heard a soft clack as it hit the bottom.

Nervously, I gazed down and propelled myself to where it had gone. I could not see it but I knew it couldn't have been that far. After a few more strides, my nose gently bumped the bottom and I found myself resting on the ground. My heart raced and my flippers shook, but there I sat in underwater darkness.

It wasn't so deep, but in fact, manageable. And the key to it all was that I was in control. I had a simple task of filling that dark space and that was exactly what I would do. I hated the darkness but was now its master, eradicating the space like a vindictive victim with draining fear.

After so many trips to the depths of that lake, the water didn't seem so frightening. Slowly, I raised the ground up and up until I could rest comfortably and watch the sunlight ripple and dance. Chul's approving grin greeted me on those days I'd confidently emerge.

On the sore, stiff, rainy and miserable days, it was Byeol who kept my spirits high and my stomach filled. Much to Chul's dismay, she'd leave assorted plants and grasses for me and even the occasional snail. Feeling heavy with guilt and worried about karma, I swore off snails and all meat of any kind during my working days. Her lovely plants were the perfect chaser to stone and sand, but it was her confident smile that let me know I was in good company.

There were days where Byeol would just perch and watch me walk back and forth for hours, smiling for support and drifting off to what looked like pleasant daydreams. Wishful and prideful thinking made me wonder if she was falling for me, but my dedication to marriage kept me from pursuing anything further. That primal, meat-devouring part of my brain also flashed shameful images of physical fantasy. And for the first time since I met her, they were regretfully not of Kalea. Byeol's seemingly fond attitude toward me only fueled this passionate vision. She had infiltrated my thoughts and pushed my dearest Kalea to the dark depths of my mind.

It was here I began to causally convince myself that Kalea was now just a memory and new beginnings were in order. There were days I tried wholeheartedly to tell myself she had moved on and I needed to do the same. But without Kalea, I had no reason for existing, and without a purpose, what was I then? If I couldn't hold on to the hope of destiny, my life would have been all for not! Still, Byeol's lure was too strong to ignore. Once again, Earl may have been right.

The stage of the final fight between me and Kalea played on a continuous loop, making it all the more clear that I'd be going home to a rocky relationship. We had both made it clear we let the passion and fundamentals slip, launching us into a boring, stale, bitter partnership.

Still, I marched on with pebbles and stone, filling and filling until the water rose up and flooded the trees and the plants that surrounded the space. It had become a soggy walkway that I could securely plant my flippers on. The end had become tedious with me securing any empty space possible until water was completely out of view. Most would have called the project finished, but on the average day, I felt I needed to spare no expense when it came to my return to home and dearest Kalea.

As I carried what I deemed to be the final stone, Byeol stood waiting for me in the patch where the lake had formerly been. I'd shake the unjust images of her out of my brain but any view of Byeol carrying out a fruitful look would instantly pop them back up.

"It has been many years since you have started this journey. I wanted to share with you a fact that will lift your spirits high."

"I had to do it. As far as I'm concerned, there was no other way. I am not special or different—in fact just the opposite."

"Oh but that isn't true. Many have journeyed into the lake and have undertaken Chul's offer. But they never lasted, always giving up after mere days. You have proved yourself. You should be happy!"

I chewed on the rock, grinding my teeth in disappointment as I scouted out the final location for the missing piece. That was not how I thought the achievement was going to feel. Guilt and confusion swallowed my heart instead.

"I have not proved myself, Byeol. I have filled a lake but that does not bring any of my friends or family back from the dead. It does not make me any more brave and deserving of life. And it certainly does not excuse my visions and fantasies that betray the very one I am yearning to get back to."

"What visions? What fantasies? Surely whatever you have thought, you can be forgiven for."

I remember mulling around a few options I could take in my head. I could tell and confess my growing affections for her or I could simply walk away. I wondered what her reaction would be upon my truthful proclamation of what I wanted to do with her. Deep inside I knew this conversation would make it all so. Maybe my purpose was changing? Of course, that is the absolute hardest piece of news one can accept. I looked back at our relationship without rose-colored glasses. Under the spell of Byeol's beauty, really, I was close to a breakthrough.

"The relationship I had with Kalea is not what is once was. I had diminished it simply by my own doing, my own shortcomings that led to her unhappiness. For the past few years I have dwelled on if leaving her alone would in fact be the best option. I could be doing all of this just to return home to resentment and fights. Regretfully though, I do not wish to let her go—she is all I have."

"Courtship is always the greatest time in any relationship; so many firsts and triumphs and excitements. It is extremely hard work to overcome the romantic stage and settle into trust and comfort. The mere planning of stealing one's heart is typically the greatest achievement in the whole process. I know I have yearned for this as well. Have you considered the relationship has run its course?"

Byeol smiled a wonderful, flirtatious little grin as she batted her eyes. I understood just who it was she referred to. I took a deep breath and listed the many fantasies I had racked up during our knowledge of each other. She did not leave nor did she wince in fear or embarrassment.

She slowly moved toward me, trembling, until her lips touched mine. Her warm cheek slowly rubbed against my face in soft, romantic contact I had not received in a great long while. I had imagined this over and over in my head, but when the moment came, I felt nothing. I pulled away and looked at the ground.

"I can't. I still feel yearning and desire for her; therefore, I could never break my promise and devotion. I'm sorry."

Happily, Byeol pulled away and gave a slight nod of understanding.

"And still you think you don't deserve her? That you let her down, and worse, you do not even deserve life? I shake my head at you if this is what you believe."

With an appreciative gaze, I let the rock slowly slip from my mouth and onto the forest floor below. The lake was covered and I was ready to go back to the one I loved. I loved Byeol too but maybe in a different way. It wasn't just her attention and caring attitude toward me. It wasn't just the mysterious mystic. It was her knowledge. Her experience. I was in awe.

The first phase of the agreement was complete. Byeol and I walked across the sand as we silently searched for a place to put the new lake. With a renewed fondness for both the past and the future, I turned to her. "What do you believe happens after we die? And why does it happen when it does? Is there a plan? A destiny? A definitive one we can't see? Something beyond…love?"

She remained silent, careful in thought and word choice. As we walked along, I stopped before a clearing where plants gave way to a sprawling little meadow. It was there I decided to dig.

"Does it matter? We are alive now with opportunities to do good and bad. When it comes down to it, this is the life we are certain exists."

"Does Chul know this?"

"That is the beauty of life—we may choose our own path and beliefs. Chul and our community work hard for one another, including myself. All I can tell you is while you can, have faith in yourself and have faith in others. In each other's abilities because as of now that is what we have. Use them wisely but truthfully; use yourself how you see fit. If it is love you want, then choose love!"

TWENTY-THREE

DIGGING THE new lake hardly took any time at all. It was quite simple actually because for whatever reason, digging came very natural to me. Perhaps it was due to my fearful escape plans that typically consisted of me digging a hole to hide in.

I started by chomping down all of the meadow grass and greenery—a job I was more than happy to complete. After leaving the ground barren and mulched, the next step was to flounder my flippers and toss away as much dirt and earth as I possibly could. After digging deep down into the ground, I'd smooth over the excess soil and spread it through the surrounding forest.

Digging daily exhausted me—but it beat walking back and forth, tediously carrying pebbles and dwelling on life problems. Here, I really had to focus on where I was plowing to and where the dirt was going to go when it was all said and done. Before I knew it, a great, empty lake basin sprawled before me—carefully circular and gradually deep. The only problems that stood before me then were getting the water there and preventing it from seeping into thirsty roots and past coarse grains.

This is where I got the idea to bed the lake floor with leaves and rock and dead bark. I'd scour the forest, venturing to dark corners looking for items to cover and secure the ground below. Much of the fighting and gunfire had long since ceased so exploring outward rarely felt like a death sentence. I'd come back with rocks rolling below my flippers and smooth bark hanging in my mouth. I layered the bottom, making the contents as smooth as I could until there were no more traces of the true ground.

With a crack of thunder and a flash of lightning, rain drenched the ground from a monsoon in the sky. The lake filled and filled until sure enough the water actually began to run over the edges and across the forest floor.

I gazed around to see Chul confidently smiling at me from across the other side. Without hesitation, he dove headfirst into the new lake and drifted across to me in an elegant stride. Emerging swiftly, he turned and nodded with approval. I was very careful to stay away from my creation so I would not poison the land again and have to start from scratch.

"Your end of the bargain is complete. Do you have anything you wish to take with you?"

I searched the forest for memories but I felt it was best to leave plants and certainly rocks and stones where they laid. I would forever taste the grimy dirt between my lips so that would constitute as my souvenir. I pondered taking flowers for Kalea but I was certain they would not survive the trip. I shook my head.

"Then let us depart. We shall guide you home."

I followed Chul to the beach where Hyeok and Byeol awaited on the shore. Rain poured down and the water bobbed with uncooperative madness. Each wave was bigger than the next and pure black thanks to the disturbance of the hissing rain. I shook and trembled and knew what would be expected of me but I remembered the lake and its great fill up brought about by my own actions. I was in control, not the foul emptiness of the Ocean. For every depth had a bottom and every quarreler had a fighting chance.

Before we set sail, the sun returned and violent winds calmed into stillness. I was amazed at the timing but remained certain fate had something to do with the sudden change. This was all finally meant to be. As I took in the view one final time before setting sail back home to Hawaii, I realized that in a way, because of the physical mark I had left, this was my home too. Perhaps these little leavings were just what I needed to make a valuable purpose for myself?

Chul entered the water first and invited me to come in next. I launched myself into the wavy coldness as Hyeok and Byeol followed. Hyeok stayed at my back left while Byeol positioned at my back right. Chul led the way as we kicked off, forming a protective pyramid able to pierce and ride past the wildest of ripples.

I thought of the sugar mission and how I would forever regret not reaching the boat with Pika. But this day was another day and I swam swiftly through the endless blue. We were quiet with our words but loud with determined spirit. I was swimming deep and far, onward with an eager smile, finally returning to my sweetest Kalea.

I kicked and paddled and flipped further than I had ever gone before. With hot sun on my shell and companions keeping a watchful eye, I knew there would be no way shadow dwellers and fanged beasts could destroy us. After settling into the stride, I'm actually proud to admit I enjoyed the swim. Watching innocent schools of fish pass below us filled the darkness as did the occasional piece of long, journeyed driftwood. Little had I known about the intricate wonders that too sailed the Ocean. The silence for once did not unnerve me. But of course this was its most cruel of tricks. It earns your trust before striking its most cruel of attacks.

It was the eye of a hurricane that gave the illusion of paradise. Foolish and underprepared, the four of us were caught in rolling waves as the storm returned angrier than before. The sky turned into a pure black until there was hardly a way to decipher water from air. As Chul swam on, all that could be picked out in the swirling madness was a bobbing boat's light far off in the distance.

"We must turn back. We must wait until the storm has passed!" Hyeok screamed.

"We can't return now; it's too dangerous. It is Akela's path—we must go forward."

"Forget about the deal, we're all going to die."

"Not unless we dive deep. We can continue on the farther we descend."

All eyes were on me to determine what to do. While I knew we'd never find our way back to land, there was a very good chance we may never find our way out of the Ocean's depths. Hurricanes had a way of turning you around and stealing your idea of direction. As the bobbing light came closer, the English markings USS Sphinx became visible.

"I have seen this ship!" I exclaimed. "Near my home just out by the docks. We must be close."

Chul frowned as the four of us fought to remain still—an impossible feat in churning, blustery water.

"If you take that ship, you will lose all that you have worked for and gained. There will be punishment."

"But it will be safe!" I protested. Chul shook his head as he swam on. Hyeok grinned at me as he fought to move forward. Ultimately, a riptide grabbed hold and pulled him back. The last I remember of him was his horrific scream echoing through the darkness. Byeol yelled his name and turned to assist, suffering the same fate. Our eyes met for the last time as she too faded into the darkness. My heart fluttered in fear as I'd never again lay my eyes on her beauty and open my mind to her wisdom.

As I swam toward them, Chul intervened and blocked my pathway with his entire body. "They will survive; you do not need to worry."

"How do you know?" Chul gave me no answer. As we bobbed back up to the surface, all I could see was his devilish smile.

"I have completed my portion of our deal."

"No! We are not there! I'm not home!"

"I have taken you as far as I can. But I have given you everything to succeed. Do not take the ship. Listen to what she told you. Listen to yourself. Or else destiny as you call it will assign you other plans."

Without warning, Chul too followed the same fate as his family and disappeared into the swirling darkness. As I lunged to follow, I stopped myself and instead swam up for gasps of air. Looking around, I could see no coastline of any kind. Only waves bigger than you could very well imagine crashing down on and around me. The only hint of civilization was the bobbing boat light.

The darkness engulfed me until I felt essentially blind. While no monster in their right mind would attack during a hurricane, the storm itself was turning into a destructive entity of its own. Desperate to swim on and complete the journey, desperate to escape the frightening winds and rain, I did what I always had done before; I lost faith in myself and headed for safety.

I clung to a dragging chain, hanging off the deck and into the water. As I lurched myself upward, there was no way in slippery hell I was getting on board. It wasn't a particularly large vessel compared to the ones I had seen but climbing aboard was a near impossible task, especially in rocky waters. The boat tipped back and forth with me hanging on for dear life. Voices in my head told me to let go and trust in myself but reason chased them out and steered me to a safer route.

I felt as though I could be lifted and cast up high into the sky—
that's how hard this boat was swaying. It also dawned on me this could
be my way in. I was certain I had seen it before and it had to be going
to Hawaii—why else was it in these waters? Earl had made a fatal mistake on our journey, locking us up in the chamber and counting on
instinct to tell us when we arrived. I'd never know if we made a stop-
over in Hawaii and just didn't feel it or if we did in fact board the
wrong vessel. All I knew in that moment was I needed to get out of
the water.

I was angry at Chul, feeling plainly cheated out of our deal—
he did not take me home. I didn't care what methodical, mystical
wisdom he may have instilled with his exercise, I needed safety. As
images of monsters flashed in the corner of my view and thunder
roared and cracked and shook the entire sky, I thought perhaps I'd
try again when the water calmed and the hurricane passed. I hoped
Byeol and Hyeok and even Chul were okay. I knew I'd be if I could
just make it on deck.

So at the right moment as the boat listed as far as it possibly could
go to its opposite side without tipping over, I let go of the chain and
let sheer force and wind carry me upward. As the boat crashed down,
so did I—skidding across the wet, flooding floor of the USS Sphinx. A
door flapped in the wind as water poured down its prevalent tower of
stairs. I slid over toward it, misjudging the force completely, sending
me skidding over and down each step in a terrible tumble.

In calming, silent warmth, I embraced the dryness but dwelled on
Chul's warning. I used myself as I saw fit—was my action my failure or
the intervention of something grander than I thought?

TWENTY-FOUR

DRUNKEN SAILORS whistled shanty tunes over spilling pints as they swayed back and forth around tables. They either cared very little about the hurricane's dangers or gave up and accepted their unfortunate fate. I scurried around, passing kicking feet and tapping toes. I slipped around in the spilled, sudsy beverage—accidently ingesting some which immediately made my poor head spin.

With nowhere to go really, I carefully watched the crew as they had the time of their life swaying with the waves. As they celebrated and drank, other maddened members raced around, trying to brace whatever they could.

I scampered from the darkly lit tavern space into a space-age world of nods and blinkers and spinning pieces. Men hard at work listened carefully into headphones and earpieces while others stayed transfixed on the bleeping green screens before them. Some raced about while some held tightly to the wall upon each waving crest.

I really can't explain to you what I saw because I never once saw anything similar to compare it to. There were gadgets and machines in every corner of that ludicrous laboratory. But never once did anyone explain measures and procedures to me. Why would they after all? They'd have to be insane to speak to me…bless Ron the security guard!

Anyway, in that moment, I was bewildered at how many buttons and crew members it took to keep a boat afloat. Without a clue on what they were doing sailing out at this time and place, I backed out slowly and looked for more adequate shelter.

There was no way I was headed back down to the waste chambers again—I was just fine meandering through the decks until we got to shore. Part of me hoped they were seeking out the coastline I had just left; only so that I could track Chul down and give him a piece of my mind.

Warm and dry and temporarily safe, I recalled Earl's warning that the vicious crew would throw me off without hesitation if we were to meet. Drunken members in the tavern room saw me plain as day—but I think they all attributed the unexplainable sightings to their drink anyway. No one did anything because each one seemed too embarrassed to be the person to exclaim there was a tropical, shelled critter waltzing about the ship floor.

I was careful, peeking behind every door to make sure the coast was clear. I've discovered most humans stare plainly at their feet as they walk—careful not to step or kick or run over something. I have no idea how you do this; you're missing the whole world as you stare down at the empty, boring ground.

Obviously, this made navigating around difficult as most people I encountered were staring down in my very vicinity. Some focused so intently on their feet, they walked by me without the slightest hint of recognition. I believe one woman actually caught sight of me and shrieked, racing in the opposite direction like I was ten times her size and could devour her in a single bite.

I couldn't move too quickly on account of my tired muscles and delayed motor skills so outrunning any captor was out of the question.

I searched and searched until an open door presented itself momentarily when a crewmember exited and left it to swing open. I made my move and entered some kind of sleeping quarters where crew curled up in puffy blankets. Others vomited in little white bags thanks to the constant rocking.

Nevertheless, it was quiet and warm and a pile of clothing presented itself in the corner of the room. I made my next move by scurrying along the wall like I had always seen Earl do until I made it safely to the laundry heap and buried deep underneath. Oh it was warm but of course my doubtful, internal voice arrived to invoke inner chills. I wondered just where the boat was heading.

Bit by bit I dragged the pieces of clothing until I was nestled in the dark underneath a bed. As snoring and sniffles echoed, I drifted off to sleep as I felt the raging waters slowly calm themselves below. I remained where no one could find me for days until water and food became a necessity. I would have to scout out some saving grace because surely there had to be plant life and, ironically, water aboard.

Now here comes the very serious part of the sailing journey—they did not head to Hawaii but in another direction; somewhere colder than I ever thought imaginable. Further and further they sailed until finally they let the very vessel drift slowly—simultaneously they listened into earmuffs and recorded information discovered on their strange bleeping machines. Rows of worried crewmembers charted findings on wall maps and discussed the lay of the land ahead.

I witnessed this firsthand as well as the sludgy, wet powder called snow. I emerged on the open top deck where it rained down upon us, freezing my very joints and inner workings as I slipped along a thin coat of ice. The crew kept warm by wearing thick layers of presumably animal-made coats. I had no such luxury and could feel myself getting sluggish and weak. I needed food, but more importantly, I needed warmth.

I had come to understand humans love the snow—playing and rolling and even fighting with the substance. Well that's all fine and dandy if you can survive in the stuff but I surely couldn't take much more of it on that journey. The temperature was unimaginable—so much so, I swore the very waters we sailed on were turning to frozen blocks of ice. I trudged through the ship, searching for warmth, but drafty, chilling air filled every room—not even my tucked away laundry nest could provide shelter any longer.

It was the wafting smell of boiling vegetables and tender meats simmering in a thick sauce somewhere down the hall that saved me. I drifted and stumbled my way from room to room until the glorious kitchen presented itself with one lonely cook chopping and stirring and concocting a behemoth batch of bouillabaisse. As they focused on the creation, I stood below with an open mouth. Ready to catch any fallen chunks, I feasted on broccoli and carrots and celery and every kind of vegetable known to man. It was paradise I tell you, particularly when the delectable dribble of meat sauce dripped off the table and into a puddle before me. I lapped it up until I saw the proprietor throw excess bits into a waste bin.

When they left the room and bin unguarded, I eagerly ran into the container full force until it fell down sideways on the floor. I helped myself to various chewy meats and hearty grains. I finally felt warm.

When the chef came back, I remember cowering underneath a stool until they opened a strange hatch that unleashed immense waves of inviting heat. They removed some crusty, panned contents and slammed it shut. I knew if I were to survive this trip that was precisely where I was going to have to hide.

Yes, I know now what the place actually was—an oven used for baking and cooking at wickedly hot temperatures. It was dangerous and foolish, but just know I was uninformed and more importantly, very cold! So I waited for a long while until the oven was in fact used again. I studied it, watching him set it at temperatures so I'd know just which one would be right for me. Eggs were delicate so I noticed they'd be placed in at a lower level. He cooked up a fancy quiche dish and left the door open as he did his best to prepare the meal and remove it from the pan.

Enticed by the heat and signaled by the always reliable timer—I made the dash inside. I tell you it was a hell of an ordeal climbing up onto the open door but determination and wild wiggling launched me up there. It was then he closed the door behind me and I was locked inside a dark chamber of immense warmth.

How did I survive? Well luckily, it was a low heat and the chef turned the machine off moments before he opened up the door. It was at the perfect temperature, actually, so I would not bake like a potato but instead just bask in calming heat. You have to understand, the snowy weather takes way more of a toll on me than the heat does. I needed something to rejuvenate my insides and this hot box absolutely got me working again. I couldn't take touching ice and snow with my bare skin—it was such an awful, shivery feeling. But of course, about an hour into my lock up, I regretted the oven decision.

You know how sometimes you just have those moments where you work so hard to accomplish something and then you absolutely realize it was a bad idea? You suddenly wake up and think what am I doing? But all too often it's too late to fix the problem? Here I banged and pushed and could in no way escape. Thankfully, the chef never turned the heat up high, otherwise I would have fried within minutes. I truly didn't understand the dangers of the oven and am very lucky to be alive. I guess it worked out in a way because I did thaw myself out and feel great when I entered.

I don't know how long I was locked up in total but it couldn't have been more than a day. Ready to escape and dive off the boat to soak in fresh waters, I knew I'd freeze into a block of ice—I was stuck there, along for the ride. I was no closer to Kalea than I had been before. It was astonishingly strange that Chul was right and I was being punished for my cowardly actions. I just wished the full punishment didn't come in the form of blistering oven fire.

Then suddenly the door flew open and the chef went to go pull out the rack. He was about halfway when he saw me—he fell flat on his face in shock and confusion. Regrettably, I think there was a bit of blood that eked out of his crown from a sharp, painful impact.

When he came to, I hadn't made it that far, and sure enough he could confirm there was indeed what he thought he saw living semi-comfortably in his oven. He picked me up with shivering hands and rushed me to the Captain, who stared at me in fear for a good six hours straight. I knew whatever was to happen next, no matter where I was cast, it would not be good.

TWENTY-FIVE

BEING A worldwide celebrity is fantastic when you are loved and respected and thought of as a real swell soul. Being a worldwide celebrity for absurd, propagandist lies is the absolute pits! The Captain did a complete one-eighty back to home shores, clutching me tight in an impenetrable glass box all the way to civilization. Again I found myself in a cold, dark room on a chilly metal slab, only this time I was surrounded by dozens of humans and not one comforting face.

Some days I was made to walk straight lines marked in bright yellow—well that was the hope I gathered from it anyway. Most days I would just stand completely still as the white-coated lab men eagerly observed. Then they put me into a cruel chamber with paths that led to nowhere. They'd crowd around and see if I could find my way out. I wondered what the point was since they wouldn't let me go free anyway; I'd end up just staying put and watching the disappointed grins and yawns fall upon them.

They flashed shattering, bright bulbs at me and scribbled down chattering nonsense onto paper pads. While I was poked and prodded to the nth degree, absent voices coming from a brand new little black box called the television warned of a communist takeover by methods of secret animal warfare. Newspapers covered doorsteps with my picture and adjacent headlines like "USSR Training Sea Life to Steal and Spy." The more the papers spun their yarn, the angrier the radio voices would get. The lab technicians were sure to have every opinion available, fresh newspaper print tucked under their arm and AM programming turned way up high.

I was often transported back and forth from building to building, which became a nearly impossible mission unto itself. Guards would sneak me out back and rush me to a sleek, black car but throngs of angry people would rush over to see me. Journalists would climb up on rickety fire escapes just to nab a better look.

And all these people, they were just so mad. They chanted and bobbed anti-communist signs as they pointed their frightened fingers. More often than not, the guards would get me into the car nice and safe; but one time this strung out, slimy-haired, grease ball of a guy yanked me from my protective entourage and held me high for the public to see.

As he made a run for it, I dizzily swayed from side to side, trying to hold together my motion sickness the best I could. I went flying after a successful tackle knocked him to the ground. Messy hands grabbed from every direction before I saw a big brute march up and sputter some hateful spit my way. The lab workers got me out just in time—but I tell you, I really felt hated!

Years later I would discover a television rebroadcast that had a disgraced, drunken slob of a man slander and yell a report in his cramped hospital room. He glared with hatred into the camera, begging anyone who would listen to go on a maddening rampage and destroy all the marine and reptile life they could.

"My friends," he remarked, "if I have no sense of decency, surely that behavior is replaced with a heightened sense of what is wrong for our country. We know this little stowaway could not simply arrive on our ship by himself. He was planted, nay, trained by the communists to keep watch and report our very weaknesses so an underlying infiltration could unfurl right under our nose. And it doesn't end with him—it is scientific evidence that animals can and will be used to break down and destroy all that we Americans hold dear. Hold on to your values! Trust no one! Not man or beast."

This in turn started a frenzy where many of my kind were unnecessarily slaughtered—cast out to sea and fed to the sharks simply because of irrational fear. Imported Chinese snappers were sent back in the ships from which they came. Varying pet shops refused to carry anything that wasn't true-blue American bred. I had suddenly been thrust into the human world after so many years of carefully navigating around it. But it was unavoidable—end of story.

If this offends you, well I apologize, but it's the honest feelings I had during this tumultuous period in my life. Humans take and unnecessarily expand their habitat—I had seen them kill, actually kill each other over land that we always thought was ours. In all my life, there were few humans who had a humble regard for the nature around them, and now that I was cast into their world (by a simple mistake I might add), they wanted me out.

They wanted the idea they perceived me to be out of their life, even though I was nothing close to what they saw. I heard words and descriptions from the chanters and haters—I wasn't a spy! I wasn't trying to ruin anybody's life. I was chained and imprisoned so people could hate me and focus their boredom on something that made them feel like, for one second, they mattered. Well, perhaps I related to that desire a small bit…but having an opinion is one thing, refusing to hear others or worse yet, projecting a false one onto someone is something else entirely. If this was my destiny, I didn't want it!

I'd find out about those poor critters who lost their lives in cruel raids years later and would think of them often. I carried their blood on my hands, wondering just how I got myself in this whirlwind of a situation and how humans could be so maddening and judgmental. But the more exposure I was given to the world—the more insane the world became.

Nightly news segments broadcast in black and white carried panicked anchors' tales about Russian intelligence and nuclear warfare—whatever the hell any of that meant. I was just passed from station to station once the lab folk figured they could make a buck and cash in by delivering me through the back door.

So every day I'd be put through scanning machines and swab tests and then I was brought to networks where belittling reporters jokingly stuck a microphone to my face and asked what my angle was. I was learning the ins and outs of the human world all right, listening to their every misinformed word. When I wasn't doing that, I mourned the loss of the lives I inadvertently took—circling back to the popular thought of what exactly made me so special and "fortunate" to be famous.

Then one day they demanded I be brought to them by a grumpy, old, hairless fellow they referred to as Mr. President—he had no relation to the mustached president that I could see. He poked and petted me on his desk but the man never felt comfortable getting his hands or his suit near my "contaminating vicinity" as he called it.

The next thing I knew, his nervous associates carried me out to the front steps of his sprawling white home where thousands of people stood in anticipation. While the people gasped as the hairless President took center stage at a wooden podium, I swear I heard a few voices say the whole world was watching—readying to break out into World War III for the prevention of nuclear animal intelligence warfare.

"Fellow Americans, this is a trying time in our nation's history," he said. "The Russians, as we know, have been successful in entering a satellite into orbit. We can evidently see they are capable of scientific advancements that are superior to our own. But now is not the time to lynch and claw and yell and bite our enemies—now is the time to show our enemies what we Americans are capable of. Let us not distrust the honest and helpless creatures such as our friend here—let us not stoop to the levels of having the honest and helpless fight our battles for us. Let us forget about battle and replace it with progressive thinking and hard work."

The next thing I knew, I was up in the air held high in the hairless President's sweaty hands. A storm of shouting erupted from the crowd, some cheers and whistles, some death threats and hisses.

"Let us not enter into panic and corruption over one of God's creatures—jumping to conclusions that blind our judgment. We have run test after test and I tell you, he is innocent! There is no trace of communism in this creature's eyes, his heart, and his very soul!"

After that the anger subsided into thin air and all the humans banged their hands together in gleeful unison. I struggled to get free as the hairless President held me by his slippery palms as far away as he could. I was close to dropping but he quickly handed me off to some associate who dipped me back into a carrying tank and zipped me back to the dreadful lab I'd miserably have to call home.

I thought after that barrage of forgiveness and change of heart I'd be freed, but it seemed the people in charge of the chaos only claimed they trusted me in public. In private it was all a little different. They simply locked me up in a lonely room—no more tests or attention administered. I'd sit all by my lonesome and wonder how in the heck I got there.

This was not the way it was supposed to go! Earl had died in vain and my years spent filling the wretched lake with pebbles was all for naught. I had been journeying for the better part of my life just to end up right back where I started. It was enough to make my blood boil...but not enough to kill me. At my lowest, Ron the security guard came in!

You see, I had been stored in the corner of this place for quite some time before the white coats decided I couldn't be in there any longer. So they put me in some dark room down the hall—and then eventually a whole other building. But no matter where I was, I was always alone and usually without any kind of lighting. I'd be lucky if they remembered to throw some food my way. As an unnecessary prisoner, bordering the lines of storage junk, I simply wallowed and waited for any kind of attention—bogged down by misery and lacking hope of any kind.

Ron was this chubby, short fellow with curly, sporadic red hair and big, black glasses that covered half his face. He usually was the one who ended up feeding me and somewhere along the way he must have spotted that I was tired and lonely. Every now and then he'd take me to rock back and forth, which I appreciated even though his rocking style resembled intense earthquakes. But he meant well and no good deed went unnoticed. I think he felt similar to me in a way and resonated with the lonely isolation. We were perfect for each other—we just didn't quite know it yet.

One day he grinned with boyish excitement as he propped the door open and wiped the sweat from his brow. He lugged in this big brown box with a strange, hollow screen in the middle. He propped it on the table beside me and yanked this long antenna until he got it just where he wanted it. With a few plugged-in wires and the fiddling of an assortment of knobs, Ron turned the box on and eagerly smiled as he left. The silly kid gifted me a television set all in the efforts of keeping me company when he couldn't physically be there. And I tell you—I was addicted from the first sight.

I became transfixed with the stream of black and white images pressed against my glass. I could see humans running around inside of it and it took me a lot longer than I care to admit to understand they weren't real. I couldn't hear a damn word because of the enclosure but at least my mind became focused on something different entirely.

Dusty men wearing thick-brimmed hats shot each other with guns in the desert. Floating doors revealed unimaginable lands while a husband and wife and their offspring enjoyed meals and time spent together. People chatted on chairs and others paced around an audience of inquisitive listeners. It was an insight into the human world that confirmed to me what I had been seeing all along—just closer and without the danger.

I'll never forget when the words "Hawaii: The 50th State" graced the majestic screen. I couldn't really read English at this point but the lone images of swaying palm trees had me enthralled within seconds. Rolling beaches stretched as the sunshine beat down upon the pretty plant life.

It was home—I knew it in my heart I really was seeing my old stomping grounds for the first time since I had left it. The oh so common sight I had seen around my journey—the fabric with stars and stripes draped in the wind as uniformed men bravely saluted. Horns trumpeted (silently to my ears) before the beating of a drum invited dancers in grass skirts to take the center view. I knew it was home— it was my culture and my people. I gasped and held back tears as the skirts waved in the wind with tremendous talent. Humans banged their hands together as a very official-looking man stood before the large, eager crowd. As he spoke the view began to shift, slowly and softly as it captured the haunting beach view. Then it stopped.

It stopped and it got closer—closer and closer to a small moving object in the sand. When the wanderer became the full view that the screen cared to offer, the image became crystal clear. It was a being just like myself—green shell and wrinkled flippers—only much bigger than me of course. Then I saw her smile filled with happiness! Then I saw her eyes filled with love! I saw her crawl along the shore just like she had always done while we were together. I finally understood what television could do! It could show you your deepest desires and connect to the furthest reaches of your heart. It was Kalea—she was alive and well. I would have known her anywhere and she was right in front of me now.

I pawed and clawed the glass, desperately trying to get to her. I screamed Kalea's name, but she could not hear me. I banged against the glass and swam in panic around the tank as the image slowly panned back to the crowd and speaker. I begged for her to come back but the television wouldn't listen. It couldn't hear me and deep down I knew that wasn't a possibility. But in those seconds, all the love I had for Kalea came flooding back to the forefront of my mind. I remembered why I was doing this in the first place. I knew now was not the time to give up. Not after I knew she was still out there. Not after I had been through this much to get back to her.

Energy flowed through my body like I was a newborn ready to take on any challenge life threw toward me. Like a torpedo, I took off through the water with my little flippers propelling me to the top. I launched through the plastic covering, knocking the blockade down onto the ground.

Guilt and confusion and pure laziness had stopped me in those recent times—I had felt like giving up because failure had come my way too often to count. But not that day! Not ever again. I warn you, never give up because of your challenges and strife, though I know how depression and doubt can act like the thickest shield of all. It may feel strong. It may feel overwhelming! But I say to you, it can be broken! My destiny would not yet be cemented in communist hang-ups and espionage conspiracy theories. My destiny was to love Kalea!

The television set landed with a splat, shattering into sharp pieces across the floor. I landed down beside it (on my flippers for once) and headed toward the door so I could slip through the moment Ron the security guard made his daily visit.

TWENTY-SIX

IT WASN'T who I was hoping. Before I could make my mad dash out of the horrid closet, I witnessed a uniformed gentleman usher in a young lady to make use of the unoccupied space I was stored in. When he got a load of me (after the frightened woman screamed in terror of course), I was stuffed back into my tank and the man played it all off as a successful routine checkup.

The lid cover was immediately replaced, and a rock, I kid you not, a rock was placed on top to keep me from breaking out. They were what I thought to be high-ranking leaders that could afford just about anything but they weren't willing to shell out a pretty penny for my surveillance. I was a distant afterthought, yet they didn't have the decency to just let me go on account I was still considered a "threat to the nation."

I was quite all right with that though because a garden rock was certainly no match against me to keep me fenced in. It was, after all, a heavy rock that was not meant to be on such thin plastic. Day by day I watched the lid creak and crack—often helping it along by pushing and rocking the weight back and forth. One day I heard the snap and luckily dove into the corner where it narrowly missed me and sunk with a thud to the sandy bottom. The now gaping hole was more than enough for me to squeeze through and I found myself back on the floor.

Simple Ron waddled his way over, leaving the door propped wide open as he came to sprinkle some awful, wood-shaving-inspired food my way. He just about lost his mind in tearful sorrow when he saw the rock inhabiting much of the tank space. I'm sure he searched high and low, lifting up every grain of sand until he saw I was no longer there. I'm sure he knelt down on all fours, crawling about as he called for me, reaching into every dark corner where I could have been hiding. By the time he put it all together, I had been long gone. I would have paid all the sea grass in all the world's tide pools to see his dumbfounded look.

I scuttled along the slippery, hard floor, staying as close to the edge of the wall as possible. The more I spent time indoors, the more I hated it. Sunshine shone through the glass panes but it was nothing in comparison to the uninhibited rays covering you on a sandy beach. The air was stale and the floor was cold.

I lurked underneath benches and chairs, watching miserable humans nod their heads at each other and walk in unison to their bland destination. When there are beaches around, why would you want to spend your time in a boxed barricade? I scuttled to the door, shaking my head as stubby fingers clacked a mile a minute over forceful buttons. I suppose it did make a rather satisfying ping noise.

Along the rows and rows of desks I went. Past the suits and fedoras and skirts with their faces buried in newspapers and minds deep in thought. I managed to get outside through a skinny, low open window but honestly it only led to further trouble.

The confusing place teased me that I was in fact back in the wilderness—fresh air blessed my nostrils and green grass tickled my flippers. But there was no way to go—absolutely no way to continue on to my journey. I'd march along the grass and find a wall sternly blocking me from going past. So I'd retreat back the other way and find a wall blocking that direction too!

I followed this poorly constructed circle and found no routes of escape. I was sealed in, and worse yet, I was spotted by some sandwich-munching woman sitting still on a bench nearby. She dropped her food and readjusted her glasses just to make sure she was seeing right. I couldn't outrun her since I could feel my body drying out and there was no exit to take. I admitted defeat and let her carry me inside where I was reunited with a beet red, out of breath Ron who placed me right back where I started.

Now instead of putting an even heavier rock on top of my confining cage, they bolted it down and padlocked it so there was no chance of me lifting it off or breaking through. The material was harder and the only foreseeable link to the outside world was a tiny hatch that Ron used to pour my flaky food inside. For once in my life, I wished I was smaller.

So there I sat, watching television and pondering my journey back to Hawaii. A stern, sweaty man spoke alongside a handsome, youthful counterpart in some sort of black-and-white conversation. A man and a boy wandered a beautiful forest, ready to throw rods in the water and fish.

Every day there was something new and if I wasn't careful, my sanity would slip and I'd lose myself again—these images just had a way of sucking you in. They also indirectly made me want to get home all the more. Seeing that little boy throw his rod in the water made me think back to all the times I watched the fishermen jet out on rickety boats to try and lure my neighbors to the shore. Most claimed they were smart enough not to fall for that trick but their hunger grew larger than their common sense, I suppose.

Oh how I wanted to shout in frustration but what good would it have done? I waited patiently for Kalea's love and the forest lake to fill—I was just going to have to use patience here in order to escape.

My attention turned to the television set that I had inadvertently broken during my early escape attempts. It still worked but the covering was chipped and loose—shards of it even remained down on the floor, sparkling under the television's glow. It dawned on me that the tank I was in had to have been made of similar material—they were both clear and glossy after all. I determined that mere glass couldn't keep me in—especially after I realized this was probably how Earl got out in the first place. He broke straight through the glass.

Now, I'm not the strongest beast in the Ocean but let me tell you every attempt makes a difference, whether you succeed or not. Every moment, no matter how soft, will eventually change as long as you keep going. So that's what I did—I grabbed a pebble and rapped it against the glass in the same spot for a month. Two months maybe! It felt like a long while and I noticed chips and tiny dents forming the longer I carried on with the project.

Ron thought nothing of it—dismissing the action as unexplainable animal behavior. Before I knew it the dent began to spider. Cracks snaked their way alongside the front face of the tank until one fateful day I heard the whole enclosure crumble from a sudden, forceful pierce. I went sliding out with the water and glass and rock, landing with a thud upon the messy floor.

Naturally, the ruckus brought attention and the door went flying open. Behooved guards pondered what had happened as they stared down at the mess. As eyes scanned and searched for my body, they discovered I was already gone so they all ran out to put the place on high alert. I was still in there, cleverly hidden behind the door where they could not find me. A man came along and swept up all the glass and water while workers raced in every direction to find my location. They couldn't, never thinking for a second to actually close the door and calmly survey the situation.

I waited until nightfall when the moonlight lit the hallway paths and clacking fingers ceased to type. I had free rein of the building and tried to be careful and not make the same mistake I originally did. I wandered and wandered, and folks, this time, I actually made my way out.

What a long, arduous jaunt this place led me on. I took a dip in some fountains first of all because I sorely needed a soak. I was drying out faster and faster in my old age. Next, I had absolutely no sense of direction—what with all the flashing lights and towering buildings. I had no clue where to go, hustling across an ever-stretching space of lawn until a slippery stream led the path to freedom.

Problem was I didn't know how to get down there…I was trapped on a bridge overlooking the water and was much too fearful to simply dive in. As I paced around looking for an entryway, I scuttled to the other side to find a pathway down. The streets were eerily silent and no pursuers chased behind me. As I scouted out my way to the watery highway leading to the Ocean, I couldn't help but see a bold light ahead. Rows of columns illuminated like a dream around this sturdy structure. A man; bold, bearded and shrouded in holy light.

I was pulled toward them like the bright beam possessed a haunting power to capture those who gazed upon it. I knew I had to find water! I knew I was mere flipper steps away from a free path! But I swear to you a godly figure appeared in the illumination; an all-knowing creator perched on a mighty chair, ready to share with me all of humanity's secrets and reasons. I had to know…I regret it, but I simply had to know.

The long trek toward him slowly revealed a still man pondering the plight and future of his nation. No, this was not the stern statue that I had mistaken for a giant of greater power—standing before the bearded boulder was the man from television. His handsome charm looked up at the seated statue with watery eyes, muttering questions as he fiddled his quivering hands in his pockets. My questions on why I was sent on this journey would not be answered that day.

Quickly made into a curious fool, I slithered back but my shadow disrupted the illumination and caused a stir. The human saw me and crouched in defense. Curiosity evidently got the better of him as he came toward me and flashed his pearly whites. Picking me up, as all humans tended to do, he searched all over until it dawned on him where it was I escaped from.

"I 'er think we're both not supposed to be out here, are we? Especially not alone. Our little secret, pal?"

His warmth was irresistible. I knew the mission had failed and I'd be brought back to the awful confines of the storage room once more, but if anyone was to do it, I was glad it was him.

For the rest of the night I was locked up in a small room where this man observed the starry night sky out of his window, murky drink in hand. There was a lot going on in this room, what with the flags and maps and papers sprawled all over a wooden desk. With no corners to hide in, a shivering maid curiously brought in a tub of cool water after a late-night request. She kindly placed it on the floor beside me and placed me inside—my drying skin was once again saved in the nick of time.

The strangest thing was she uttered, "You're welcome, Mr. President."—before scurrying away. I wondered just how many people in this world were named Mr. President. Everyone I met had this bizarre name that seemed to strike fear into those who addressed them. A common name I thought, much more than Akela.

To differentiate, I mentally noted he was the handsome President—out of all the humans I had encountered, this one seemed the most calming to the eyes. Under his watchful eye I sat in my tub while he paced around before plopping down and sprawling out on his cushioned couch just mere steps away.

"You don't know just how much trouble you caused, little fella. The unrest has finally died down and you want to shake things up again? Make hell for me, is that it?" he clucked with a laugh. I certainly didn't intend to create any hell or trouble for the handsome President, or anyone for that matter. All I could do was listen and stare ahead. "I know, it's not your fault. It's the people…they believe what they want to believe. Oh, to be an animal…to live in your own world and worry only about your next meal. I hope you're happy."

He sat up and gave me a good, hard stare. His speech was slurred, though naturally it had a few eccentric sounds. But I could tell he was worried; nervous about something or someone. His troubled eyes looked down into his dark drink. "Does everyone of your kind get along? Some are greener than others, maybe, but you're all still the same species, aren't you?" He stood up and set his drink down on the desk, peering out of his window with his back toward me. "That's our biggest problem—not spies or bombs or political strife. It's all right here…happening now…and I worry for the future."

He stopped himself and turned. With a skipping pace, he bounced to me and petted my head as I floundered in the provided tiny tub. I wish I could have given him more comfort that everything would be all right—to hold him just as he held me. But I drifted off to sleep that night and awoke in my old tank in the closet the very next morning.

I didn't stay locked up for long—it seemed I had made a friend in the handsome President. On his loneliest of days, he would call for his top people to come fish me out and bring me to the little, portable gray tub. Then he'd go on for hours, ranting to me about "Castro" this and "Jackie" that. He'd walk me around his grand house, showing me artifacts from the mythical men before him.

I'd just tune him out because I hadn't the faintest idea of what he was saying. I know he desired some strange ring that belonged to a fellow named Roosevelt which contained a strand of hair from a man called Lincoln; that did ring a bell but I was positive it could not have been the one I had once held in my possession. But during these political soliloquies and confessions, I'd often plan out my escape. With nowhere to go, a vessel was provided when he fearfully hid a white bag found next to the couch.

In a bid to hide this puffy pouch, his clammy hands stowed the sack away by his desk—right in the vicinity of my reach. With a lurch forward, I put all my weight on the edge of the tub till I could scurry out and over—to my delight the purse was open. As I made certain my body was fully concealed within, I heard him pick up the telephone contraption and order someone to "quickly and discretely deliver the handbag to her this instant."

I tell you, the handsome President must have rambled the whole day because he closed up the bag and unknowingly sent me on my way. I thumped and bumped around as little hands carried me on a rapidly paced journey further than I had gone in years.

I finally saw the light of day when hands came rifling for one of the many pointed contents. The bag dropped to the floor with a thud as the owner of it screamed a high-pitched squeal. I poked my head out to see a perfectly lavish and clean indoor haven and a buxom body that was solidified with the blondest of curls and the most definitive of curves.

"Good heavens!" she shrieked, her hands clinging tightly to her cheeks. As I shimmied out of the bag and toward any available open window, she climbed up atop the tallest chair to avoid any contact. "John, what on earth are you trying to do to me?" she howled to herself.

After a fit of giggles and a feast of white little dots, she summoned the courage to throw me off my pace and pin me down with her bare, wiggling foot. With her free hands, she dialed the telephone on her desk. "Well hello, Mister…I know I'm not supposed to be calling you. Then again, you're not supposed to be putting little critters in lady's purses, now are you?…why yes, I have him right here in my room… well I can't just wait around all day, I have a screen test tomorrow and… all right, all right, midnight it is. But if you're not careful I might just let him go into the nearest river."

With that, she lifted her leg and slammed down the phone. I huffed as we both stared toward the room's picture window, and I knew my chances of getting out were slim. I looked up to see a toothy grin glaring back. "Well, if I can work with a monkey, I can surely work with you. You're not my usual soft and cuddly idea of company but you'll have to do!"

And so we spent the day together. Keeping me tucked in her left arm as she tromped along in skyscraper-tall shoes, we ate at the fanciest of eateries where she fed me salad from her own stock of served food. Then she had to get her nails smeared with sparkly red paint and her hair extra curled. Then we'd just wander up and down the streets, basking in attention.

I'm telling you, everywhere this woman went, crazed humans would flock to her and request pictures and signatures. It was a lot more pleasant than the crazed mobs I had faced in my past. They'd scream for her to look one way or to pose over some drafty grate so her dress would lift. Of course they all had to point at me and inquire just what the heck she was doing with me in her company.

Even I couldn't escape these scrutinizing questions—dogs on leashes leaped on by and did double takes when they saw me clutched against this woman's bosoms. I'd just smile and shrug because I didn't have an answer. Most of them just barked with hurtful hostility anyway.

"What is that dreadful green slime doing out here on our streets?" they'd shout. "He must be compensating for something if he's out and about, taking one of the most popular humans for a walk," others would mutter.

By the time we made it back to her room, I was exhausted way beyond the river swimming days. The handsome President awaited her but with an entirely different look. I actually didn't know it was him until he somehow shed his hair and glasses. With a playful laugh, they went right in for a passionate session of lip rubbing. Clothing was shed as I wandered the perimeter, looking for an escape. The building was too high and I was returned that night, still smelling of nail polish and tired from the scrutinizing attention.

Not long after, there was this other grand escape adventure, where by the miracle of fate I was in the handsome President's care when Elvis Presley strolled in for a visit. I had seen this hip-swaggering human on my television set when I came across a program where he strummed an overgrown ukulele on the beaches I knew oh so well.

This Elvis fellow hopped around in familiar, flowery shirts along the beautiful shores I once called home while all the while his name flashed over and over so watchers knew just who this important being was. I wondered if he too called Hawaii home—I became desperate to find out, eager to hitch a ride if I ever could.

With all the commotion going on in the handsome President's office that day, I could have easily walked out of the room if I possessed the skill to open up doors. He had brought me in to simply show me off to the curious "king" before shoving me off to the side. Upon our first meeting, I will admit, I was a bit starstruck. After all, his confident charm radiated through the screen somehow and touched millions more than just myself; I was just really confident he was finally my ticket home.

While handshakes and photographs swirled about, I climbed up and into the unwatched suit coat lying on the couch. I managed to hoist myself up with a surge in neck and jaw strength, pulling on the thick fabric and dragging my way to the top. I nestled, uncomfortably snug, in the inner breast pocket while all the commotion had this Elvis Presley eagerly wanting to get out and on with his day. The extra bulging weight didn't seem to cross his mind one bit, so once again I found myself out of the confines and into the world.

After a few muffled comments from people about his evident weight gain and a long, wondering wait in the dark (I had become an expert at this by now) the clothing's fabric gave way and I came skidding out on the floor.

He was playing music and singing at that point but I had no clue there were that many fans cheering about and listening to him from surrounding risers. Elvis laughed in stunned surprise as hot stage lights threatened to cook me right then and there. An echo of deafening laughter erupted as another man ran out and picked me up in mid-escape.

"Well, what do we have here?" he inquired.

"I don't know, Ed. Looks like I took a bit of Hawaii back with me," Elvis softly chimed back. With laughter and banging, the crowd went wild as the other man ensured the people they'd be right back after a word from their sponsor. Elvis gave a little bow as he cradled me back into his arms. "Thank you very much," he muttered before rushing away and immediately returning me to the handsome President and my dungeon.

We only saw each other one more time when, as a nervous, sweaty wreck, he hid under his desk with me clung tightly in his arms. We'd only peek periodically at maps on his desk that he'd occasionally add little markers to around the same spot. He'd ask me what should be done as his quivering hand gripped a curious piece of paper.

"Tightening the knot of war..." he would say over and over to himself. After a long look into my glazed little eyes, the man sighed and tightened his attire as he climbed out from under the desk. A quick call was made requesting I be picked up and returned to holding for safety as he made his way to the door. After clearing his throat, he stopped one last time and turned to me, awaiting pickup on his desk. "Still, I 'er feel you have caused me more trouble than the Soviets," he said with a smile. "Thanks for listening."

That was the last time I ever saw the handsome President in person—I suppose he just got too busy doing other things to care about me. You know, I really felt bad trying to escape on him all those times because his friendship really was appreciated. He just wanted open ears and a mute mouth to spill all his secrets to.

I was getting more and more restless by the day to get out. But all these defeats continually wore me down to the point where I felt like throwing it all in and just claiming the closet as my new home. Of course, by now, you should know me better than that. Sheer determination to prove everyone wrong, mixed with memories of my sweet Kalea, kept me mobile. If only the handsome President had truly studied my face and taken me where I desperately desired to go. I only saw him again for a brief period on television—his face covered the screen for weeks on end, interrupted only by teary-eyed newscasters and a constant replay of scuffling men headed down a hallway.

All in all I carried out fifteen escape attempts from the room, getting more and more confident and crafty with my methods. I faked my own death one afternoon by simply refusing to move. A foolhardy Ron threw me out with the garbage, and suddenly I found myself out wandering in faraway sludge. I was free and actually in nature for once. I navigated waterways and ate my weight in fresh grass until I did in fact hit the Ocean.

I was discovered only because of the peculiar marking sprayed on my back—the unfriendly new management seemed threatened by my friendship with the handsome President while his associates worried about my frequent darts for the door. They were certain some secret spy organization had something to do with my desire to flee so more unwelcoming tests were completed. They took a can of black permanent spray and went ahead by marking my shell with a giant X—just so I could never get mixed up or go unnoticed.

I would have gotten away free if I hadn't run into some drunken politician who recognized me in the midst of a card game on the beach. Amazed, he snapped me up and returned me after all the journeying through the wide waterways. It had a much cooler feel—I assured myself it was the wrong Ocean anyway.

Peculiar Ron had always been a misfit but most obviously was a product of his time. Hair grew from all sides of his face while the scraggly ones on the top of his head grew long. I never saw him positively socialize with other workers—he was usually taking the brunt of ranting rage. To defy his employers, he must have let his appearance falter. To escape from his misery, he visited me and drank himself silly with an array of bottled beer. He'd point to my back and assure me I was the perfect pet for the space program—sheer incoherent nonsense like that.

Together we'd watch nose-wiggling women on the television until one too many drinks made him drift off asleep. Often he'd take me out and give me full body pets, and luckily, this was one of those times. The only problem was that the door was closed and there was no way for me to reach the handle.

My plan came to me vividly and quicker than ever when I surveyed my options. A plastic, six-ringed device used to string together his beverage containers fit perfectly around my neck. This gave me added height and I was able to rope the door with the towering plastic and pull with all my might until it opened.

I ditched the ringed tool and made a run for it—trying to make it to where I originally meant to go before getting distracted by the statue and its godly glow. It was morning however, and I didn't go unnoticed by all the incoming staff arriving for work.

My guardians had had enough, and yet another man known as Mr. President (I referred to this one as the angry President) saw to it I was locked up in a max facility with double-plated glass and high-end tank coverings. Poor, incompetent Ron was placed in a chair in front of me to see to it I could never escape again, let alone come out for visits and attention.

Out of options, I soon realized my only way out was going to be addressing the poor, lost soul directly—he had a thin brain but a thick heart. If anyone would listen to me and hear my plea, it would be Ron the security guard.

TWENTY-SEVEN

I HAD been on this journey for nearly the greater part of my life now. Kalea had become a distant memory—just a flickering speck of hope that wavered in the wind. But I yearned to tell her everything that had happened; the people that I had met and places I'd seen. I don't think she would have believed me in the slightest. But I'd insist on proclaiming every detail because it was all for her. Every lap swam and mountain climbed. She was the one who gave meaning to my life after all—my purpose…my destiny.

But then I reveled in long gone memories of my old pals launching an attack on the sugar ship to turn the water all sweet. Oh how I had spent eons of hours waiting for mere seconds to talk to her. It was these times that were worth fighting for. Perhaps going back was no longer just about feasting my eyes on my sweet Kalea—it was to travel through time and return to a long gone portion of my life that had turned to memory.

My new tank was impenetrable by any rock and unmovable by any thump or bump. Ron was thoroughly instructed never to take me out or show me the slightest bit of attention. For if he did, he would not only be dismissed from his duties, he would be imprisoned for going against his people. I gathered most of this through Ron's forlorn stare at me through the glass—I could plainly see he wanted to so badly pet me but couldn't for the sake of his own security.

Humans are funny, you know. I had been wrapped up in human life for quite some time now and I had witnessed them love each other physically and witnessed them kill each other until nothing remained but a bloody pulp.

The more and more I got to know humans, I could plainly see they were all different. But I was never clear on why this was the case. All I could see was each one sought validation and respect just like me. Yet, internally, they couldn't bring themselves to do it. They could not tell one another what it was they truly felt so they turned to me, a creature that could not respond to confide their inner secrets. I was sorry I couldn't do anything for them so they wouldn't just live their lives with secret feelings buried deep inside. I understood this feeling, but after fighting to break through and profess my desires, I won over my darling Kalea.

Society, this sprawling tapestry of towers and buildings was a foreign concept to me. Food was readily available as was love and companionship, yet nobody seemed happy. I used to spend the better part of my day searching for food and shelter and certainly others to share my life and feelings with. But humans isolated themselves in metal boxes and papers that covered their faces.

I'll admit to you, I had trouble understanding what it all was I had witnessed. Rooms and objects that had no definition in my mind, along with tasks that seemed to have no link to pure survival—yet it was what most humans seemed to occupy themselves with every day. It felt like a cold world—a lonely world—and I appreciated my beaches all the more. I cursed myself for spending all that time alone, buried in the log hole as a young offspring. If I could do it differently I'd talk to every passing fish that swam my way. Lonely Ron seemed the spitting image of me as he rocked back and forth in his chair, fighting off the urge to sleep or the opportunity to talk with passing co-workers.

Ron the security guard seemed as though he was becoming all the more unhinged the further and further we went along. Frequent clashes with nasty co-workers left the man in a miserable funk. The all too frequent body slam or undeserved scolding left his eyes looking upwards and his hair wavering down to his shoulders. A scruffy beard grew to seismic proportions until you could no longer see his smile. He was bored guarding me all day, perhaps plagued with a case of the "what's it all abouts?" The television was no longer allowed to help either of us pass the time. But secretly, late in the day when all other workers made their treks home, Ron would stay and reveal his over-grown ukulele.

He'd strum a tune and mumble lyrics as his eyes would flutter with passion for the music. Some days I'd see him just stare at a pho-tograph with a girl—long-flowing hair that displayed a variety of col-orful flowers. I knew that look in Ron's face—I too had felt the weight of love all those many years before; I still did. But I also knew the for-lorn look in his face and the sighing silence that crippled any chance of these two becoming lovers.

The last thing I remember about Ron in those days was that every night before he'd leave, he'd flash two fingers at me before slinking away into the darkness. It was a symbol for something that unified a lot of people—I would see that later on in the great open street of Haight-Ashbury. Ron would jitter as he said this destination over and over in profound excitement while we drove. Until that day—I knew I was going to have to help him get to that point first.

I am absolutely positive the burning question on your mind has been can animals talk? Well evidently, we can talk to each other (and in our own languages I might add) but we lack the proper skills to com-municate with humans. I am told canines possess the most advanced skills to talk to you while various birds can actually utter several differ-ent phrases. I could never do that, adhering to a specific animal pol-icy and simply struggling with the many ways to form words. I just could not find a way to speak human—it's incredibly hard to move my mouth like you seem to do without any effort at all.

With other animals it's easy—we all have various, different types of language but it's of course easier to adapt to. Different dialects depending on the region as well! I had slowly understood more and more English during my time spent with all you people but it was in no way fluid. And being cooped up in a watery glass box surely didn't help my communication skills any.

During long nights after a full day of work, Ron would hang around after hours and strum the big ukulele until his heart was con-tent. Instead of beverages he pulled out these little papers and rolled himself an uneven cigarette. What he was tucking up in the middle was a green substance I recognized from the Good Time Gang all those years back. I remember my flight with those wonky vultures—light transcended into feeling while evidently inanimate forest objects spoke to me. Obviously, something was very wrong with that plant. Ron's glazed faced tipped me off that he was enjoying the mind-bending effects of this same strange substance.

So it hit me—if anything seemed possible while digesting the preposterous plant, my communication skills might just shine enough to get me freed. If I were to manipulate the situation just enough with my broken English, this sinister sprout would take over after I got Ron's attention.

So there I was making funny faces, holding my eyes open wide to try and get Ron's attention. For weeks I did this because he smoked this shrub more than once—but he really just wasn't paying attention to me at all. He'd wobble around and stroke various soft furniture sets or appliances in the room, but he'd never look at me and take note of what I was doing.

It wasn't until he took a puff of his freshly rolled papered plant and prepared to sprinkle in the flavorless food, opening the tiny latch to feed me, that I was able to poke my head out of the water and give him a good stare. I was desperate by now, trying to show him all my vulnerability and inner desire.

I opened my mouth as wide as it could go and forced out a slur of sounds buried deep down inside. Perhaps it was deep frustration that had built up over the years that was finally ready to come out to those who would hear it. Whatever the case, he dropped the jar and stared back at me in absolute bewilderment. I was certain he somehow heard me speak the name "Ron." His plant had worked and acted as an inter-species translator.

"Yes?" he stammered.

"Ron!" I proclaimed.

"No! No! This can't be happening. I got to go home." Ron turned to leave.

"Ron! This is no place for me. This is no place for you!" Ron stopped.

"What do you mean?"

"Let me out of here. We can both go to where we are meant to be."

"Where?"

"To the Ocean."

"To…Haight-Ashbury?"

"What?" I said in confusion. That was oddly specific.

"Haight-Ashbury—San Francisco! Everyone's going west! Every-one's going to the coast! The Ocean! This is a sign. Right? Right?"

"Yes, Ron! You are not meant for this place. Take us there…take us—" Ron didn't hesitate any longer. He yanked and banged on the tank lid but couldn't get it to budge. His trembling hands went for his massive ring of keys but his eager twitch didn't allow him to enter one into the hole.

In a confused fit of self-discovery, he picked up the stool he so often perched on and threw it directly at the tank. The glass shattered instantly and a wave of water carried me out onto the floor, soaking poor Ron who stood with both arms raised in the air. As he picked me up in his arms, we both glanced at each other with a loving look that was long overdue.

"The photograph…the one in your pocket…" He pulled out the very one with the girl who had flowers covering her hair. "Go to her," I said. "Tell her how you feel."

With a triumphant stride, Ron smiled from ear to ear as he made his way out the door with me in hand.

The next thing I knew I was chucked into the front right side seat of his teal-colored car. He nearly slipped as he came back to hook some kind of belt around me so I wouldn't slide from side to side. We were both obviously confused about what was happening to us as the mind-bending plant somehow worked as a translator between us. Unsure if I was really talking and making sense or Ron was just going insane and hearing what he wanted to hear, we chugged along down the road at a frightening speed, blaring music about lighting fires.

"This can't be real. This can't be happening. This is only because of the—why didn't you tell me you could talk?"

I wobbled from left to right—thankful the belt kept me safe from Ron's erratic driving.

"At least tell me your name," he cried.

"Akela," I answered.

"Wow, man…what a trip. Akela…who are you? Where have you been trying to escape to? The coast? San Fran? What is this?"

"Just keep going. Find your girl and tell her everything. Never be apart whatever you do! And just take me to the Ocean."

With watery eyes, Ron wiped his tears as he steered the car right on a sharp curve. "Screw the government. Screw Johnson. I spent way too much of my life working for those fascist pigs! No more though. We're going west. Peace and love Akela; that's all we need."

We sped up and down, veering every which way as Ron banged on the wheel in front of him with both newfound freedom and frightened anxiety. I didn't expect him to break the tank like he did, and I don't think either of us had considered the consequences of stealing me and heading out on the run. It was in the heat of passion and Ron was making damn sure he wasn't going to blow the biggest chance in his life to kingdom come.

Parked halfway on the street and on the front lawn, he simultaneously straightened his hair and unwrapped some chewy, white block after he felt dissatisfied with his breath. He looked at me for reassurance and evidently, I must have given him a resounding yes. He bounded out of the car, leaving me strapped to the seat as he screamed Veronica's name, tripping over various rocks and obstacles on the ground.

Lights flickered on and dogs barked threats and questions while the distraught guard tried to catch his breath, huffing and puffing outside the door. Sure enough, a window slid open and the flowery hair flew about—Veronica was even lovelier in person. Her curious eyes and sleepy smile were no match for her thin negligee that caught poor Ron off guard. He turned to me in a panic.

"Ron?" she inquired unexpectedly.

"I can't do this! This was a mistake."

"Yes!" I cried. "You have it in you. I've seen the way you look at that photograph. I know you fantasize about her every day. Her effect radiates off you. Tell her that! Tell her!"

Ron straightened up and cleared his voice. He shifted his weight from side to side as he planned out just what it was he wanted to say. He stopped and stared and mumbled and greeted her about seven times, but after another look back at me he sighed and went straight for the truth.

"I love you, Veronica. Ever since we met I've been crazy about you. You're beautiful and kind…your energy is inspiring. You make me feel good about myself. About life! I quit my job Veronica—no more government work. No more working for the man who brings us down. No more taking the easy way out! I'm going west. San Francisco! Akela told me that. He told me to go. I'm going to start living. I'm gonna do it right. Get out on the road. Adventure! And I want you in my life. So, will you come, Veronica? With me? To San Francisco? Please?"

"Yeah, sure!" she said in a high-pitched squeal. Veronica shut the window and disappeared as an out of breath Ron laughed giddily. He turned to give me some sort of a signal with his thumb before looking up at the starry night sky. Veronica eventually skipped out with a bag swinging off her shoulder. With a hug and a gentle lip rub, they walked hand in hand to Ron's car. He opened up the back door behind me to let her in before he took his own seat.

"Veronica, meet Akela," he said with a grin, gesturing toward me as I remained strapped to the seat.

I spoke nothing further. The air remained silent as Veronica feasted her eyes on me, studying me for an eternity.

"Far out," she finally said with a nod. Ron giggled and started the car—music blared again, only this time it professed the love of a joyful man feeling so happy they were together.

TWENTY-EIGHT

THOUGH I had seen cars and vehicles speed by me, I'd never actually been, to my knowledge, inside one until that day. It was spacious and comfortable and when Ron wasn't zooming around like a maniac, it was actually kind of fun. Somehow the trekking speed at which we journeyed calmed me and provided assurance all would be well. As long as you kept going, you would reach your destination.

We switched places obviously and I was set up in the back seat with a tub of water. It was funny because it seemed as though that tub was the very same tub the handsome President had kept me in. The only difference was I could hardly fit—it just barely surrounded my body, which prompted me to think all the years of inactivity were going straight to my belly. Never once did it occur to me that I could be slowly growing like I should have done all those years prior. After living nearly a lifetime, who in their right mind would think their teenage growth spurt was finally happening?

They'd sprinkle food into my tub daily—and none of that flaky, processed stuff either; this time it was fresh, handpicked sea grass from real water pools. Ron and Veronica would yak away until a song they deemed good came on. They'd nod their heads to the overgrown ukulele strums and play along.

Some days Ron couldn't quite face what it was he was doing and would stop the car to run out on the road and get some air. Veronica would run out and comfort him, hugging him and rubbing her lips all over. We'd continue on the journey right after, once Ron regained his smile and confidence in himself.

I'd spend my time perched along the windowsill, taking in the country like I'd never seen it before. We were going so fast the other cars passed by like bright blurs; sometimes I couldn't even tell what they were, they had come and gone so fast. Other times I'd stare at the stretching fields of gold and lush forests of green. It took Earl and myself years to wind our way through the rivers. Here I was trudging past it all in a matter of seconds.

This time it felt real. It felt like I was actually going to get to the Ocean and nothing was going to interfere. Not boats and their crews, not mistaken turns or silly tasks in exchange for directions. Not even my own fear of swimming into the great wide unknown. I was in good hands and now all that stood between me and Kalea was a lengthy swim—but I felt ready.

All that would remain to prove I did in fact take this journey would be my memories and the spray-painted X on my back. No matter how hard Veronica scrubbed, she couldn't remove the government marking for the life of her. There was still a chance I could be recognized but the further away we drove, the slimmer those chances would be.

Those were some of the most freeing days I had encountered in a long while. Sometimes we wouldn't drive and I'd be okay with that. The deep, inner me wanted to get en route as fast as I could and enjoy what little time and life I had left with Kalea. Another part insisted I listen deep to the music I was hearing.

Ron and Veronica had little money to fuel the car (or themselves for that matter) so we'd make the occasional pit stop, plant ourselves on the sidewalk, and sing away with a little jar out front. Passersby with flowers in their hair and flowing dresses would throw coins their way or often just sit down and sing with them. Actually, some people hitched a ride with us some days and would offer the infamous green plant as payment. I had to sit right next to them and I can tell you the smells protruding from some of these people were just downright awful. But they all seemed fascinated by me and would spill their life stories as they gave out full body pets.

The humans in suits and fedoras did not spare a dime, though it seemed as though they were the ones with dimes to spare. They'd simply ignore us or give us a scowl—Ron would just shake his head and keep strumming. It didn't matter; we were free. Free to swim together in the lakes we discovered together. Free to sprawl out and sleep all together in the backseat of the car. Free to be free and explore what we desired.

I remember actually going to a few diners with them where I'd anxiously await under the table for any shared food to be dropped my way. The funniest one was labeled "The Tiki Bar" and obviously paid homage to my homeland. Waitresses wore grass skirts while fire dancers entertained to drumbeats. I crawled around the sandy floor and was assumed to be part of the decorations. A wave of homesickness came over me but I was comforted by my new friends. I wished for them to come with me and see the real place—the absolute Hawaiian treasure of course being Kalea.

We drove and drove over the winding stretch of highway I laughably identified as Route 66. I'm positive we even drove over the same stretch where Earl and I tried to once flag down a car. And out in the desert I was certain vultures flew in the distance along the sunset—I wondered whatever became of the Good Time Gang.

Ron was sure to stress the importance of the "mother road" to us all. It was on the infamous road where my journey was once again changed. Not by a roadblock or an enemy, but a simple, flat voice that interrupted the radio's music.

"We interrupt this broadcast to bring you a special news bulletin. American civil rights activist Martin Luther King Junior has been killed. He was shot earlier this evening at the Lorraine Motel in Memphis, Tennessee. King was taken to the hospital and was pronounced dead at the scene. The gunman is still at large."

Silence. The radio for once played nothing but pure silence as tears and sniffles filled the car cab. Ron was so distraught he had to pull over and turn the car off completely. Of course I didn't know who Martin Luther King was and how these two knew him, but the man must have affected them deeply because they cried in sorrow and anger the whole night.

This news put a damper on the trip and Ron and Victoria hardly spoke, let alone strummed the overgrown ukulele. The whole journey seemed nearly pointless to them now as our speed to the Ocean severely decreased. Anytime a news bulletin came in over the radio, they'd have to turn it as loud as it could go to find out if the killer was caught or the rioting had ceased. We were parked in the lot of some drive-up burger joint when I finally caught wind of their ongoing conversation. Between meaty munches they'd share their deep, internal gems about life.

"But he was nonviolent," Veronica would protest. "I don't get it—what danger was he if he was nonviolent?"

"I don't know what this world is coming to. You ought to know this was the government's doing—putting the guy up to it."

"Was it?"

"I don't know, but it seems like something they would do. They feared him and everything he stood for."

"Which wasn't anything to be afraid of in the first place! Peace, equality, opportunity—he gave his life for others, man. To fight the good fight. So did Kennedy…"

I don't know what this world is coming to became a common phrase Ron would utter over and over as the drive went on.

"Makes you wonder if you're doing enough, you know? Like if I'm living life right and trying to do things for others."

"You've done lots." Both Veronica and Ron turned to glance at me at the same time—each with a confused grin on their face.

"I've saved an animal from confinement—trust me, I haven't done enough." With the throw of his burger and a few yanks of the steering wheel, we all once again found ourselves in the presence of one of Ron's infamous fits. As he cried and sobbed and sniffled and coughed, Veronica snuggled up close and patted his back. "I know I haven't, Veronica. I've been greedy—just living for myself. All I ever wanted was you and the road. Now that I've got those things, I've got to be better. I've got to do more. I can't just selfishly get everything I want. I have to do the same for everybody. Share the love."

Impressed with his wide and heavy heart, Veronica crawled right up onto his lap and began another rip-roaring face rub after they barely finished chewing up their meals. I, on the other hand, was stunned.

I pondered that perhaps learning English wasn't the greatest for my goals after all. Because my heart broke into a million pieces that afternoon when I realized just what it was Ron was talking about. This King fellow and Kennedy fellow and even Ron himself had done generous things. It seemed to me they had sacrificed their own needs to put others first. And when they didn't, they worried about not helping out enough.

I saw this firsthand as we rolled along—Ron was eager to give rides to just about everyone until the whole car was filled up with takers wanting to head west to the Ocean. And then the crew would talk about how they helped others and would communally use all coins raised to feed each other or give to some other passerby down on their luck.

Once we finally reached the much anticipated and talked about Haight-Ashbury, we discovered a slew of people like that. They shared everything from clothing to shelter—even the green, magical plant was passed around from lip to lip. Heck, I saw some people actually share their own beloved spouse with another.

I'm telling you it was a shock to see so much love and generosity and…hair! But it also showed me just what a selfish and miserable curmudgeon I had been. I never helped out Earl—I in fact blamed him for getting us lost and for having his own struggles of loneliness and self-destruction. I bitterly resented Chul and Byeol and all the lake dwellers who innocently struck a deal with me for information. Because of me, they might have possibly been drug to the bottom of the Ocean. And my dear departed friends Kaimi and Pika—all they ever did was help me search for my mother and win over Kalea's attention. Then of course Kalea…a whole different story…I manipulated her into loving me and failed to deliver my promise of being a devoted husband.

Bottom line, I was selfish. Everything I had done was to advance myself and for my own personal gain. I had never once stepped up to help someone, particularly now because I always had one goal in mind. I wanted to get back home and give all my love to one being. And I only wanted to do this because I was hopelessly addicted to her all-around beauty.

I had now seen what a wide world it truly was and that it takes all of us to contribute in order for others to live wonderful lives. This had to have been why I had never made it back home. This had to have been the reason for the whole journey in the first place. It was a mission of self-discovery and I in that moment discovered I did not deserve Kalea. Not for the reasons I had always thought but instead because I had much love to give and few outlets to give it. Almost on parallel with dying Earl, my inner doubts knew I had not done enough whether there was an afterlife or not.

For the next few days I listened to music, hanging out in record stores and watching flat, round discs spin and spin. I ate fresh green vegetables and found myself passed around and around to everyone who was eager to give me a full body pet. It made them happy so in turn it made me happy.

I was stage-side for several performances of a rather loud band that claimed they were grateful to be dead. One wide-eyed wonder offered Ron and Veronica memberships into his exclusive family burgeoning out in the desert. If it wasn't for a lack of water for me, they claimed they would have gone. And I even managed to make a furry friend from the animal kingdom—a rather cocky white rabbit who insisted a local band had written a song about him. There certainly were a lot of colorful characters out there on the coast.

I suppose getting through to Ron to go on this journey was a start and I liked the feeling of setting him on his path. So it was then and there I renounced my entire goal of making it back home. The looming swim and the sanctuary of my beloved beaches were a dream now; one I had clung to all my life. But it was time to wake up and give back to repay those who had helped me along the way. It was time to put my efforts not into traveling forth but into doing some good. This sounded like a worthwhile destiny to me.

Of course this was all talk when I was put to the test during a much anticipated day at the beach. Ron and Veronica and their newfound friends frolicked unclothed along the sandy shores. The beach could not be compared to what I knew and loved—the lengthy stretch of imported sand contained few plants and all humans.

But waving right in front of me was the open, deep blue water that could lead me home. I had done it—I had overcome tanks and locks and finally arrived to the final leg of the journey. I scoffed when the only mass in sight were tiny boats sailing out into the distance. I certainly learned the hard way I should have never hitched a ride on one and bravely swam ahead. If only I had done it, Earl would have still been alive.

I trembled out of excitement and fear as I crawled over the sand, away from frayed beach towels and to the wide open where nothing of any sort could stop me. All I had to do was swim, swim to freedom! Take the first step into the fresh, refreshing Ocean and head through the great wide open to where I belonged. But the change in my heart chained my flippers to the ground. I tried to bargain with myself, assuring I'd do good and spread love and good deeds as soon as I got home. I tried to convince myself to test out the waters and see just how the San Francisco Bay felt.

I huffed and puffed in moral frustration, inching forward and yet cowering back. The moment from my dreams had come and they had always assured me I'd run safely to the Ocean in a freeing, mad dash. I had imagined this moment a thousand times, but never once did I account for a moral reshuffling and Nia Walker crossing my path.

The distant sniffles of a little girl ceased when she saw me pondering my future on the beach. With sticky, open fingers, she wiped her tears and waddled her way toward me with an eagerness to grab and shake. I was fine with controlled adults but children were another story. I was scooped up and shook like the day Hawaii came under attack. She giggled and said "fishy" over and over as she spun me around, pretending I could fly.

As the world shook, I took the little girl in, noting her jet-black, little dress twirling in the wind; only a shade darker than her skin. Her hair was braided and dangled all the way down her back. And there was loving life in her eyes like nobody I'd seen. In that moment I was all that this little girl cared about or wanted in her possession. Ron, of course, saw this and rolled up immediately after realizing he'd forgotten to pay attention to my very well-being.

"Hey, little girl, you found my friend I see. Thanks for saving him, otherwise he might have ran away. But be gentle with him." The girl ignored Ron's request and began to twirl faster and hold me as high up in the air as she could. "You know what, you better give him back."

As Ron's concern grew and his hands reached out to take me, the girl's face scrunched up and tears instantly welled like a waterfall.

"Nia Walker, what do you think you are doing?" her mother yelled. "Taking things that don't belong to you?"

Nia froze in fear and dropped me instantly. I, of course, landed smack on my back. As Ron bent down to flip me right side up, he looked at the distraught mother. She, too, was wearing a dress as black as night, only hers contained a fluffy hat with a dark veil that drooped down over her face. Ron grabbed me but froze, my legs twitching in midair. I saw him gaze at both of their outfits—a humble understanding was obviously reached in his mind.

With a hard swallow, he set me back on the ground and stood up tall, smiling as he rested one hand on Nia's shoulder. "You know what, why don't you take care of him for me?"

"Really?"

"No, uh-uh, that's the last thing we need," Nia's mother protested.

"I think you could use a friend and by the looks of it you two seem to get along swell. Go on! I bet he'd be happiest with you."

Nia giggled with delight as she clutched me tight in her arms. Ron stifled his own tears as he took one last look at me and smiled. To this day I don't know what became of him; whether he was ever tracked down by the government or thought our conversation was more than just an illicit hallucination. Whatever he's doing I just hope he's happy.

He deserved a good life because he always seemed like a good person to me; ready to help me out and give me comfort, even in the earliest days of our relationship.

Yes, I knew this was a step in the right direction. The simple joy this girl received from my presence was irreplaceable. I trusted Ron that she and her mother were fitting owners, despite her mother making absolute sure she didn't come in contact with me. Oh, she tried her best to convince Nia to leave me at the beach but her heart was set. I would be going home with them and making sure tears never fell from her little eyes again. I gave up my journey and accepted my true destiny of selflessly bringing joy to another.

I took one last look at the peaceful water that met with the sky. Ron turned one last time and told Nia and her mother that my name was Akela.

TWENTY-NINE

I'LL NEVER forget the shaggy, faded orange carpet that tickled my skin—brown from all the years of dirt deposits that flew off Nia's shoes. I'll never forget the dark wood cupboards or the dim lamps or the cushy, circular chair she'd curl up on alongside me. Smooth trumpets would softly blow from the record player and the kitchen would smell of sizzling meat. It was cozy—a perfectly sized place for me to roam as I could never seem to get lost. There were four rooms, though I spent the majority of my time in Nia's; I always felt comfortable and never once did I try to escape.

Her mother looked nauseated every time she glanced at me, and it was a rare occurrence when she would actually make skin to skin contact. If anything, it was with her toes in order to move me along—usually if I came too close to her vicinity. But the smile Nia would have when she'd kick off her shoes, throw her bag down, and run to me after a long day in the world…it was something else, I tell you! Her mother noticed that too, and I certainly believed that is why I stayed.

My first day at this lovely establishment was nerve-racking for us all—but Nia quickly made sure I was acquainted with every single item in the place. She introduced me to stuffed animals, some that were made to resemble my kind and some of wild critters I had never even seen before with big ears and lengthy noses—I doubted they could be real. She pulled out every frilly dress she owned and tried desperately to clothe me in them until it finally sunk in I was just too misshapen to wear what she did. Her misshapen tube that spawned glowing red orbs was a source of entertainment for hours. I witnessed every record album and made note of the prominent people she chose to hang on her wall.

I tried to utter a thank you when she set up a dish of water and food for me in the corner of her room, but she was too jittery to have ever noticed anyway—I think she assumed I was to be kept like some yappy, little puppy. She was always trying to get me to retrieve thrown items as she inquired if I was happy and a "good boy." What confused me the most was the little jar she carefully brought down from the mantle.

Over a brick-encased, roaring fire sat a picture of a stern man with thick, dark hair. Her trembling hands clutched a rounded vase that presented some sort of poem. I pondered for days when she claimed that this was her father. I had been overwhelmed by showcases of human life for years, but this claim I simply did not understand.

As days passed, I gathered Nia and her mother were on their own and saw they would stop occasionally and glance at the prominently displayed vase by the picture on the mantel. Her mother would lovingly look at the picture of the man—there were almost always tears when she did so. Slowly, but surely, I gathered the father must have been inside that vase one way or another. In any case, that's all they had left of him.

Life is funny. I had gone through considerable loss throughout my journey. There were times I felt jealous of everyone's apparent lack of loss and yearned for a life so loving and populated as the others seemed to be. But no matter who you are, you lose somebody. I saw this with

Nia and her mother, and I understood their pain. Often, I'd hear Nia ask exactly where it was her father went and her mother would simply confirm heaven. I never did get a clear cause behind his absence, only hearing the act referred to as "the riot" when it was brought up.

But still, they kept on—we all did and all of us in this world continue to do so because it's all we can do. As they found themselves discussing his absence, I found myself looking for heaven around the house as if I was going to be the unsung hero who brought him back. There was no luck on that front, prompting me to wonder if he and Earl and my siblings were all comingling in the same place. I wondered if it was the faraway land the old gator talked about.

Though in no way could I replace her father, I felt a protective bond forming between us and I cared for her and kept a watchful eye. Nia filled her void with me and with television; a golden, glowing screen played pictures all day long across from her cushy chair. After she'd greet me and spin me around, she'd click the television knob onward, sit back, and watch a group of bickering people escape from the jungles of what looked to be my own Hawaii. She watched this show for hours; her other favorites were a scantily clad woman in pink garb emerging from smoke and a man pretending to be a bat alongside a brightly colored, masked pal.

Oh! The kicker was that the television we feasted our eyes on in a daily ritual had sound. The television Ron had given me was always muddled from the glass and water; I could never actually hear what they were saying. I was in my glory humming along with tremendously catchy jingles about how the *Brady Bunch* became the *Brady Bunch*. Sound gave those watching television much more of a reason to watch, whether it was some profound news of daily world events or a quick blurb about purchasing canned ham. We were enthralled, and to tell the truth, it was what we'd do together most of the time.

After Nia's mother put her off to bed, she'd sneak me back to her room and entertain me with some story that included her miniature fake animals and fake humans—usually with me involved and bent on world domination (for whatever reason she always insisted I came from the moon). She'd get too rambunctious of course and blow the whole operation—her mother would storm in livid and loud.

I was staying in the family bathtub, which in all honesty I didn't mind. After years of being cooped up in a supposedly impenetrable tank, this was a welcomed hostel to hang my hat. Generally, when either of them went to use the tub itself, they'd place me outside and do their business (stand there for ten minutes and waste precious, dribbling water) and then fill it back up for me to splash around in. They were even so kind to put an accessible step beside it so I could come and go as I pleased.

I remember little Nia tried joining me a couple of times but her mother couldn't get over some uncomfortable facts she termed as "disgusting." It was there she witnessed my bullet wound for the first time that she would gently try and nurse to no avail. No matter how hard she scrubbed, the X on my back never did come off.

I didn't mind the shared bath at all except for the fact that we were a tad cramped—my shell felt bigger for some reason, grazing both sides of the tub. Nia certainly wasn't shy either, running around daily in only her skin. I had never seen anyone quite as dark as her before in all my travels. Few folks of that shade worked in my confinement, but I supposed in all my years, I had never paid much attention to the color of anyone. There were no humans that came in my shade of green and that's as much thought as I had given to that subject.

Nia left routinely early every morning, long after her mother had begrudgingly removed me from the tub, did what she needed to do, and prepared a meal for her daughter before heading outside. Nia would refill the tub after standing under the faucet and made sure I had plenty of flaky foods to eat while she was gone.

I only left that building once by her choice when Nia thought showing me off to her peers was the best idea she'd ever had. Sticky little fingers clawed and pawed at me, desperate to get a feel as a queasy adult watched me from afar. Nia did this against her mother's wishes and so I was forced to wait inside her messy, paper-filled table all day until she could sneak me back home.

I enjoyed going out and seeing what it was Nia did; it turns out a lengthy day of learning geological landscapes and word spellings was what filled her outside life. I was proud she was doing this and learning about the world around her. Her mother was less than thrilled that she took me out into the world without permission.

For the rest of the days beyond that one, I'd emerge from the tub after breakfast and wander the home of my lovely owners. I'd usually greet Nia before she left—typically by watching her devour a morning meal and eagerly parade around in possible outfits to wear. For a young child, she certainly had a great sense on how to run her life—brushing and cleaning herself and locking up the place when she left without ever seemingly being told.

To fill my time, I'd investigate everything from the kitchen sink to the remote control. I remember being so enamored with the toilet—I spent a whole week trying to climb up and get a good look at the water within. I was lucky that day; had I been any smaller I could have swirled away down the looming hole into the dark abyss. I remember Earl fondly telling me that was his preferred method of travel—prompting our lengthy stay in the ship's sewer tank. It looked pretty tiny to me, and I had no idea how he did it.

My other pastime was to simply watch hours and hours of television equipped with sound. Before you judge too hard, just listen to what this brilliant invention did for me. The machine taught me everything I know about the human world and it's how I can relay my story to you now!

It all started with the debut of this colorful program of stuffed monsters who happily gave the letter of the day to eager viewers. They'd start with "A" and move to "B" a few days later, always giving ample examples of words that start with the corresponding letter. It wasn't the most riveting television, but I was hooked because no one had ever taken the time to actually explain to me letters of the alphabet and how to spell. So with years of diligent watching came the fluidity and understanding of how to read and write. Old images of words like Hollywood, Plymouth, and USS Sphinx suddenly resonated and meant a whole lot more!

I'd even practice with a nearby pen and drew what I learned on the nearest wall. Of course poor Nia took the blame for that as no one in their right mind would believe I did it. Well, Nia did because she had a wondrous heart of gold but there was no way of convincing her mother of my talents.

Nia would often have to spend evenings cleaning my work, angry but always certain to tell me never to stop writing. While we occasionally proposed silly questions to each other like what our favorite color was, I never once requested to be returned to Hawaii. Anything longer than two words was royally illegible.

One day, curiosity got the better of me and I scribbled down an innocent question that had been burning in my mind since I had arrived. Without giving it a second thought, I wrote down "where is heaven?" in hopes of getting a final answer.

As I waited to hear if Earl in fact had gotten himself there on good merit or not, Nia's mother was the first to find it. She scrubbed the walls and chewed her fingernails in a nervous twitch for hours; she couldn't look Nia in the eye when she first got home. Finally, she broke down in tears and professed that heaven was all around us in infinite beauty. I didn't understand and refrained from writing anything on the wall again in an attempt not to cause an emotional stir.

I instead turned to the prevalent parade of advertisements that described for-sale products that humans were supposed to desire. Lucky for me they always gave a demonstration and a lot of these items like cigarettes or coffee or food were lying around the house already. So I knew what they were now called and what they were used for. This didn't solve the mystery of every single object or occurrence I had stumbled upon, but it sure helped. With time, the scripted images I witnessed made me feel all the more cultured and part of the world around me.

My favorite film was this picture called *Love Story* about a doomed romance of a young couple—it really gave me an insight on human relationships while appealing to my very own problems. Nia's was regrettably the horrific *Exorcist* which we watched on repeat. I'd usually have to leave the room when she played it.

The highlight I'd say was when this old-fashioned western came on and a rough-and-tough man by the name of John Wayne rode his horse and wagon through a dusty desert. In the background a flock of vultures flew on as opposed to the regular circling they always did. I could only think of one vulture group that would do such a thing and one distinct set of vultures that flew through a movie set all those years ago. I squinted as tightly as I could and found a square blotch where one of them was carrying me. If I could find it again, I'd watch that scene over and over just for a shimmering glance of Earl living one more time.

As Nia got older, she'd bring home more and more work to complete and tire away at her bedside desk until it was ready for the next day. I will admit I helped her a few times after taking a gander at what it was she had to do—I found the occasional question sheet blank and took it upon myself to figure out various math problems or names of countries she forgot to label.

I remember the moment I saw the world map for the first time, gleefully pinpointing lonesome Hawaii in the middle of the Pacific thanks to my newfound literate abilities. It was a holy discovery to find I could retrace my steps and see for myself where it was Earl and I ended up. Though I'll never fully know, it seemed like we overshot Hawaii completely and ended up over somewhere in the Orient. I diligently tried to understand what country there had bloody warfare cover its ground but a map could only tell you so much. Japan seemed like the most obvious because of its Hawaiian proximity, but I vaguely remember heading North in all that stormy commotion and something about the geography just didn't feel right.

All the talk on TV those days was about Vietnam, which I could safely rule out as one of the choices. It seemed humans were fighting yet again but something about this battle particularly angered just about everyone in the country. But at least I could now safely say I had been and was currently in the country of the United States for much of my journey. Evidenced by the map, there was a lot more to see.

Little aha moments would pop up during my stay—one in particular happened when Nia's mother's friend came to visit with a pile of brochures on a desert town trip she wanted to take. The brochures made their way to the floor, where I was lucky enough to read all about Las Vegas, and right there on the cover was a picture of the flashy Flamingo Hotel.

It looked different as many buildings had sprung up beside it, but I knew for a fact I had been there before. This was the first inkling inside me that proposed the idea I had in fact traveled to somewhere special. This inkling popped up again during the raging opposition of the Vietnam War—recognizable, hairy faces lined the San Francisco streets in front of buildings I entered with Ron.

I witnessed a man, whose name I can only recall as the disgraced President, flash his fingers and board a helicopter to fly away. His undoing stemmed from authorizing a building break-in, which, some years later, I would learn was all my fault. He had caught false wind that I had been spotted somewhere in this infamous hotel, and so he sent his men to go have a look.

I felt sort of triumphant that they never gave up the search for me—and I had evidently had the last laugh by outsmarting them all. The disgraced President apparently refused to look like a fool, what with his ridiculous act of utilizing unlawful amounts of manpower to catch a lowly "communist" sea critter. It was blamed on rival spying and left at that for all the history books to come.

Always behind him during his television addresses were the white doors to the building I had so often entered for visits to lend a listening ear. The looming tower and godly stone figure that halted my escape were prominently displayed next to it. I had called this area home for some time and only now understood the importance of the place. And from his hospital bed, a fellow named Joseph McCarthy blasted some reptilian creature for causing a communist stir. It was some sort of retrospect and it took me way too long to realize I was the creature in question. I began to wonder, as these answers popped up more and more, if all of these locations and landmarks were important, what did that make me?

While I'd ponder my strange fortune in this world, Nia began to rely on me as a confidante like so many others had before. I had noticed changes in her demeanor—she gradually had little interest in watching television with me and all acted out stories involving me and her stuffed figures had ceased.

She was more focused on the lengthy art of styling her curled hair or painting her face with powder and markings. Every time she'd bang little sponges against her face, a cloud of dust would poison the air and close my windpipe—I'd be momentarily blind during the haze of it all. But with really no method of convincing her to stop (she wouldn't have listened anyway), I'd just hide in the farthest room while she carried out this morning ritual. I tried to tell her my displeasure through writing on the wall, but for some reason, she had even lost interest in communicating—dismissing it as a former childish fantasy that couldn't have been real.

Late at night though, she'd sneak into the bathroom and lock the door behind her. In the pitch darkness, I'd feel her hand stroke my shell and gently wade through the water. She'd sigh and ramble on about a cute boy at school that showed her no attention or a girl who made a rude remark about her hair. I had no control over any outcome and just listened to her stories the best I could. I found myself intrigued and haunted though whenever she came to visit me with her mother on her mind.

"I wish Mama didn't have to work so hard. She's gone twelve hours a day and we haven't even eaten a meal together in a month. I never get to see her—it's not fair. I wish we had money so…so Mom could spend time with me. Or maybe she's doing it because…because she doesn't like me. What if she's embarrassed by me and just wants to get away? Then who will I have?"

I wish I could have harnessed the ability to tell her right then and there that I had seen her exhausted mother come home from work and spend all her free time watching Nia sleep. I wish I could have told her she wiped her tears while running her fingers through Nia's hair. No matter how hard I tried, I still couldn't form a coherent English sentence and notes were out of the question because she wouldn't believe me.

It finally dawned on me that this family needed a provider—someone to support them financially and lend a helping hand so more time could be spent on bonding activities and memory making. Thanks to hours spent watching financial reports on stock market rates, I understood the value of currency. I had seen coins exchanged but had never fully understood their value and worth until that time. I made it my business to collect as many coins as I possibly could so that Nia and her mother could have substantial extra income.

Hell-bent on following through with my earlier aspirations of being selfless and doing good, I would give up television and my daily world lessons to sleep and soak. I'd sneak out every night once Nia and her mother went off to bed by pursuing an arduous climb that thankfully got easier every night I'd attempt it.

I'd push my tub step out into the kitchen and use it to climb up onto a chair and then use that height to wriggle up onto the counter. The window was the easiest part of it all because it was loose and easily slid open and I could squeeze myself out and fall into the garden below where a soft variety of flowers cushioned my landing. Getting back in was just a matter of pulling myself up a vine with clenched teeth and a wriggling will to climb up.

While out in the world, echoes of lightning quick bangs crackled through the hazy street. Vicious dogs howled while roaring mufflers demanded attention with their conversation-halting intrusion. It was an unnerving neighborhood, certainly unlike one I'd visited before. Screams of distraught victims preceded sobs that went ignored in the shadows. Passersby paid no attention to me but I worried what kind of attention Nia and her mother were receiving. If I were to raise enough money, I could successfully move them to a much safer place.

So every night I'd roam the streets for loose or dropped change, collect what I could, and bring it back to Nia and her mother. Some nights were a complete bust while others might as well have been a gold mine. I'd find simple pennies and dimes in the gutters, which always at least amounted to something if I dedicated myself and looked hard enough.

The repetitive action reminded me of filling that lake for Chul. It started with endless searches that would result in a little pile Nia's mother would perplexingly find on the corner of her coffee table. It was enough for her to think something strange was occurring but it certainly wasn't enough for a new house.

If I were to make a difference, I would have to take donations directly—a risky confrontation style that would evidently put me in harm's way. Lucky for me there were a lot of cash transactions occurring on this street—with patrons purchasing anything from candy to mere powder. While I wasn't yet brought up to speed on what this merchandise was, I assumed it was some kind of medicine as the recipients always looked to be sickly and weak. Folks of all makes and models itched themselves uncontrollably, twitching and shivering as they counted out the bills to their hooded supplier.

Now I couldn't just outright steal the money from these folks so I was going to have to play their game. It was a racket that looked insanely profitable and actually attainable when I spotted Nia's mother hoarding an entire covered bag of the stuff in her kitchen. She'd use it for baking Nia cookies or to sprinkle in her morning cup of coffee, but no matter what the house always had a replenishing supply.

So I took it out with me one night, considering it an investment for the family, and began a successful operation on their street with the common kitchen goods. On my first night, I accidently wound up with a little taste of it while trying to open up the bag and realized it had been sugar all along; the very powder that shipped from the Hawaiian Islands and won over my darling Kalea. I missed her so in that moment but reveled in another "aha" discovery; this is where the shipments of sugar had been going off to for all those years—to be snorted and sold on the streets.

So that's precisely what I did; I'd sprinkle the stuff in lines like I had seen the other humans do and stand fearlessly in front of them.

A few confused souls would wander on by and do a triple take at the bizarre site before them. Eagerly, they'd all lick their lips and dive in for a snort but I'd maintain my stand and block their heads from going in. Confused and frightened, they'd always back away until I gestured to the small pile of coins I'd bring with me.

A typical human would probably cut their losses and leave right then and there but for some reason these poor, sick folks desired the sugar enough to actually comprehend I wanted money. So half convinced, they'd throw a few bills my way and snort a line. If they went back for another, I'd either gesture to the money or chase them off. Some would be there all night seeking the sugar's benefits while others would begrudgingly carry on. Beyond Nia's mother scolding her for using up so much sugar, I was seemingly in the clear.

Both Nia and her mother would awake to stacks of several hundred dollar bills each morning and quiz each other about its origins. Neither of them possessed an answer and since Nia's mother was older, she was the caretaker automatically in the right. So she blamed her daughter, at first believing she had taken on a part-time job to earn cash. But the cash earnings had become so grossly massive that the possibility of a supporting job was ruled out. Nia's mother switched from concerned to angry—she assumed her daughter must have gotten it criminally. Poor Nia, throughout the daily interrogations, protested her involvement to no avail.

"Nia, I want you to tell me, once and for all, where this money is coming from. I didn't earn it—it's not mine and I know you ain't working for the money."

"Mama, I don't know where it's coming from."

"Are you stealing?"

"No!"

"Don't tell me you're doing what I think you're doing. You'd break your mama's heart if you let strangers come—"

"I'm not doing anything! I'm telling you, it's not mine! Maybe it's Akela's."

In that moment, tremendous rage shot through her mother's whole body and exited the fingertips of her left hand. In one steady strike, she slapped Nia across her cheek as tears streamed down both of their faces. Nia fell to the ground while her mother trembled—I knew I had to intervene.

As her mother preached about the use of drugs and how her daughter needed to stop at all costs, I bolted to the kitchen chair with my stool nudging along in front. The intermittent scratching along the floor was enough to break their concentration. Both were absolutely captivated as I made my artful escape out the window without any trouble at all. I scanned the lawn for any sign of money, witnessing two fellows bounce quarters off the brick wall. Without missing a beat, I scampered toward them, apologetically took a quarter from them and scooted back to the vine that would pull me back home. They just watched in amazement, not even caring I had just flat-out robbed them.

Upon my return, Nia had ice pressed against her face while her mother jumped at the commotion of me making my rushed way back inside. I headed straight for the coffee table where I dropped the quarter in the usual delivery spot. Both girls had wide-open mouths and wide-open arms. Nia's mother embraced her daughter, begging for forgiveness and vowing never to harm her again, let alone let her go. Neither of them truly understood what just happened but all I can say is the mood lifted to a giddy one where the money was counted up and celebrations were quickly put into action.

The money had accumulated to a life changing amount, but thankfully, it was the mother-daughter bond that would lead them to a better life. Nia's mother vowed to take less hours at her outside line of work and they'd spend time together doing activities they loved. I received more full body pets than I was ever entitled to that day while all of the money was quickly stashed in a box safely stored out of view.

For the first time in my life, I felt as though I had accomplished a completely selfless good deed for others and was on the road to becoming the best version of myself that I could be. Life was truly sweet.

THIRTY

WELL, IF you're expecting things to stay just peachy keen in my story, you are sorely mistaken. The more I meddled in the human world, the more I fuddled life up. It would seem some unhappy gentleman heard rumors of competition on the streets and learned that the culprit was in fact not the same species. When Nia's mother began to use the money for food and furniture upgrades, these sudden changes sparked a special interest.

One dark night, not too long after I got out of the sugar selling racket, I awoke to the door ripping open right off its hinges. Two very determined masked men pointing guns searched around every corner until the pile of money I had earned was uncovered in a counter pot. As they swiped every penny, I emerged to investigate the commotion and froze upon seeing their startled gaze. After overcoming the sudden surprise, they picked me up and took off with all of my hard work. I bounced around their back seat as one of them counted out every bill—there was no concern for my safety as I rolled around, banging into every side of the car doors.

When we arrived at a dark, unwelcoming den, a marked-up man with black ink decorating the majority of his skin unfurled his hood and pointed his pistol in my direction. I perched on his broken desk as he paced around, kicking and throwing chairs to portray his power and displeasure with me.

Of course all of his followers looked at each other like their boss was insane—the way this particular situation must have looked was beyond them. Humans don't talk to animals (seriously anyway and especially not in front of others). But here was this frightening beast of a man, pacing up and down, throwing cigarettes at me and telling me to stay off his turf. Oh, I understood completely—this guy couldn't handle competition and so he had to threaten me out of it, which I thought was a little immature. But he had weapons and a temper that I didn't, so after a quick carving of the letter C into my shell, I was taken back home and warned never to sell my sugar again. Obviously, I was going to have to start again from the bottom.

The door in Nia's home needed repairs, as did various furniture pieces that were toppled over in all the madness. When Nia's mother found the money missing, a fit of panicked crying overtook her until Nia was able to calm her down. It had helped them get ahead a little, but now there was no chance of moving and finding a better place to stay.

Naturally, their scowling faces turned to me after they had internally accepted I was the one who brought the money to them. The evident crime scene made it apparent that I was also responsible for the theft and break-in. Neither of them knew of my kidnapping nor did they ask if I was all right. I attempted to make back all the stolen money, but I knew sugar selling was out of the question. I was swiftly out of products and too exhausted to hunt for loose coins.

Life was worse than ever before inside the Walker household— particularly for me because Nia had reached an apparent age where she was able to hold down a job like her mother after classes. So I was all alone during this time and the two of them hardly saw each other.

When Nia was home, she'd not only close but lock her bedroom door so no one could get in. She'd blare her ear-bursting music and act like I never even existed. I was once again lucky if my water was ever changed and if fresh food was sprinkled out for me in the tub.

Determined to vie for Nia's attention, I hid in her room all day when she was gone and buried under a pile of clothes. Cleaning her space was definitely one of the activities she was not completing while spending her time locked away in there. When she came home, I was shocked to see a familiar sight—the green, magical substance that broke the conversation barrier for me and Ron.

Nia calmly spread the stuff out on her desk and rolled it up in white papers. She'd turn up the music, lay back, and smoke it until the supply disappeared. After careful diligence over the days, I noticed this was Nia's nightly routine. She'd lock out her mother in favor of the plant and smoke away, neglecting any work that was awaiting her attention from inside her backpack.

It was my conclusion that though this substance made the impossible happen, it was ruining my owner's life. And all the sugar I had been pushing, along with the medicines I had witnessed around the neighborhood streets, was ruining people's productivity and true behaviors. I hated seeing sweet Nia this way, a giggly and tired mess that refused to move from her bed. I had to act if I wanted to save her future.

So as Nia and her mother worked shift after shift to make ends meet, I'd break into her room and fish around for the hidden greens. Usually carefully stowed away in the bottom of a sweet, tiny pink chest, I'd unearth it, bite through the plastic bag it was stowed in, and eat it all before she could get to it. When she got home, I'd carefully take out her textbooks and display them on her desk—reeling in colorful nausea from what I had ingested. I tried throwing it away in the garbage, but Nia would find it there and avoid her mother to greater lengths than she was already.

The toilet was the next best choice but no matter how hard I tried, I couldn't get the seat to activate. Nia would come home and angrily scream when she found her greens missing. She'd replenish them almost instantly, but always discovered the plant collection missing when she returned home after a long day. She'd hide them in different areas, but I had endless spare time on my side—no matter how hard she hid it, I'd always scout the stuff out, eat every leaf, and reap the "benefits."

This was not good for my health—I don't know how Ron and Nia did it for all those years because I just felt sick and immobile. Finally, Nia figured out I was responsible and locked her door from the inside so there was no way for me to get in. I had witnessed Nia sneak in during the late hours of the night through her bedroom window. She used to give me a sheepish smile and a signal to keep quiet when I caught her. I tried to get in from that angle, but there was too much danger in balancing on a tree branch for me. I'd wobble and shake without any good grip at all, and if I were to even make it to the window, she always locked it tight so I couldn't get in. I was failing in just about every aspect of supporting this family.

Nia actually took me aside one day in a hostile moment that I mistook for an impending apology and long overdue series of full body pets. Instead, she gripped my head between her shivering, painted-up fingers and glared at me with more intimidating intensity than I'd seen in a human before.

"Stop it! Would you stop trying to look out for me, okay? I know what you're doing! Stay out of my room, stay out of my stash, and just stay out of my life!"

I was hurt—I knew I wasn't wanted and could easily leave but there just wasn't any place I could go. I had vowed to spread goodness and joy and selfless acts but somehow everyone was getting upset with my actions. So I wondered if it was me and if my total misconception of human life was to blame. Perhaps letting Nia live her life the way she wanted was what I had to do. So for the coming days I'd sit off in the corner and watch the silence and anger and emptiness in the house take over.

Out of sheer boredom and false hope, I'd continue to take out Nia's textbooks and display them somewhere so she'd remember her schoolwork. They were almost always accompanied by letters addressed to Nia's mother, along with papers marked up with alarming red ink. One day I flipped through the book to take my mind off life and discovered it was thicker and more advanced than the ones previous.

I came across an entire chapter on nuclear testing—on how it was brought forth by a familiar looking man in a wheelchair named FDR and how a disturbing clash of cultures and ideals led to a cataclysmic fight. Nuclear weapons could put an end to all that and evidently, they did. But the effects were unknown, so animals were collected to understand exactly what they'd do. Pigs had similar skin to humans so they were a no-brainer. Marine life were also brought to research labs, particularly those affected in the Pearl Harbor attacks in Hawaii.

I found my answer through casual glancing; earth-shattering attacks rumbled Hawaii many years back and some humans decided to take the survivors and see how they felt. This was why I was taken from my home and set on this long-winded course—because of human greed. Through meddling...pure meddling in a business that didn't concern me, or any human for that matter.

My heart shut down. My eyes saw nothing but clouded darkness ahead. My extremities shook as my mind drew a complete blank. I had never been so angry in all my life and it was at this moment that I simply could not go on. I had become so enraged my body began to shut down and no original thought was allowed to pass through. I blindly flapped my way to Nia's room, surprisingly unlocked, where I knew I could hide deep in her mess where no one could find me. Any disturbance was going to result in a vicious backlash that was unprecedented, no matter the victim.

So there I sat, the dulling pierce of my ringing ears encompassing my empty shell, taking the place of anything close to rational thought. Hours must have gone by, maybe days. The only noise—out of sheer annoyance—to bring me back to the world was the repeating of the word "no."

With no sense of patience, I emerged to find Nia pinned to the bed by some brutish, sloppy-faced male. They rubbed faces but anything carried out by his wandering hands had Nia squirming and repeating her protest. As they became more frantic, his movements became more frantically pronounced and Nia could no longer struggle. Of course the warning Nia uttered, demanding I stay out of her life, kept me grounded and still. His hissy quivers shook a nerve in my brain that made me want to savagely harm every human I could. He happened to be in the path of my anger so it was he that was going to feel my wrath.

Nia's well-being didn't strike me during the mission—her clothing suddenly came off in a tearing peel. The man muffled her mouth and both their huffing breaths pierced my head as my vision turned from black to red. I shuffled myself onto the bed by climbing the sheets with the power of my jaw. Before I rationally knew it, my mouth was then filled with flab as I bit down harder than I ever had before. The man left out a chilling scream and he landed with a thud on the floor down below.

Nia screamed and crunched into a ball as the door flew open and Nia's mother fiercely faced the foe by pointing toward the front door. "Out!" she screamed as the man hobbled his way up on foot and out the door in mere seconds. Nia looked down at the ground as her mother glared at her. With arms crossed—no flying fists or a barrage of disappointed lecture points were used—Nia's mother simply said,

"Whenever you're ready to come out and talk, I'll be there," before stepping out and closing the door.

As Nia sobbed on her bed, all she had beside her to give any source of comfort was me. Her quivering hand gave me the first full body pet she had gifted me in years. With a sigh, she shook her head, dried her tears, and smiled at me like the little girl I once knew used to do. "Oh, Akela," she whispered.

I laid at Nia's feet as she cried for hours into her mother's shoulder. They both sobbed and apologized to each other, citing no admirable excuse for the drifting apart. At the same time, their heads went to the missing man's portrait—the father and the husband that had left them all those years ago. With a sniffle and a sigh, Nia's mother shook her head and asked, "Where did my husband go?"

Nia clutched her tight and assured her "heaven," just as her mother had once done for her. After a long, hard stare through the kitchen window, sadness turned to sternness. "For everyone's sake, I hope so. Otherwise, what have I been working toward?"

"The journey there's supposed to be hard, Mama. But at least I got you looking out for me."

Nia went to bed not long after that. Her mother stayed up late that night, clutching the portrait of her dear departed husband close to her chest. Her attention drifted to me, and for the first time since I knew her, she lifted me up to the couch and sat me upon her lap. We stayed awake, both of us, until the sun nearly came up for the next day. We watched Mary Tyler Moore until she drifted asleep; Nia's mother had drifted off to sleep with me held tightly in her arms.

I didn't stay with Nia and her mother for much longer after that night. Like when I hatched that fateful day, I again had to leave the nest in search of adventure. Nia was full grown and had to leave the nest in search for adventure and life herself. She finished her schooling that year and was absolutely ecstatic to find out that she had been accepted to further herself in her very own chosen destiny—that of hair design (a subject I know almost nothing about). In doing so, she would move away and leave her mother to focus on herself and her own dreams. She too would leave that old homestead behind and find another place of residence in a calmer neighborhood.

That meant I could no longer be a part of their lives; Nia was simply not allowed to bring me with her while her mother, though a fondness had grown, could not bear to take care of me. I understood—I was Nia's pet. But it didn't make the goodbye any easier when the time came.

As luck would have it, a few miles down the road sat some renowned aquarium where animals were not imprisoned and researched; they were treated like royalty and fed luxurious meals every day. At least this is what Nia told me on the ride there, blathering away, unaware I understood.

I had no clue what I was getting into and glass walls made it feel reminiscent of all my years in the government tanks. I trusted Nia to make the right choice; I just wished it was the choice to take me with her. But the moment was swift and just—she and she alone handed me over to some eager staff member who trembled under the increasing weight of my body in their hands. Nia waved goodbye; I could see her watching me the entire march out the doorway until she disappeared out of my life for good. After all of the effort I put forth to protect her and steer her onto the right path, abandoning me was her way of payback.

I wondered if human life and animal life was at all equal—humans seemingly controlled animal life far greater than we controlled humans. As I watched the news in all those years during my literate phase, I learned of animal attack incidents that were interspecies quarrels. Perhaps that's how I was perceived by Nia and her mother; my efforts were misconstrued or worse, negative. The robbery would never have happened, that's for certain.

I had traveled across an entire country, an entire Ocean, been present in various wars, and met a slew of people who I'd seen grace the television screen. I looked back at my life and back at my journey and measured my attitude at every angle. I was not most animals and certainly I was not like any human. I had suffered and endured long enough—longer than anyone I knew.

Despite my best efforts, destiny or what-have-you could never seem to lead me anywhere close to my dreams. I was robbed of Kalea and my home and a decent calming life. I was robbed of a true purpose and a fruitful destiny. Even in my honest efforts to spread love and peace, my destiny was a dud. I still had no answers on what I was supposed to be doing and what happens after death. Everything was conflicted and muddled and open-ended. If the journey was supposed to be hard as Nia said, then I must have been owed the whole world.

THIRTY-ONE

YOU KNOW, as far as enclosures go and the variety of con-
finements I have been kept in, the aquarium might just have been the
swankiest. Below the water's surface, I could twirl around in a glass pool
to the delight of pointing onlookers. Above was a hot and sticky space
meant to encapsulate home. Honestly, it took some adjusting as I had
been acclimatized to softer sunshine. I could feel my throat battling
against the heavy air, gulping in breaths like it was a sip of water.

Exotic plants I once lived among surrounded me in an acutely
decorated sequence. A shallow pond was best for lounging while a
hollow log was the best hang out to get away from it all. That's where
I stayed for most of my initial time there. The staff were concerned
that I wasn't entertaining guests enough, who waited for hours just to
get a glimpse. I didn't care—I didn't even realize that was going on.
All I could see in front of me was betrayal and the blinding darkness
of misery.

Sometimes I'd stare out at the thick, impenetrable piece of glass
that kept me confined. I thought about all of my failed escape attempts
through the years. I had spent the better part of my life maneuvering

ways out of Washington but somehow I had always ended up getting caught.

It felt like I had been drifting in an endless Ocean for all my life, swimming against the current to the best of my abilities, only to be brought back farther than where I started. I never harmed anyone or wronged anyone—I only perused wholesome goals that pertained to true love and family. I deserved better, far better for what I had been put through.

So I bitterly grinded the sea grasses the staff fed me as I'd stare before me in despair. I jealously peeked out at families, blessed with eager offspring and fortunate smiles. I buried deep in the sand, once again searching for a new mission statement. Only this time, instead of doing favors for others or looking for an escape route to further my jaunt to the Ocean, I drew a blank. I was tired of planning and weary from thinking about the embarrassments and setbacks of all my days.

It was my opinion then that there was no meaning to it all—no destiny for love or second chances or hope for reunions after you die. You are born and you die and in between you try your damndest to survive for no reason; this was the way of the animal kingdom. You were there to become food and it was inevitable that would one day too be my fate. Humans didn't know how lucky they had it.

Fate on the other hand, blew with a mighty wind a familiar object that had once been a successful tool for momentarily freeing me. Wavering in the exhibit's corner was a six-ring soda can holder. Strong and stretchy plastic could easily slip down my neck and extend my grasp a few extra flipper lengths.

So I decided to use it, only the plan was not about unlatching any door handle with the device so I could run freely out the front door. The plan was to hook onto a lengthy branch I could spot, just high enough I could barely reach it with the extension. Then I would push a small rock just below a piece of sturdy tubing that vented in the hot air. I would hop onto the rock, slip the ring around the tube, and kick the rock away so I'd dangle. I'd dangle and hang and twitch and flop until the vigorous motion and hanging by the throat would cut off all air and eventually squeeze my neck shut. I'd suffocate to death and finally be at peace.

With the plastic rings in check and the rock in place, all I had to do was summon the courage. Convince myself to climb on and attach to the tube. For hours I did this, nestled in the exhibit's back where plants blocked everyone's view of my activities. I thought of everything in that moment, from love to Hawaiian sunsets and even my days locked in the experimental New Mexican laboratory. Most of all in that moment, I thought of Byeol.

Strange isn't it—the thoughts that cross your mind before imminent death? You'd think a more poetic or significant moment (or your dearest and sweetest love) would act as the triumphant banner at life's end; something that you were most proud of or certainly something you regretted. Painful fear is one of the feelings you experience before dying, a shooting pain that alerts every cell they are about to be no more. I fought past the pain and filtered through the highs and lows of breathtaking views and regrets.

But the silky, soft skin and fluttering eyes of Byeol occupied my mind as I stepped forward. Inappropriate fantasies flashed atop regrets that they never came into fruition while the shimmering lake I created rippled below. I thought of her flippers, and her shell, and her smile. I thought of every bit of her that I could, but her wise words are what pierced through my darkened vision.

"Use yourself how you see fit," she uttered, and certainly, I was doing what I saw fit in that moment. But it dawned on me that I had the freedom to do so anytime I wanted. I had the freedom to stop my mission or keep going; it was on me to get the satisfaction through the effort I put in.

Many consider the ones they will leave behind and disappoint in the wake of "checking out early." I couldn't put myself out of my misery and potentially arrive to black nothingness—pain and suffering is absolutely more attractive. In every situation, I had used myself as I saw fit and it would have been foolish to end it there, rendering all that came before that moment useless time. In other words, I opted out and backed away from the rock as far as I could.

Disappointed in myself, I cried and cried in an uncontrollable fit. My breath wheezed from the onslaught—I couldn't believe I had come that close to leaving everything behind. Instead, through an aching heart and blubbering tears in a flooding downfall, I searched for a door handle to unlatch.

The only problem was I had come out too far from the landscaped brush. The plants no longer shielded me and I distinctly remember the frantic points of children who fearfully banged on the glass to give me assistance. My violent emotional fit must have given the illusion I was choking while the plastic ring around my neck must have given the illusion it was the culprit. Staff members fumbled with the door as they ran toward me and yanked the plastic off in a lightning fast motion. And as quickly as life changed for me in that moment, someone grabbed the camera that hung around their neck and snapped a photograph. I distinctly remember the light it cast blinding me right before the staff members reached my shell.

Well, the infamous photograph was printed up and shown just about anywhere you could think of. Magazines, newspapers, and every six o'clock news station had the topic as their leading story. Giant blowups of the image hung between my cage with a written demand for all people to cut up the plastic rings or ban them all together. Now, if I had the ability to explain it was all a big misunderstanding to them, I most certainly would have at that time, but there was a lot of wild and crazy perks being thrown my way.

See, this simple, little image of me crying with the ring around my neck began airing as an advertisement to clean up garbage that could harm marine life. Often they'd have me as a guest on television, some interviewers cheekily asking if I was okay after the big ordeal. I made the rounds between news stations again, appearing on a show I even used to watch that was hosted by Mr. Johnny Carson. He eagerly showcased me to the audience but kept his distance. There was no way he could hold me, and for some strange reason, it now took at least two to three people to lift me up off the ground. I knew I wasn't moving around much but my shell was feeling even bigger, which certainly couldn't have been a by-product of weight gain.

I appeared in PSA commercials where they zoomed a camera right in my face to evoke some kind of sympathetic emotion. It was for that new hip channel, you remember the one with the bright colors flashing and the music playing. The name escapes me but I remember it was a big deal because it was all the rage.

For a short while I had my own show where I accompanied some music enthusiast and "helped" introduce videos of popular songs. Television production wasn't as magical as it always seemed to be. It was a lot of waiting and repetition—it wasn't like I could say anything anyway. I was just there for show.

Yet another President got in on the environmental craze by posing with me for pictures. This President was tall, towering with a leaning limp and jet black hair. I overheard him talking as he motored on away, dismissing the whole movement I inadvertently started—I guess the whole thing was a photo op to appease potential voters. He had a charming, toothy smile and told me about my alleged "distant cousin" that had ruined one presidency (and remained still at large). I was relieved he didn't take the time to look over my x-marked shell. I could tell we had little in common—I missed the handsome President.

I was everywhere, and in return, people from everywhere came to see me. Though my size was not a tremendous feat, nor was the rarity of my species, people had seen me on the television or the newspaper or some animal safety advertisement on the side of a bus. They came to see me just so they could say they saw me. Cameras flashed and kids cheered as I delighted them with flips and swirls in the diving tank.

How strange it was how I once gained fame through the media as a communist-trained spy, causing havoc and violence and distrust against the animal kingdom. Not too long after, I became the face of animal rights and humans worshipped me by simply sympathizing through a misguided picture. Never in my life did I imagine that happening or that I would receive endless amounts of top-of-the-line sea grass from adoring fans who wanted desperately to give me a full body pet. It didn't take long for all the residue of my suicide attempt to vanish; I was now a celebrity star living a sweet life.

As a celebrity, you often feel alone even when you're surrounded by hundreds of adoring fans, peeping on you day and night to get a good, reassuring look. They didn't want me as a pet nor did they worship me as a hero for my former escape attempts or my lengthy travels. That's what hurt the most, but their constant love for me did tend to enter my head to block all that self-doubt out.

Years prior, I would have ached immensely from wondering why they chose me as their amusing spectacle. I would have doubted my abilities and my life, but now their bombardment of reassuring interest saw to it I wouldn't have to think deep thoughts again. In order to avoid any emotional pain, you just have to believe the exalting faces awing in your direction every day. And you take advantage of every perk thrown in your direction because on a very vain level, you think you deserve it. I wondered if every zoo animal experienced this intense bout of self-love like I did.

I was eventually paired up with an array of interesting roommates when the aquarium staff felt like I was getting lonely. At first leery to share the spotlight, I was shocked to discover I was indeed the largest of the bale. Two of them, however, were lovely, young vixens who had heard of my legendary life—they were in awe of every word I spoke. It turned out I was the only male in the whole vicinity.

I had given up my dreams of heading to Hawaii and thrown out to the coral any plans of escape for a better future. I had found it now— who in their right mind would have ditched all the fandom, lust, and glory for a dangerous slog through the Ocean? Some days I even managed to convince myself this was the very meaning of it all and where my life had been leading to through all those dastardly years.

And to answer your naughty, impending questions, I mated with the two females—hundreds of times throughout my stay. Kidding! Of course I was tempted; they fawned over me day and night with their illustrious, googly eyes. But I still had vows to adhere to and they would not be broken, even in the longest and loneliest of nights. Not even when the staff brought me and one of the potential lovers to a secluded circle to mate. She was willing but I refused. Their plans faded away like a burst balloon and no matter the badgering, I wouldn't budge. I remember they were fascinated and recorded their findings like uncoordinated lemmings on sugar.

Something deep inside halted me, even though I had given up my plans to return to Hawaii, and I felt ashamed for even considering doing the deed with the groupie-esque gals. My fear of loud lovemaking also kept me grounded, as I worried the excessive volume would disturb, offend and possibly even kill the other elderly occupant.

Oh, she was a miserable, old, wrinkly bag before I spoke to her. All she did was occupy the log or angrily hide in the bushes near my hanging attempt. Every now and then I'd see her withered, disapproving eyes beaming at me as I swished around the tank water in a choreographed performance for the fans. She'd shake her head when she witnessed me watching the other two females rubbing faces to entice me through sleazy mating rituals.

The shining reason I nearly threw away my vows for them was to finally create offspring—but the feelings simply weren't there and it never felt right. There was only one who I desired to bear my offspring; even if it couldn't be so and I would never get to see her again.

The frail, old shell would never join us for fresh, hand-fed sea grass; she'd pick the weeds herself and judged us when we feasted. During occurrences of show and tell, she'd hide deep within the enclosure as I eagerly volunteered myself up to the children for a glance and feel. I didn't get her shy motives then, but I began to understand it was to avoid heartache and hurt.

The crowds began to dissipate and my choking posters were swiftly replaced by an abused ape. It became a rarity for me to be taken out and displayed for eager eyes; the neighboring koala took all the focus, despite rarely even moving a muscle. Angrily, I'd watch the docile marsupial steal all my attention, giving him the most menacing look I could muster. He didn't care, nor did the people who used to come show me attention.

I was forgotten, and my ladies later lacked lust. They too were relocated, one to a nearby tank and the other to…I have no idea. I regretted not mating with them to some degree, disliking the fact my fatherhood future was fleeing far away and the wild chance for debauchery would never again arrive. At least my conscience was clean.

I was left alone to wallow in self-pity once again, only this time the old, crusty senior remained to nag about my choices. For a gleaming moment, everything felt okay and that I was receiving what I deserved. Attention and worship numbed my inner strife, but as the viewers vanished, I knew my doubts were never cured.

I wondered if my exhibit mate was in fact the old, crusty Flora Pika had found for me all those years in the past. She looked similar but it dawned on me that had been more than a lifetime ago and she must have been long dead. I could barely remember her snooty, disapproving image, but I could clearly see I was morphing into an elder now myself. The good old days had now passed. Upon this realization, I overindulged in sea grass and cried myself silly. This was as good as it was going to get destiny wise.

"What a pity. A shame, really. There's a sea grass shortage for some and you go and gobble up more than you have a right to just because the ten o'clock tour doesn't fill up like it used to."

In my belly bloating woe, I turned to see that the old, miserable dinosaur had actually tromped over my way.

"Well, are you going to help me, or did you just come over to gloat?"

"We get what we deserve. I've been watching you. Overindulging in just about everything there is—love, pride, sex, food. Nothing's sacred to you! Are you even happy?"

"You don't even know me."

"Who doesn't know you?"

I gave a triumphant, little smirk and glanced back to where my old, anti-littering poster used to hang. My head hung in shame when the reality of its absence sunk in and rubbed the present in my face.

"They blamed you for a communist takeover. I remember seeing you on television; they smeared and defamed our kind. We lost thousands when the witch hunt led to pet flushing and shipment dumping and yet, you did nothing. I lost friends. And you let it happen."

I shivered, thinking back to those days of complete panic. "It was all just a misunderstanding. All of this has been. What could I have done?"

The old, feisty senior glared with sagging wrinkles and a half-shut eye. I knew there was no convincing her. I was in the wrong and I wore those savage deaths like a heavy coat. All I felt I could do was change the subject and diffuse the anger.

"So, you watched television too, eh? I thought I was the only one." It worked. She smirked. I knew I was opening a portal to where I would be in the clear. "What was your favorite program?"

"Oh, some oldies I'm sure you didn't see; it was a different time. Jack Benny, Lucille Ball, *The Dick Van Dyke Show*. Humans were better then—I don't know what happened."

"You flatter me, ma'am. I guess I'm a lot older than I look. I used to watch *The Honeymooners* every night before bed back when I was stationed in Washington."

Her eyes lit up with a smug flame. "The communist days I assume?" All I worked for was for naught. I sighed and gave her a nod.

"Look, ma'am, I have a past, all right, and there's a lot I'm not proud of but it happened. So I'd be appreciative if we just dropped that portion of my life from the conversation."

"Fine. Fine. It's just not every day you meet a celebrity or even an animal of any sort that's visited Washington. Where else have you been? Tell me, I'm curious."

Oh, damn her smugness. She knew just how to get under my skin and within microseconds, I fell into her webbed trap of self-discovery. "Everywhere, ma'am. From the Pacific Rim to the scorching sand of Death Valley. Why, I've even spent a lengthy stay on a couple of boats around Hawaii."

"Hawaii! My, my! Well, it sounds like you shouldn't be too ashamed of your past at all. Sure, there are ups and downs, but—"

"Well, what about you, huh? I'm sure you've a past that you regret. Ever been to Hawaii? Ever been anywhere but a cushy aquarium? How'd you come to watch television anyway?"

The fossil hung her head low; I could see tears forming and words frothing at her mouth as she kept it all back. I apologized but she still gave no response. Finally, a nod and a sigh guided her into her story.

"I've been to Hawaii. Beautiful place. Beaches like soft silk and a glorious sun that glistens off the bluest of waves. I've seen it. Met the love of my life on those shores. But again, it was a different time and the men went their own way after mating. I never saw him again, though I bore our eggs deep within the sand. Loneliness struck me but so did a bloody battle. Troops stormed the beaches, swords in hand and intentions to overthrow Lili'uokalani—a once dear friend of mine who governed Hawaii in its last triumphant hurrah."

"It will pain you to know it is an American state now."

Her eyes rolled. "What pains me more is the troops who blocked my return to the beach with utter chaos. As they stormed the island for the queen, I was slowed considerably on the day my hatchlings were to awaken. I could not protect them from the gulls. I could not save my children's lives."

Now I could not just blurt out precisely what I felt in that moment, because situations like those are delicate. The whole situation rang through me like a deafening case of déjà vu. But as she sobbed at the memory of her lost one hundred children, I decided to press no buttons or propose no accusations. My heart was palpitating like a rock and roll drumbeat and I sweated and sniffled like a wild, uncivilized creature. I wanted to talk this situation out, but in an effort for sheer kindness, I went up to the elder and placed my face against hers.

"I'm Akela."

"Makuahine." She smiled.

We didn't look back or resort to petty squabbles after that day— the two of us were inseparable in our endless yakking. I'd tell her my captivating tales on where I'd been and what I'd seen. I painted for her the most accurate portraits of Earl and Ron and Nia.

Makuahine told me all about her time spent in Mexico and how deep-sea divers rescued her from a net during a chance encounter. Wounded from the struggle, she had spent her life at the aquarium ever since. I couldn't accurately peg how old she was but I knew she most certainly lived light-years longer than I.

In all that time I didn't want to ruin what we had by popping the question of family trees; deep down I think the two of us knew the answer. We were happy. I was happy listening to her astute mind recall all the changes she had witnessed throughout her life. It seemed as though Makuahine had lived through quite an uproarious time. And her fondness for Hawaii never wavered; she could describe every sand pebble on the beach where I once lived and every shade of coral down below.

Hearing her passion reignited something in me; her vivid memories made me feel like I was there. The warm winds and taste of fresh pineapple—I had long since forgotten these perks but I felt I was closer to home than I ever had been on my travels.

"And your love? Tell me about her," Makuahine demanded sweetly.

I hung my head in shame as it took me longer than ever to even recall her name. The image of her was no longer crisp. I shook my head. Simple features were no longer obtainable to help describe her nor were my deafening feelings of love toward her. I beat myself silly over the impure thoughts of the fan girls and unnecessary weeping over the loss of fame—it was a natural feeling but still I felt ashamed.

"You made a mistake today, giving in to your inner anguish. I know you have made many in your life but who among us haven't? I made mine abandoning my post for better food and fertile males, only to find the journey back a slow and difficult one. I lost my children to gulls because of greed and inner desires. It's been my challenge through life but also the lens in which I see it. These losses make us stronger and these mistakes make us grow. It was not the first mistake nor was it the last. We are animals and just like humans, we give in to faulty desires. I thought I was destined to be a mother—that bearing offspring was the only position in life I could hold. I was crushed to learn it wasn't… at first, but it sent me on a heck of a cross Ocean journey to the right one." She took a pause and proudly gazed upon the enclosure. She too had her moment in the spotlight and I believe she too made peace with what life gave her.

"I wish these mistakes and misfortunes didn't have to happen," I said with a sigh.

Makuahine smiled. I'll never forget that smile. There was more love, sympathy, and understanding than I'd ever seen in another being before. It made me feel as though everything would be okay. "I am older than you. I have seen and experienced more. The minute you stop searching for a purpose or holding on to what you think gives you meaning, you will find it. These 'mistakes' are what get you there. Now tell me, what is her name?"

After a long pause and a recollection of my sweet love, I smiled. "Kalea."

"What a beautiful name. Do you know what it means?"

I shook my head, stunned at the fact I had never questioned it. I had always associated Kalea with the love of my life; she was a definition in her own right. I grinned as the image of her became clear again. Some sort of feeling in my body held on to the memory of her. Shocked, I looked to Makuahine's reassuring face for an answer.

"Happiness," she said with a smile.

THIRTY-TWO

MAKUAHINE AND I had our rituals; we ate sea grass together at every meal, did a few laps around the exhibit to stay fit and mobile, and then delighted the eager onlookers with a choreographed dance through the aquarium tank water. We'd gently float in opposite directions; I was always impressed with the force the old girl still had in her. She could dip and twirl around me as I'd pause and pick one of the children to look at directly in the eye. They'd always squeal and shiver with delight—some were too frightened by the intensity and went running behind their parents.

I wasn't doing the show for glory or attention now; I was simply doing it for fun, to bring delight and excitement to viewers, but most of all, to spend time with my brilliant tank mate. We'd gab the whole day through, whether it was working hours or a busy, routine tank cleaning. It seemed as though we always had something to say.

Makuahine would always share some piece of sage-like wisdom before bedtime, assuring me I was no screwup for falling into the traps of fame and temptation. She'd assure me one can only love another after loving themselves…but of course there are limits to that philosophy. She familiarly claimed to me that the journey was supposed to be hard. That's what made it worthwhile in the end. And she'd softly remind me that feeling an array of emotions is a gift we must cherish.

I just about died of a heart attack when she claimed: "You know when you find love. You'll do anything for it. Love means never wanting to be apart." Turns out that quote was a family heirloom passed down from her great-grandmother Naheeni and was uttered by her many siblings who patrolled the open Ocean around the Pacific. I told her about Flora, and wouldn't you know, Makuahine had an elderly aunt who had the very same name. Coincidence or destiny? I'll leave that up to you!

There was an earth-shattering discovery when we performed one of our diving shows. I believe the energy and movement breathed new life into Makuahine's body and spirit. I became distracted by her energetic summersault and twirl and a familiar sight caught my eye. On her right shell side, a birthmark in the shape of a crescent moon hid among years of wear, tear and fading from sunlight. I had seen it before and I had wondered for years just what that marking meant. I tussled for days, wondering how to bring it up as I worried the answer may contain a life-changing story, hidden within a wall of touchy history. Makuahine, it would seem, beat me to the punch.

"What is that marking on your shell?" she inquired.

"Which one? The nick was during a human war over in the Orient. I got shot with a bullet and luckily it only left a dent and scrape. The X has to have faded by now, but in those communist days, the government wanted to keep track of me so they permanently marked me with some kind of paint. Unfortunately, it worked damn good too because it foiled some of my more brilliant escape attempts. The C-shape, I guess, is some sort of gang—"

"No, no. You've told me about those ones," Makuahine claimed. "I meant the one on your back right side. The one that looks like a half-crescent moon!"

Well, certainly my face went as white as a cloud. I at first thought senility was setting in. "No, Makuahine, you have that marking. I have seen it before along the coast of Hawaii. I assure you it has given me many days of wonderment, but I most certainly do not have it."

Confused, the elder zeroed in her vision on my back and nuzzled me right where she said it was plain as day. Without a word, Makuahine wandered to the back bushes of the aquarium and returned with a wet and wrinkled old poster.

"In case you ever wanted to look back," she said. "I was jealous and concerned for you, but there also was a part of me that was proud." She unfurled the poster and, sure enough, my choking photograph covered the surface—anti-littering messages had never looked so real.

I suppose out of fear in finding faults, I never looked at it very closely. Perhaps my eyes were drawn more to the plastic ring around my neck and what it represented. But sure enough, on my back right side, just bordering the very top of my shell, was a crescent moon nestled within the green-and-white speckles I had always known and dismissed.

Not to my knowledge did anyone ever bring any attention to it. Kalea never spoke of it or asked why it was there. Earl gave no ribbing during the long river swims nor did Chul assign some sort of mythical meaning. And never throughout my life had I seen the back of myself until that day. I simply lacked the ability and had gone off sheer feeling and the occasional glimpse in Nia's mirror.

"How could I have not seen this?"

"You must not have been looking. Why would you?"

"But, I don't understand. Makuahine, you have one too!"

Curious, she wiggled her bottom until she got the vision just right in the glass reflection. A sweet smile overtook her face.

"Well, would you look at that. Even at this age I can still surprise myself."

The surprise in her eyes was fake. She knew it was there and she knew what mine meant. She played it off well but I could see the true maternal relief in her eyes. Letting your vulnerability show often leads to the vilest of scars. I scampered to her. Now was the time to say what needed to be said. I could tell she wanted so desperately to believe but she was not allowing herself to revel in the relief.

"In Hawaii, I saw you before the blast. Before the mustached President placed me before Kalea. It was you all this time. And you saw me too, I know you did! But you didn't stop. Why? Why!"

"I was in Mexico, Akela. I was at the coast. It couldn't have been me." She was telling the truth. "I didn't want to get hurt. I never went back to the island in all my days. I didn't want to raise my hopes that one survived. I had to move on."

The only other logical option: there was another. Another had survived.

"What is it, Makuahine? It can't just be a simple birthmark. What's the meaning?"

Face to face now, we let our tears flow and our noses touch. Through the ever-growing blubbering of sentimentality—something you'll find happens with age—we celebrated.

"Family."

Moments of sheer delight were clouded by one dreaded little fact that had not been aforementioned but still caused a big stir inside me.

"And my size?" I asked. "It makes no difference to you?"

"If you believe it does, then I worry about the size of your brain. To me, Akela, you are perfect."

After days of rejoicing and soaking up every second of time that we could, a little idea popped into my brain that required a serious showdown with fear. To my knowledge, it had been just about half a century since I had been home and I thought I was certainly well overdue. It was even longer for Makuahine and seeing the reactions on her face when old stomping grounds were rediscovered, well, I just couldn't resist mapping out our route.

And besides, with the knowledge of a possible sibling running around, I couldn't just up and leave them without a family. I'm sure they were just as eager to meet me as I was to meet them. So after nervously rolling around the exact words in my head for a longer time than necessary, I finally summoned up the courage to pester Makuahine by her bed in the bushes and tell her just what I thought.

"It's been an awfully long time for the both of us and I know, I'm scared too—petrified really. But we've become such strong swimmers, and if you can zip on over all the way to Mexico, well Hawaii shouldn't be much of a problem for you from here. There's more family waiting for us and I think we have a responsibility to meet them and let them know someone shares the same blood. And Kalea…it's time I see her. I can't wait any longer. I'm not saying it's going to be easy but if we search together, I'm sure we'll find another with a crescent moon mark. What do you think?"

Silence. A lengthy silence. More than I was ever accustomed to when I was in Makuahine's company.

"Makuahine?" I whispered in confusion. Still nothing. I called her name another time. Once more. My voice trembled in the last utterance. And then I nudged her. The blotch of skin I contacted felt cooler than ice water. It jiggled in the most uncontrolled and unnatural of ways. I fought past the brush to look into her eyes and only a short glimpse told me everything I needed to know. A week went by before the staff figured out there was something wrong and came to collect the body.

I numbly watched the passersby through the glass, unsure of my next move. It was a strange feeling, you know, because it was likely the biggest loss I had ever suffered—yet, I knew she was old and the time we had together was never planned.

Perhaps the most comforting fact of all was that I was not alone—somewhere in this world another family member swam and breathed and ate and lived. It was my mission to find them and tell them what I knew. I felt it in my gut like never before in all my travels. I was ready to face what was ahead no matter what horrors came toward me. I was ready to face my past and finish what I started. I was finally ready to go back to Hawaii.

With a burst of determined energy like never before, my escape couldn't have gone better. The creative juices flowed like a waterfall and I took a keen notice that the staff members performed a monthly duty where they straightened each plant and took every ornament out for sanitation. This meant every rock had to be hauled out to some shop for a hose down and most of them could get pretty brown and filthy after I was through with them. So it didn't take long for me to find a puddle of sloppy, gloppy mud and roll around until I was completely covered.

Staying perfectly still was the hard part, but they were one hundred percent fooled when they came in to haul everything away. I managed to tuck my legs and arms beneath me in a painful ball while my head just seemed to give the rock a small, asymmetrical feature. They bought it and carried me away in a quick struggle between three lifters.

By the time I popped my eyelids open, I was alone in a wide-open storage facility among running hoses and dead rocks. I pitter-pattered my way across the bathing room and out the door, leaving tiny, muddy flipper prints behind. If the sanitation worker would have taken out the massive music muffs that covered his ears, he may have heard the scamper. He was too focused on his song and his rock before him, so I made it out the wide-open door without a hassle of any kind. The rest of the way was plagued by tourists but I still contained enough mud to stop, plop, and fit in with my surroundings.

Oh what a rush I had ladies and gentlemen, what a newfound sense of energy indeed. Busy feet wandered to and fro but no one seemed to question the mud-covered rock that was seemingly in every corner. I zigzagged behind trash cans and behind every perfectly gardened palm tree until I came to the lovely dock that extended over the mighty Pacific. I was certain it was going to be a much longer journey to get there but those geniuses improperly designed the aquarium right next to the Ocean where the marine life could easily escape.

I froze as I teetered off the edge of the wooden planks. I couldn't get over it. There was nothing stopping me this time. No chasers or enemies and certainly no guilt of any kind. Oh how I wished Makuahine was coming with me; I knew she'd enjoy the sights of home. But I still could see them and that's what mattered. I had a mission and I always had a goal to get back to the ones I loved.

It was time, and so with one last push and a wink to a bewildered young child who couldn't believe his eyes, I hit the cold Ocean water and felt the mud instantly float away. Clean and clear, I kicked my flippers and swam forth. Relying on instinct alone, I began my journey back to where it all began.

THIRTY-THREE

SLOW AND steady was the preferred method as the sight of land drifted further and further from my view. I veered past fishing boats and massive tankers coming in to dock after a long voyage. The sounds of the cheerful beach crowd dissipated into thin air; their joyful screams induced by icy water echoed through the bay until I could hear no more. Only the chirps of gulls circling for an afternoon snack kept me company. I was much too cumbersome for them now so they knew well enough to leave me be.

Below me, the Ocean floor sat somewhere in the deep dark; I couldn't make anything out except the direction my frantic dog paddling took me. Familiar feelings came upon me and my eyes spotted sights that were not really there. Monsters crept while the unknown darkness swallowed my depth perception whole, sending me into a dizzying spell and a frightful panic. I had to turn back.

It was then a flock of six greasers swam up and gawked. For those who might not know, it's quite popular for the ruffians in the duck kingdom to dip themselves in spilled oil in an attempt to look tough. I always thought it was quite foolish but they did improve on their overall toughness as their slicked feathers swam by.

"Hey, now. What do we got here?" one quacked.

"Got ourselves a new friend, don't we boys?"

I tried to play it off cool and look as calm as I could. Thoughts of monsters and drowning darkness disappeared as I swam in a confident strut past them. They followed of course, taunting me with insults about my color and my situation of traveling alone. After a few good emotional jabs, they realized they were not going to get a reaction out of me so they just continued to swim on. In this however-many minutes span, I didn't think about my imminent death once; I focused on my sheer annoyance and overall demeanor to look unbothered.

After the confrontation, I was in the open Ocean, further than I had ever reached by myself. Upon this realization, I huffed and puffed in fear. But a few calming breaths kept my eyes on the prize while my brain instantly went back to Byeol. No, it wasn't her illustrious pep talk or her delicate bodily features; it was her stare. Her haunting, watchful eye as I carried the pebbles back and forth to the new lake.

I remembered that feeling, each step I took to the Ocean down the matted path of weed and dirt (careful not to let my fear show in her presence). My mouth felt as though it was full of pebbles and all I had to do was let go. I opened my quivering lips just a smidge and felt a figure ease its way out to freedom. After bubbling silence, a satisfying, tiny clack rose up through the water.

The figurative rock hit the literal bottom below, and just like that, the dark unknown wasn't quite so unknown anymore. I had journeyed to the depths of that lake, exploring every corner as I built. I had no reason to fear those depths. I knew they were safe. Every dark unknown had its dark end. As I opened my mouth to let every imaginary peddle dribble out, I knew I was in control. My eyes opened wide and I swam on in full stride.

I had a plan of action from then on to swim forward and distract my mind with questions and scenarios and memories of the past. I compared water, debating which stream was a better swim in all my different journey locations: the American river system through the Southwestern desert or the steaming mysteries of the undisturbed water in the Orient? Did any of this compare to my native Hawaii? I could feel the water warming around me—it was slowly becoming more and more like I was home.

I thought about the Good Time Gang and what other weirdly wondrous deeds they did for other struggling creatures in need. Did they kick the habit of munching on the mind-bending greens? Ron seemed like he was dependant on the stuff.

And where had old Ron gone to? I hoped he was safe but I had a sneaking suspicion the relentless government would have sent out a search party to track him down too. It was a big country though and Ron could have been anywhere. I hoped he settled down and married Victoria. If anything, he was strumming his overgrown ukulele and watching television like he always did.

Nia on the other hand would have finished her hair design school and no doubt opened her own shop. She hopefully kicked the smoking habit as it seemed to encompass all of her energy when she did. I burst out laughing when I thought of her, wondering whatever happened to the partner I bit in that fateful night of anger. I felt a little guilty for doing so but he was simply in the wrong place at the wrong time. Was anyone still dealing sugar in that old neighborhood of theirs? I hoped it had become their old neighborhood—I always felt like my next trip outside would be my last. I was comingling with a frightening bunch of fellows, mind you. I just wanted the best for her. As much as she may not have externally showed that she appreciated me, I felt as though she was my own.

My mind raced from person to person, animal to animal as my trip unfolded again and again in my head. I thought of climbing mountains and watching the glowing sun set over the empty desert. I thought of my mad escape attempts and getting lost in the pentagonal court-yard. I wondered what became of Elvis Presley and that busty blonde bombshell who inadvertently took me out into the world. I thought of fame (both the good times and the bad). I thought of Makuahine's wisdom and how I feared and loathed her before we conversed. I winced in fear as bullets flew in every direction on the bloody battlefield, and I gagged at the return of the foul stench I was subjected to while Earl and I stowed away in the steamer. How in the world did I not burn to a crisp in that oven?

As the calming waves carried me up and down, I'd catch glimpses of the horizon; bar none, the best I ever saw. The sunlight shimmered off the water as it gave way to the stars. Whenever I felt anxious or lonely, I'd count every speck in the sky, never coming close to the actual figure. How lucky was I to witness such a natural beauty—a transcendent sight of such radiant light as it were. The only word that came to mind when I looked up at the never-ending beauty around me was heaven.

Then, just like that, I was reminded of one of Earl's many songs. I'd repeat all of the ones I could remember him belting out during my swim.

If you're feeling alone and blue,
Then there's only one cure for you!
Crane your neck up to the sky,
Look way, way up high,
And know that the cosmos are true.

Each has a story behind their shine,
Days of struggle like yours and mine.
A transcendent sight of such radiant light,
One day my friend, your stars will align.

Oh Earl—he was always crafty with his words. Crafty with careful clicks of his tongue. In reality, his mouth never seemed to close. I hoped wherever he was, he was now at peace and forgave himself for past grievances. I still can't confirm or deny to you whether he made the trip over to the place of peace he spoke of. Same went for Makuahine and the handsome President and Kaimi and Pika and all the beings I had met years and years prior.

All I knew was they were never really gone, not while I had the memories of sugar raids and river swims and aquarium shows. As long as the memories persevered, they lived on inside me and never vanished completely. Perhaps this was the afterlife Earl spoke of. Perhaps his fear of love and positive lasting impressions secured his immortal spot in his acquaintances' heads. Even though he was not present, I still told him he succeeded immensely.

I believe all of that upriver swimming in my past made me fit and ready for the slog back home. Not that the traffic was excessive in the open Ocean, but I found myself passing other Greens and Leatherbacks while paddling at my normal stride. Some would just give a slight nod as I passed (an action I confusedly reciprocated). Others would come over in a frantic swirl and beg me for directions, as they had no clue where they were. I guess I had a tranquil look on my face that led me to radiate an all-knowing aura. It dawned on me that I had absolutely no knowledge of where I was either.

The only compass I had to rely on was instinct. I knew I wasn't heading north because I wasn't getting any colder, and I wasn't heading south because I wasn't getting any warmer. It's common sense and after years of heading every direction, my brain somehow retained what temperature was what and where. If I had gone too far east I would have hit the Orient, and if I would have gone west, well, I would have known it by now.

Hitting such a small target in such a massive waterscape was worrisome for most, but a deep underlying scent of sugar and pineapple seemed to lure me in a steady direction with a gentle list to the left. The old me would have panicked over finding the precise path, but now I seemed to possess the nonchalant confidence that I'd find my home eventually. I seemed to wholeheartedly believe it was destiny and my abilities as a swimmer blocked any creeping thoughts of doubt.

I'd pass the occasional steamer blowing its horn on a lonely journey to the deep south of the world. No birds flapped above me as there'd be no place for their weary wings to land. You'd think I'd be lonesome too out there, but I was in good company with my bank of memories. And when I had a job to focus on, I'd face it with full attention.

When I got hungry, I'd start a lengthy descent to the very bottom where untouched sea grass grew in shaggy fields. You didn't see very many residents down there as the darkness blinded us both from knowing each other's presence. Maybe that was a good thing; I knew of various, sharp-fanged dark dwellers, mostly from hours of nature documentaries at Nia's. They looked horrifying, able to rip me to shreds in only a few gnashes. But my stomach rumbled so fiercely some days, I licked my lips at the thought of grit and gristle.

Nevermore did I feast on the living, though—there was too much guilt behind each bite. I instead savored floating greens so life could continue for the easily eaten. I pitied frequently consumed critters smaller than I. It wasn't fair but it was life. I tried my damndest to be the change I wanted to see. That all too often led to a great reminiscing period of the slug that briefly accompanied Earl and I—I wondered where he had gone and what kind of life the poor little thing had lived.

Sleep was another frightfully important component I grossly overlooked when I made my mad dash to the water. I couldn't just float in the water all night and I certainly couldn't hold my breath in the Ocean depths—I needed a flat surface to use as a cozy bed for a good night's rest. Let me tell you, there were no island stops whatsoever on the swim and on about the fourth or fifth day, I was ready to fall apart. I hadn't slept in all that time, and I knew I was way too far out to return to the mainland for rest and reassurance. I had to keep going in hopes of a savior that would keep me afloat.

My legs ached like some enemy had been pulling at them all day, desperate to rip them right off me. I wouldn't have been surprised in that moment if they did just plainly fall off and sink to the Ocean floor. My heart fluttered, and my vision was blurry at best—my eyelids could hardly remain open to begin with. My stride slowed essentially to where my knotted arms only rotated clockwise once a minute. This was not enough to propel me forward, and so despite giving the journey my all, I'd fallen and drowned halfway between California and Hawaii. Not an ounce of panic touched me though—I was either too docile or too nostalgically sentimental to care.

It was a great blue, bluer than the surrounding water that lifted me back up for air. For the first time in four or five days I could rest and let every muscle relax in a sudden, freeing drop. I had no idea how Kalea or my colleagues did it for all those years. Maybe they received help from wondrous, big-eyed, gentle giants as well. But in that moment, all I knew was a kind whale helped me rest and carried me throughout the night. We never said a word to each other as I was too exhausted and they were too big to form an understandable language.

It must have been hard, I thought, being so big you couldn't go where you wanted or love who you wanted to love. You couldn't ever truly hold the one you wished to hold dear, and some places you could simply never visit because you couldn't arrive. I pitied them, but I understood the moral of the story as they left me, rested and ready to continue on to the next leg of the swim. External size does not matter, only the size of your heart. They could have swum on or devoured me in less than one bite but their heart told them to help instead.

Some critters (and some humans) have hearts smaller than what's visible to the naked eye but all the looks and adaptable features to get by without a scrape. That morning I took pride in the ever-growing volume of my heart and gave thanks for those who listened to theirs as well.

As luck would have it, a log went floating by a few waves up ahead. I swam over and noticed a lengthy leaf protruding from one end. I had asked over and over to some higher being to please give me a place to rest, and along had come the whale. This was just overkill in the best possible way. For the rest of the journey, I gritted my teeth and held onto the leaf with all my might; the log would sail on down behind me.

At nightfall, I'd shimmy up onto the log and list gently with the tide. At rough seas, I'd hold on for dear life and ride the rocky waves to the highest crest, marveling at the speedy fall downwards I'd immediately find myself tumbling in. For a few split seconds, I felt like I was flying; flying high up with Kaimi over the swaying palm trees and bubbling lava pits. I knew he was with me during every roller coaster ride down each wave.

I screamed until only saliva flew from my gaping mouth, but this time is was in sheer delight. If I fell off the log, I knew I'd tussle around the water and eventually resurface. I could always climb back up and do it again, and believe me, I wanted to. I wanted to brave each wave that came at me, ignoring the skyscraping size that loomed ahead all for the thrill of the fall. You may not understand it, but a great friend once told me "the higher the risk, the greater the reward." When you're up as high as you can go, nothing can be closer to the truth.

I was not mad at Chul for breaking his deal nor did I think he actually ever did. I knew what he meant when he claimed only I could go forward and take myself where I was destined to go. Climbing aboard the little spy ship was only cheating me out of the great adventure that was ahead. I wouldn't have wanted to miss those waves or the unfiltered view of the sky for anything.

Chul knew this is what I'd face—this and more. More internal growth than I ever knew possible. The satisfaction of facing my fears head-on by conquering them with a furious stride. It was he who helped me conquer my fear of the depths in the first place. I understood it all now, kicking myself for boarding that boat to escape meager rains.

It rained half the time I sailed over to Hawaii and ships happened to pass in temptation as I swirled about on my log. I thought of Chul and thanked him for his wisdom—no way would I cheat myself out of my adventure's end result. My time in captivity was a just punishment, but as time went on, I wouldn't even see it as such.

I remembered back to my wide-eyed, innocent days as a youthful being. I thought specifically of the day Kaimi and Pika found old, crusty Aunt Flora on the beach. That day I told myself I wanted to get off the island and see new sights and experience wild adventures. I wanted to fight for love and know my mother and prove to the world my size meant nothing. In all those quiet days beside the tide, I yearned to get out, yet I had spent a lifetime trying to get back. In doing so, I got what I always wanted—adventure and purpose, even if I didn't realize it at the time.

Now I wince at the amount of hopelessness I wallowed in, the trivial complaints that left my lips. We never really do take it all in at the moment, do we? We never really realize what we have until it's gone. But those struggles and seemingly impossible situations are right where we're supposed to be, albeit we are determined to get to a "better" place. The self-labeled failings are not really failings but only a juicy part of life that shows us what we are capable of. Why did I not cherish the moment? All I could do now was cherish the memory and marvel at the markings on my shell.

I cherished the memories of Kalea; every single one I possessed from our first conversation about birthdays to our relatively silent meals of snails and sea grass together. The relationship was never a mistake nor was it a wasted effort to fight for it. We had our downs but the ups are precisely why we live. The face rubbings and long walks in the radiant moonlight on the beach…our confessions of hopes and desires. We exist for each other, whether it's for partnership or traveling or giving someone a push to reach their potential or experience surprise siblinghood.

I rehearsed daily what I would say to my brother when we were once again face to face. I would recognize his half-crescent moon anywhere and most certainly lead with that line to establish a bond. How lucky was I to discover all life had not been vanquished in that terrible gull raid and more than just one went on to experience life? We had much to discuss—both my sibling and I, and of course, Kalea and I. Days of catch-up stories and nights of deep appreciation for the lives we've lived. Some days I couldn't help but jitter right out of the water in anticipation—the journey dragged when all I wished to do was see them.

Suddenly, I could see a waving palm tree in the distance. And then another and another. I could see the towering rock that culminated in a dramatic point and loomed over the city with its smoldering lava—I could not believe the thought actually crossed my mind to jump in after a silly argument. Boats and ship traffic became steadily heavy as did the arrival of the reef. Every shade of yellow…pure, unfiltered blues…fuchsias and byzantiums and carnelians…you get the picture. Fish of every size and shape wafted around in a lazy daze.

There was no need to rush onto the Hawaiian shores. I was home all right and with a slick push, I eased off my log and let my sea grass stash sail off with the tide. I paddled forth, taking in the layout of the very place I once called home, taking in the residents, new and old, and navigating around the noisy chaos that had become the mustached President's harbor.

As I craned my head to scope a path around an impending propeller, a jolting force knocked me to the very bottom of the reef. Thankfully hitting only my strong shell, the hungry attacker slithered through the water and sharply turned, on the way over for another strike. As it did so again, I was not as fortunate because the beast latched onto my right front flipper, taking a chunk of flesh with it between its blood-soaked fangs. He was fast—outswimming him was out of question. I could barely keep up to sneak a peak of his ghostly white eyes and scaly sides. The beast was old and eerily familiar, covered in thick spots of algae—believe me, there was fight in him. As he came back for a third attempt, I knew I could not hide. I had to take a stand against injustice and fight back.

I was capable of a forceful smack just like him, so instead of cowering away I latched onto his puffy, pursed lips until I was shaken off. Confused, he came back for yet another tear at my skin, but I rammed the top of my head into his bottom with all the force I could. Angered, he came back and pushed my body down as he bit every which way. Some were successful and drew blood while others only consisted of water. But there was no way I was swimming on now—I had to see the fight through to its very end and plead with the assailant to rethink their actions.

I wanted peace and I wanted reason. And yes, I very much wanted to swim away. But you can't just do that! You can't run when others challenge and harm you—you must show destroyers the very blood that flows in you has history, and there is no way it will be an easy match. You must fight for everything you hold dear and not cower when danger calls; for if you let injustice become normal, you will never grow and you will always lose. But you also must give thanks for enemies as they are the ones who put you up to your greatest tests and make you question where it is your heart lies. I desperately wanted to refrain from bloodshed and death, but after gaining no momentum with reasoning, I had to question if I wanted to die as a peacemaker or live on as a fighter.

I could feel my movements growing heavy—heavier than I ever knew them to be. Swimming in any direction took effort but surprisingly the wounds were spread far across my body. The beast's nicks were scarce, only a few missing chunks from his fin slowed his stride. He had energy and determination to finish me off, so with every lunge, I'd tip forward and feel him clunk into my shell as I'd bite whatever nearby piece of him I could.

He grew tired as did I. He relented into the darkness as I sailed on, only to periodically return with the element of surprise. Blood poured from an array of wounds, snaking its way to the open Ocean in a dark red stream where larger mouths craved the taste. I swam on the best I could, but shadows drew close—ones I could no longer hold my own against. Three, maybe four, surrounded me as jaws opened to show teeth bigger than I. My earlier foe did his best to clamber away, but the great white to my left snapped him up in one gulp.

I did not run, nor did I relent. I stared them all down, looking deep inside the soulless black eyes that studied who among them would make the first move. I didn't say a word but neither did they. It was an oceanic standoff of the highest order. I was cornered as each one wiggled their fin in delight, daring each other to try and snap me up first.

Slowly, as the blood poured, my eyes sealed shut. I was weak and knew whatever movement I made would spell catastrophe. I could only muster enough strength to make a single movement now anyway, so whatever it was, the motion would have to be wise. I could not go forward or backward or side to side—I was fenced in by the hungry hellions. So I chose to spend my final seconds on reflection. I had done what I set out to do and made the journey back. I was lucky in every aspect of life and grateful for the time I was given.

My eyes jolted open when it dawned on me, in all of this, I had never brought back a single gift for Kalea. No souvenir besides my ramblings to show my love or where I had been. I had all that time to look or collect, but I just never put in the effort. Guilty, I looked around for nearby inspiration and a shimmering shell poked up beside the rock and sand, a familiar golden ring with oval-shaped glass taking every ounce of my attention; the mustached President's gift.

With a happy-go-lucky smile I nodded and began my descent to retrieve the lost treasure. All four jaws opened wide and lunged in rabid warfare for the opportunity of having me as their meal. I felt the life drain from my body as I drifted gently toward my old, forgotten possession. I couldn't get over how I had found it again. How lucky was I?

THIRTY-FOUR

AROUND ME, there was only blinding white light. It took some time before my eyes could adjust, but eventually the sandy shore revealed itself in all its peaceful glory. The soft nudge of the water pushing itself against the rocky coast welcomed me home as I craned my weak little neck as high as it went. Above me was a radiant sun that blanketed every bit of my weary self.

I remember the clang when each shark made their move to lunge toward me—gentle listing carried me to safety as all four crashed into each other in a raging whirlwind of blood and teeth. As far as my blood went, I know I should have been nearly empty but some sweet barnacles intervened and closed up my wounds as I drifted away after battle. They saw to it not a single drop more was spilled; the waves saw to it that I safely arrived at my beloved home. I nodded at the sweet barnacle clan as they let go one by one, returning to the Ocean. I shakily made my first stand. It had been weeks since I last walked.

Trembling like a newborn, I stumbled through the sand as every muscle in my body ached. Though it seemed to take more energy than ever before to go forward, I noticed an obvious difference in my stride, and certainly, in my view. As I swiveled back to take in my healing wounds, I could see my back end was further back than I ever remembered. My flippers were further down in the sand, and my gaze could see a smidge more than I was used to.

I couldn't dismiss this as just wishful thinking anymore—I had grown to my species' full size and then some after all that swimming. I had felt a peculiar growth phase over the years but not one so obvious and rapid. I felt as though I was a behemoth giant that could squish anything that got in my way. Perhaps I was just finally growing out of my childish phase—a mere late bloomer that arrived at his full potential after all; I was much too modest to attribute it to a brutal journey well done. Beside me sat the golden glass ring, still glistening like new after all those years. I gripped it between my lips and marched on, ready to return to my sweet Kalea.

My thoughts about my size were confirmed when a group of human children ran straight toward me and began to gasp and scream at my very sight. Parents followed, clicking a plethora of cameras with blinding flash bulbs (you'd think after all those years in the aquarium I'd have grown accustomed to it but evidently not so. This group was more bewildered and swarming by the minute than ever before).

Everyone tried their best to get in a pet while I tried my hardest to just keep going. I'd been on a journey for over half my life and I wasn't going to waste my welcome on fanfare and admiration. I had to get reacquainted with my old home but throngs of beachgoers made that a nearly impossible feat. An authoritative man in red ushered the wave of humans back but even he was aghast at my unusual size.

I, on the other hand, was aghast at the unfamiliar sights I saw. Sprawling buildings stood high in the sky as thousands of frizzy-haired humans took to the beach. It was so loud I could barely hear myself think, what with all the childish screaming and splashing and booming music going around. Groups marched out to the Ocean, armed with flat boards, while others took up every bit of the beach by just lying there without any regard for others. Food fell atop the sand while fruity, sugar-filled drinks made their rounds by an army of platter-carrying workers. I couldn't get over the lack of trees and forest—all of it was replaced with concrete and glass.

No, this was not what I knew or cared to know in the first place. I chuckled at the brightly colored shirts and flowery humans that wore strands of carnations around their necks. As happy as could be, it reaffirmed my old thought that you simply can't be sad when facing a carnation. But there were no other Ocean dwellers in sight. No other animals crawling around the sand beyond a pair of employed parrots posing for pictures.

At first concerned I had not reached the right island, I knew and could sense it deep in my heart the land had changed without me. The entire aspect of Hawaii had shifted to accommodate leisure seekers, while steamers filled with pineapples shipped out more frequently in one hour than they used to do all year.

And I refuse to discuss with you all the traffic that now zipped on through paved roads that completely cleared away our old jungle homes. I was looking at a completely different place and could not find the appreciation in what was new. So I marched on through the proverbial runway, feeling like a scrutinized model I had seen on Nia's television. Everyone had to take a picture and gawk as I made my way toward the only palm-treed section in nearby view.

After cooling off in a relatively remote beach, I came across a section that had not a single human at all. Blocked off by threatening signage and poor fencing, I found myself alone and transported back to a time when I strolled the beach daily and waited for love to find me. Here I was reminded of my lonelier wasteful days waiting for life to begin without putting forth any kind of effort. As peaceful as it was, the memories of bitterly hiding with the tide were much too painful to relive.

Thankfully, the horrid sounds of bloodthirsty, attacking gulls interrupted my thoughts and drew my attention elsewhere. In the distance, a band of the bullish-beaked bastards boldly beelined a barrage toward movements in the sand. After scuttling forward a tad farther, I recognized the commotion and identified the sandy twitches. They were babies, fresh from hatching below in a birthing pit. With no one to help them and only a clueless march to certain death, I knew there was only one action I could take.

After a madcap race across the beach, tripping over dirt clumps and buried crustaceans, I arrived to the massacre in motion where a group of gulls fought each other over the rights to eat a floundering newborn. Blood again soaked the ground as feathers floated gently across the breeze. Struck by the atrocities that were being committed by such villains, I uttered the only word that made sense to end the situation. Every gull stopped flapping and yapping as I bellowed, in a newfound baritone voice, "STOP."

Affectionately, I gazed upon the lovely little newborns, struck with awe and wonder as they looked at me with curious hope. One saw its chance and began to shimmy toward the water right under a gull's flat-forked feet. One by one, each gull's eyeline turned to gauge the fleeing newborn.

It was then I barreled with all my might into the ghastly gulls, knocking some across the beach as if they lacked any form of inner control. This time there would be no slaughter of my kind in a senseless raid to satisfy hunger—this time I would make it cease. Frightened by my size, some immediately took off in a panicked flap while others tried to take a snack for the road.

Every gull that took a single nip at a youngling was subject to a swat that sent them whizzing up through the air and away from the scene. Other brave (or foolish) ones took a stab at me but could not for the life of them pierce my shell. Instead, they were treated to a slam and a cautionary reminder not to eat little ones as their wings jammed underneath my weighty body. I remembered late-night lessons taught to me by the Good Time Gang. My flippers flipped high in the air as all the commotion I could make began to force them all far away.

Careful not to aid the babes along too much, I assured them everything would be okay with kind, inspirational words. But I did not touch any of them; I let them work it out on their own by fidgeting and tumbling on over to the water. Without the intervention of the gulls (I kept the rest away with a fiery look), they poured into the water in droves, splashing about in pure joy as they discovered the wondrous Ocean for the very first time. Hundreds were born that day as I watched them march on, even those who lagged from acting as launching points deep down in the pit. How fortunate was it that I had made it then and there on that particular day and at that particular spot. Destiny, perhaps, played a little role in my intervention.

One, and only one, could not get out of the birthing pit no matter how hard they tried. I'd watch them crawl and push against the sand, only to flip over again and again. Finally, it landed square on its back and was left to die without any sympathy whatsoever.

"You can do this," I explained. "I know you think you require help, but I'm here to tell you struggles like these will only make you stronger. You can get through it."

It twitched and flopped as the beating sun slowly sizzled its underbelly and all energy was exhausted. I urged it to continue on and go forth, but no matter how hard it tried, the babe could not turn and climb out of the birthing pit. So with much hesitation, I looked to make sure no one was around to witness my helping hand.

"You're lucky," I claimed as I picked it up between my flippers and cradled the newborn all the way to the water. It gazed up with fresh eyes, nestling softly in what seemed to be total comfort and trust. I knew this one would face a lifetime of hardship and struggle going forth because of my actions, but I knew of course that they would overcome it all. As it hit the fresh, freeing water, I concluded they were absolutely lucky indeed.

I triumphantly stood guard and pondered the fine future our kind would have in the coming years. I wondered what they were thinking as they took in every feeling and object that surrounded them. By now they knew danger but they would also know love, something I was privy to in my first moments thanks to the kind hands that threw me from the shore. I wondered if they questioned where their mother was and had that same burning determination to find her that I did. Their journey to cross her path would be a lot shorter than mine. In that moment, the matriarch frantically scurried her way toward me from across the beach.

"Hello! Hey! I'm here! I'm here!"

I knew that voice.

"I am so sorry…I was only gone for one minute. I didn't think they would hatch until tonight."

Words spoken in a tone of pure sugar, pleasure, and bliss.

"Is everything all right?"

I couldn't give her an answer. As she huffed and puffed and proudly gazed at her young, all I could do was look upon the one thing that had kept me going for all those years. My sweet Kalea was standing before me with no separation—unconcerned with any other being around her. Her beauty still radiated. Time had been kind to her and hardly any wrinkles or sunspots showed. Excess weight led to a drooping belly but the same sweet female I fell in love with still encompassed every bit of her shell.

I blatantly stared without any hesitation, waiting for eye contact, waiting for her to realize just who I was; waiting for the blessed moment of our reuniting face rub. The warmth of the sun paled in comparison to the melting spotlight I felt when her eyes shifted to me.

I found myself feeling just like I did when I met her—out of words but full of hope. As she blathered on and looked around, that hope, however, slowly faded.

"Parenting today, I tell you. My mom wasn't even present when I was born. Gone to a completely different island. Now you're expected to be right there with them to make sure they get to safety, which is great, but it is a lot of pressure. Did I miss it then?"

It dawned on me she was indeed a mother. She bore children, obviously with a suitor that was not me. She had moved on and forgotten all about our vows. But she had now become the very thing she had always dreamed about being—a proud Mama to an array of stunning children. It was bittersweet but at least she seemed happy. I choked as I opened my mouth to answer.

"Yes, but they are safe."

"Yeah? Well hey, thank you. I can't tell you enough how grateful I am for your help. You were so brave back there. I saw you chasing away those gulls like nothing. Really…I…thank you. You're so…big and strong! My babies, they'd have all been eaten if not for you. What are the chances?"

I saw it in her face—not the slightest register of familiarity or recognition. It was like we were meeting for the first time. She smiled at me, looking me up and down and then back at her beautiful children listing comfortably in the bay under the bright blue water.

"I'm Kalea," she said. "Nice to meet you."

I swallowed hard. With it went pain doused with heartache and a chaser of reality. I knew—I had always known—there was an overbearing chance that she would move on. I wanted her to be happy and that mere desire kept the real bite of the sting away. It took every fiber of my being to not blurt out my identity, but it was not the right moment.

How could she not recognize me? I didn't understand. Anger began to overtake the joy of seeing her again. But I could see by the look in her eyes my face was showing every kind of festering emotion. I wrestled internally with whether to tell her the truth—but as her plump partner waddled his way to her side, I knew there was no possible way I could tell her.

"Everything okay? We lose any?"

As Kalea stumbled over her words, I eked out as much reassurance as I could muster, eyes pointed as far away from him as I could get them to turn.

"I got to them in time."

My gaze was brought back to his earnest, little, trouble-free smile. Relief overtook him as he sighed and snuggled in close to Kalea. I saw his gargantuan hanging belly and his pristine, little waxed-up shell. I saw into his clear, painless eyes and his swaggering, straight stance.

"Well hey, thank you so much there, partner. Glad you were there to help. You don't know how many we've lost over the years because of attacks like that. And you really chased them off?"

I nodded. I saw the calm, uninspired laziness in his face.

"Now I've always wanted the best for my kids, but those gulls, they'd eat me and Kalea right up if we intervened. I've just been petrified of 'em all my life. I'm not good with confrontation. Good for you, pal, good for you!"

I saw the half-crescent moon sagging on his left side.

I saw my brother for the first time up close, understanding a mere fear of interaction kept us from meeting prior. I could understand that from an earlier perspective but I was sure glad we no longer shared that fear. In the nearby pool I saw my reflection. I was bigger—bigger than both of them. I was scared and beaten and aged by the past, but damn was I filled with stories and thought and perspective.

Of course Kalea didn't recognize me; I was not the Akela she once knew in the slightest. In the thick of this cruel, Shakespearian twist of fate, I began to smile for the first time. I began to look both of them in the eye, directly in the eye, and carry on the conversation. I was not in the position to judge or lecture or reveal anything to Kalea that might hurt her or her new beau. I simply leaned in to get the full inside scoop.

"So how long have you been together?" I inquired.

"Oh, years and years," he answered.

"We met long ago right here on the beach. Stuck together ever since."

"How? How did it happen?"

After a loving look at each other, he gave a sweltering sigh as he looked down upon the sand. He couldn't make eye contact with me.

"Well you see, I was born without a family. Gulls ate 'em all up when I was little. I had stayed tucked away in the birthing pit so they never got me. I always thought someone survived though so I scoured the island to find them. When I did find someone, I was always too shy. Found this one by the waters pining over a lost love on my search. Knew I had to do something—"

"And I haven't cried since."

A pause.

A long pause.

And then a breath.

In and out.

I smiled.

"Well, I think that's lovely. You don't see a lot of true love these days either. Couples are just about an ideology of the past."

Kalea and my brother looked to each other in confusion on that one like I had spoken a completely different language just then.

"Really? Everyone here is married and has armies of children. Where are you from?"

"All around really—just spent the last few years on the coastal United States." I smiled at Kalea, remembering fondly the days when I eagerly awaited her return from that exact place. I knew a connective spark would ignite with the clever mention of her old stomping grounds.

"Oh, how nice. I haven't been there since—gee, I was hardly grown up."

I was in shock! We planned that trip for years but ultimately never went on account of my floundering, fearful disability.

"Really? You have never gone back?"

"Not once. It's just too dangerous and tiring. And once you have kids you just honestly want to stay put and put all your energy into raising them right."

"And me," my brother said with a smile, "well, I've never even been off the island."

"You don't say!" I gasped. "Never even once?"

He shook his head. It made sense. The more I drank him in, the more I could tell he wouldn't have lasted a day on the open Ocean.

"I don't know. What else is there to do or see? There's nothing out there but danger. Besides, what could beat this? This place is paradise!"

I looked around the towering hotels and heard the gross misplacement of reggae music protruding from a boom box. I cocked my head and gave a little smile. I found myself unable to agree.

"Well, you must! There's so much to see beyond Hawaii! The Grand Canyon and Las Vegas and San Francisco and even the White House when it's all lit up on a summer's eve. Now Korea, I really think you'd adore Korea!"

Again, I had switched to a completely different language. Kalea and my brother glanced at each other in quick reassurance to dismiss what I was saying as false craziness. Of course they had never heard of any of these places—they lacked television or books or the very opportunity to visit such a place.

A lengthy silence drew the conversation to a close. I wasn't angry and finally every fiber of my being wasn't telling me to pounce gleefully on Kalea to give her a good nuzzling. I saw, quite simply, we had changed. We had changed and it was for the better. I had hundreds of reasons to back me up on that claim and they were all gently resting after their big journey into the water. And they were only the few that I had apparently met!

"I'm sure you are great parents. You should be very proud."

"Oh, we are," Kalea said with a loving sigh. She was at peace, comforted by the tranquil life she had created with my brother. My view gently listed to the half moon on my brother's side. I had been sure to hide my moon side, carefully pointing it away so it couldn't create a stir.

"I'm sure your mother is proud of you," I concluded.

I turned. I knew it would be the final turn and the final time my sweet Kalea would enter my view. I had dreamed about the moment over and over and when it finally came, it was better than I could have ever imagined. She was not hurt or saddened by my absence. She had not withered into nothing or died trying to find me. She lived her life, the one she wanted, and that's all that mattered. It was a victory in my book. Besides, I received something most never find in their lifetime: closure. Our marriage was not meant to be but that did not mean life could not continue. There was more to life than just our love. We were destined to find each other all right; only the outcome was not what I had ever thought. And that was wonderful.

"Well, what about you?" inquired sweet Kalea. "Tell us more about you. Who are you? What do you want in life?"

I smiled, giving one final turn as I gazed upon my family. I had known the answer to that question once. Well, I only thought I did. I had been searching for an answer to that question for the past century. Again, a strong breath in and out and she was gone. With a smile as pure as they come, I squinted and cocked my head to the side. In the distance behind them, three familiar faces watched from high atop a mound of sand. Hyeok grinned while Byeol flit her flirtatious eyes. In a single motion, Chul gave a nod of sheer approval.

"Kalea. That's a pretty name. Do you know what it means?"

Not surprisingly, she shook her head as she lifted her gaze from the sand and directly to my eyes. It almost felt as though she knew me in that moment. That she found something there that tipped her off on just who I was but it was too late to act on it. I fell in love with her all over again with that look; that honest, anticipating, hopeful artwork of a look.

"Happiness," I answered her as I walked away.

"Wait!" she exclaimed. "Does this belong to you?" The sparkling golden ring shimmered in the sand just beyond her flipper. "It's beautiful," she said, hypnotized by its pure radiance.

I simply returned to the cool, endless wonderland that is the Ocean. I did not look back but I could feel their perplexed stares penetrating me, even long after I exited their view. Hawaii was no longer a recognizable home for me, nor did I want to live among the partying beachgoers who guzzled daiquiris daily without a care or a goal. Of course the memories of it would live on inside me. Though I wasn't there, it would remain as my home until the end of my days.

You know, if given the choice between being an animal or a human, I'd pick animal every time. I was free to go wherever I wanted without the issues of currency or acceptance. Humans always seemed to feel the more they expanded, the happier they'd be. I merely needed to see the land—not own and fight over it. Perhaps they hadn't discovered what I had—that we live on in thought and memory. Perhaps all this was a built-in attempt to be immortal—so legacies could live on forever through high structures. Perhaps they were so hung up about heaven they put all their energy into getting there and missed the point of it all. It's just all so primal, it really is.

I couldn't help but think about all the sights I witnessed on Nia's television that I had not yet seen in person as I wandered over to the bay. There were the African plains where the elephants roamed and the Australian outback where Earl's cousins surely hailed. I wanted to see the colors of India and the towering coliseum in magnificent Rome. I had much yet to see and more to live through and surely no time to waste. Age was just a number while destiny was on my side.

Upon a brief residency in the south of France, I discovered some nincompoop who buried his face in a mobile computer instead of studying the brilliant surrounding sights. He had rented a small villa where every night he'd fall asleep on a patio deck chair with the computer slowly falling from his lap. I'd emerge from the water and open a word document to write this very book, clacking away like the typists back in Washington had done. This wasn't as satisfying however—no *ping* noise at the end of a line.

Intrigued by my first few words, he would curiously leave the computer open and running on the table each night. He'd try his best to catch me in the act but I'd never go if I could see him obviously spying in the curtains. It took some time to get back into the habit of writing but I feel I did all right with it, all things considered. My flippers had grown immensely, which slowed my precision quite a bit more than I'd like to admit.

My hope is for him to take it to some publishers after it's all said and done so people can read about what I have seen and who I met. I'm not trying to be boastful or make anyone jealous or confused. I wasn't aiming to concoct a tell-all about my days as a celebrity nor was I using the project as a method to work through my issues.

I just wanted to proclaim to the world the one fact I had been striving toward all my life—the very notion that became the object of my desire in all those years of journeying and adventure. The mere achievement of it left me wanting to yell it from the rooftops of every village I passed and let every passerby know everything was okay.

Though I had failed many times over, I was no failure. Shame and unhappiness no longer accompanied me. If there's one mantra or theme or endnote I want people to take from my life and bring into theirs after it's all said and done, it is simply this:

Akela found Kalea.

ABOUT THE AUTHOR

Ryan Uytdewilligen was born in Lethbridge, Alberta and raised on a family farm. He studied broadcasting and worked as a creative writer for a radio station, which really kick-started his passion for the written word. After studying screenwriting at Vancouver Film School, Ryan optioned two feature films and published two nonfiction books, *101 Most Influential Coming of Age Movies*, *The History of Lethbridge*, and a YA novel called *Tractor*. He has judged the NYC Midnight Writing Festival, written for various blogs and magazines, and continues to obsessively watch movies while writing in many different mediums.